IMAGINE

A TALE OF FAITH AND COURAGE IN A DANGEROUS WORLD

F J MESSINA

Blair Brooke Publishing

ISBN: 978-0-9998533-7-5 (Soft Cover)

PCN: pci1503

❀ Created with Vellum

1

ashington, D.C. – Thursday, December 24th

W It was almost like being rocked in a cradle, the sensation—soothing. The sound of the subway car clicking over each new piece of track created a hypnotic drone in his ear. It pleased him.

He was on his way to work; he needed to put himself in a particular state of mind. It was essential that he perform at the highest level tonight. Closing his eyes, he took a deep breath. Silently counting to ten, he let it out in a tiny stream between his lips.

His eyes opened. It was no surprise to him that the normally crowded carriage was less than half-full. At eight o'clock on Christmas Eve, most people were already gathered around hearth and home with family and friends, ready to enjoy some oft-reprised, memory-laden meal or the sharing of traditional drinks and sweets. Beautifully wrapped presents sat under countless decorated and twinkling evergreen trees, waiting to be opened this very evening, or perhaps the next morning.

In years gone by, people would sing songs celebrating the birth of Jesus, the Savior. It bothered him that in more recent

times, it seemed the babe that had come to save the world had
been relegated to a spot under the tree or on a mantle. There, as a
colorless little figure, he would be surrounded by a ceramic Mary
and Joseph and three gift-bearing fellows dressed in turbans and
robes—men who hadn't actually arrived at his side for many
months. For the most part, the whole straw-filled scene would go
unnoticed by those who were ostensibly there to celebrate this
singular birthday.

The train came into a station and stopped, the sliding doors
opening with a whoosh. He reached down, grabbed his guitar
case, and stood, waiting patiently as an elderly woman pulled her
collapsible two-wheeled grocery cart through the doorway, out of
the car, and onto the platform. With a quiet, "Excuse me," he
stepped around her and headed for the stairs which led up to 13th
Street.

Stepping into the crisp night air, he knew the city streets
would not be as empty as the subway car when he walked the
two-and-a-half blocks to his destination, the site of the evening's
gig. Instead, he had to tilt the instrument case all but vertically to
weave his way through the thickening crowd of people. The
excitement in their voices, the smiles on their faces, lifted even
his own spirits. He felt surrounded by a sense of celebration, one
that had little to do with the reason for the season.

The collar of his dark blue peacoat pulled up to his ears, he
maneuvered his guitar case around men and women, singles and
couples. He ducked his baseball-capped head and buried his
chin into the warmth of his gray plaid scarf, confident not a single
person he passed was even slightly aware of him.

Approximately three minutes after he had emerged into the
chill of the night and the buzz of the crowd, he stopped. Staring
for the briefest moment at its sad and darkened edifice, he
stepped briskly up five concrete steps and into the lobby of the
Foster Hotel.

The decades-old odors of cigar and cigarette smoke filled

his nostrils, along with the smell of recently used lemon cleaner. He paused in the well-lit yet shabby space, fully aware he was being recorded on rarely watched security video. He gave its future viewers plenty of time to note his diminutive frame, the lush blonde hair that fell to his shoulders, as well as the tight jeans which hugged his thin legs, the peacoat which hid his butt and hips, and his pointy, ankle-high women's boots.

After a long moment, he walked past the tired leather couches that sat on either side of an even more distressed area rug and headed toward the elevators to the right of the front desk. Simply nodding in response to the greeting that came from a young man behind that desk, he passed the elevator and took the steps to the third floor. He didn't want to be stuck in a small wood-lined box with people who would cordially and stupidly ask, "So, you play guitar?"

Stepping into the narrow hallway, he turned to his right and walked toward the front of the building. Turning right again at the end of the hall, he stopped in front of room 311, pleased he hadn't encountered any other guests or visitors.

The key he retrieved from his coat pocket unlocked the door to the room which had been rented by someone else several hours earlier. Turning the ancient handle, he stepped into the dark and musky chamber, closing the door behind him. He pushed the upper button on the old-fashioned light switch just inside the door and filled the space with a yellow, sickly glow. It pleased him that the staff had drawn the floral curtains closed.

Checking his watch, he got down to business. He placed the guitar case at his feet. He removed his ball cap and the blonde wig he had worn under it, then arranged them carefully on the floor inches from the doorway. Slipping off his leather gloves, but leaving on the surgical-quality latex gloves he wore beneath them, he grabbed a wooden chair that had been left in the room specifically for his purposes and dragged it to the window. He separated the curtain just barely enough to make certain he had the view he expected.

Retrieving the guitar case, he placed it on the floor next to the chair, then sat. He bent down and quietly snapped its locks open, then lifted out the frame of his Remington Defense CSR, resting it on his legs. He reached down again, picking up the weapon's barrel and spinning it into the frame until he heard a satisfying click. He flipped the protective lid and checked the built-in telescopic scope. With one outward pull, the buttstock was engaged, and he held his instrument of choice—a highly accurate compact sniper rifle. Capable of placing ten rounds in a four-inch grouping at five hundred yards, it was more than adequate for the eighty-nine-yard shot he would take sometime in the next thirty minutes.

He reached down one last time, lifted out a small hand-held vacuum, and placed it on the floor at his feet. Since entering the room, he had walked only to the wooden chair, then to the window. He hadn't touched anything but the chair and the curtain. He would have to lift the exterior window, a feature left from the construction of the Foster in the 1930s, but he would come in contact with nothing else.

After he had taken his shots, he would close the window, disassemble and repack the weapon in less than one minute, return the chair to its original location, then use the vacuum to retrace his every step in the room. He would pay particular attention to any stray hairs from the wig lying near the door. After slipping his flowing locks and cap back on, he would vacuum as he backed into the hallway, tuck the small cleaning device inside his jacket, and leave two minutes and thirty seconds after his second shot. He would appear to be just a working musician headed to another sad Christmas Eve gig—probably in a bar surrounded by even sadder patrons with nowhere else to go on that festive night.

He waited. He peeked out through the curtain. He waited longer. He peeked again, then again. Finally, eighty-nine yards away, his target appeared on a balcony, looking down at the crowd that had gathered in the street below with hopes of hearing a few words from their new hero.

He carefully slid the window open, then picked up the rifle. He leaned in, pushing the curtain aside with the gun's barrel, resting it on the windowsill.

The rifle's bolt felt comfortable in his hand as he pulled it back. One 7.62 x 51mm round rose out of the weapon's magazine and he slid it into the firing chamber as he gently drove the bolt home. He knew he could repeat the process in less than two seconds, and he would be certain to collect his brass from the first shot before leaving—the second still sitting empty and smoking in the weapon's chamber.

He stared through the telescopic scope; his eye found its quarry. *Slow breath in. Hold it.* The bright orange crosshairs located center mass on the target. *Release the air. Squeeze, don't pull.* BLAM!

2

CRASH! Startled, a large black man in a well-used chef's jacket looked up from the industrial cutting table in the brightly lit kitchen. "What the . . . ." Before he could move, he heard laughter erupt; he shook his head.

Stepping around the other kitchen fixtures, he walked through the swinging door and into the simple dining room of Pecos Bill's Bar-B-Que Shack in Shiprock, New Mexico. Facing him were six significantly inebriated young men and an upended table, its plates and broken glasses scattered on the floor. Before he could say a word, the boys sheepishly hustled out the door, half-mumbled, half-giggled apologies following them into the night.

"I've got it, Gus." A slender twenty-year-old dressed in jeans and a Pecos Bill's T-shirt headed for the mess. She had straight, long black hair, dark eyes, and skin colored with her Navajo ancestry.

"No, no." He raised his hand. "I'll take care of it. It's almost eleven and we're closing up."

"But we've still got to clean and prep, don't we?"

"Listen, we're going to let it go. I'm just grateful you were willing to work Christmas Eve for me."

"No problem." She picked up some glasses from another table and headed toward the kitchen. "There's really no one here for me to spend tonight with anyway." She turned her back and pushed through the swinging door. "My roommate, Kai, went home to see her folks."

Putting the glasses down, she looked surreptitiously in the direction of Gus and the dining room. Quickly, she slipped scraps of meat into a Styrofoam container, filling it to the brim. She spoke loudly enough for him to hear her through the door. "And with the road through the pass closed for the winter, it would take me a couple of hours to get all the way around the mountain to my mom's place on the reservation." She snorted gently. "I'm not making that drive tonight. Glad to help."

Gus pushed through the swinging door, a gray plastic bin full of plates and glasses, some broken, in his hands. "Still, I appreciate it and I'm sure the other kids do as well." He chuckled, "Anyway, with only a few tables all night long on a Friday, it's pretty much cleaned up already, right? Plus, we're closed tomorrow; it's Christmas. I'll stop by in the afternoon and prep for Sunday. You get out of here."

"Thanks." Wiping her hands with a stained cleaning rag, the young woman pulled on a heavy wool coat and picked up her purse. With her back to the man, she slipped the container inside the coat. Turning, she gave him a tender look. "Thanks, Gus. And Merry Christmas."

His eyes on a pile of dishes, the words slipped sadly from his lips. "Merry Christmas to you, too, Abby."

~

ABBY WALKED into the frigid night and straight to her old, dented, Chevy Malibu—once a pretty nice car, now strictly transportation. Sliding behind the wheel, she pulled the Styrofoam container out of her coat and laid it on the seat next to her. She turned the key, and the engine coughed to life.

Backing out of her parking space, one of only two cars in the lot, she drove onto a snowy and nearly deserted main street and headed for the area that posed as downtown Shiprock. After only a mile or so, she pulled to the curb, opened the door, and slipped out of the car—Styrofoam container in hand. A few steps down the alley between an empty retail space and a twenty-four-hour convenience store, she leaned down. "It's a cold one tonight, isn't it, boys?"

Two men looked up at her from the base of a faded brick wall, where they sat on a long piece of discarded cardboard. Their faces half-covered by scarves, the steam of their breath escaped in puffs as they spoke. "Cold enough," said one, his voice barely audible. The other added, "Colder than a . . . you know what I mean." His body shook with an apparent chuckle.

Abby pictured the yellow smiles hidden by the tattered rags. "Well, here's something that might make it a little warmer for you, roast pheasant under glass."

The twin heads bobbed while one spoke. "No, girlie, but I'll bet it's some of that Pecos Bill's barbeque, ain't it?"

She smiled. "You got me. That's exactly what it is. Now, how 'bout I go inside and get two large hot coffees. Sound good?"

"Wouldn't hurt," answered the scarf on the left.

Without another word, Abby stepped inside the convenience store and returned a few minutes later with two steaming cups of black java. "Which one of you ordered the caramel macchiato, no whip?"

A gloved hand raised. "That would be me." The man tossed his head in the direction of his colleague. "He's got to watch his weight."

Abby bent to hand them their coffees, then pulled three lottery tickets out of her pocket—holding them up with a wink.

"Bought us a few shots at a better life—one in honor of each of us. Let's hope a little luck comes my way. If it does, I promise I'll be back to share some of it with you. Sound good?"

The scarf on the right answered. "The way I figure, it's about time we had a little luck, and it'd be no surprise if it came through a sweet girl like you."

She stood. "Well, then, let's hope I'll be back in a couple of days with the keys to your brand-new motor home." She grinned. "That way you'll have a warm place to sleep *and* be able to go anywhere you'd like."

She looked around, taking in the men's grim environs, then bent down to put a hand on each man's knee. "You guys have a Merry Christmas, okay?"

A cough rattled in the chest of one of the men while the other responded, "You, too, girlie. Merry Christmas to you."

Abby knew the luck she was talking about was not likely to materialize, but she gave them one last smile, turned, and walked to her car—wishing she'd left it running with the heater on full blast.

hiprock, New Mexico - Friday, January 29th

S Abby blinked. Consciousness returned as if it were morning. She looked around at the blank brown walls, the rows of theater seats, hoping no one had noticed her drifting off. Unconsciously, she checked her chin. *I wasn't drooling, was I?*

Full consciousness took hold. She realized the droning voice of the man at the front of the small lecture hall had, for all practical purposes, put her to sleep. Behind the podium, the speaker's black turtleneck and gray tweed sports jacket were the perfect complement to his short salt and pepper hair and neatly trimmed, graying goatee. The undulating sound of his well-rehearsed presentation, meant to engage and enthrall his audience, had the opposite effect. A stream of seemingly irrelevant images on the screen behind him had only worsened the situation. Three words came into Abby's mind: *Death by PowerPoint.*

Dr. Ansel Wertz had been invited to speak at the Shiprock South Campus of Diné College, the multi-campus college system of the Navajo Nation, located in Arizona and New Mexico. He was addressing students in a comparative religion class. His topic was,

"Western European Justifications for the First Great Crusade, 1090-1096 AD." She'd let out a long, silent breath. *Fascinating stuff.*

Though Abby was a mildly serious college student at best, she had decided a class in comparative religion might be more interesting than some of the other elective courses offered on the campus she attended. She was certain that in today's super-connected world, everyone was more likely to wind up interacting with all kinds of people. Wouldn't it be nice, she felt, to understand a bit about what they believed—even if only a bit?

She pursed her lips. *This guy is too much, rambling on about the first crusade. It's making me crazy.* She raised her hand.

Hers being the first response from the brain-numbed audience, Dr. Wertz stopped his speech in mid-thought, smiled, and directed his attention to her. "Yes, young lady with the black hair and the red sweater. You have a question?"

A thought shot through her mind: *He comes to speak to a group of Navajo students and he thinks identifying the young woman with black hair is going to narrow things down?* Pushing the thought aside, she spoke. "Excuse me, Dr. Wertz, but are you trying to justify a bunch of people a gazillion years ago believing it would be pretty cool to walk from France all the way to Jerusalem to kill the folks who lived there just because they worshiped a different God? I mean, what's the big deal? What if there is no heaven you can get into just by killing a bunch of infidels? Come to think of it, what if there is no hell?"

Wertz was only slightly taken aback, his years of experience in front of rooms filled with captive audiences on full display. Smiling and rubbing his hands together, he said, "Ah, I see we have a bit of a John Lennon fan in the room." He paused as if waiting for laughter; none came.

He continued. "Well, that's an interesting idea, isn't it? And certainly, there are those—agnostics, atheists—who would support that position, wouldn't they? But the vast majority of the peoples in the world do believe in God—some God. They believe in some sort of religion, in some version of heaven and hell—in the possibility of some type of afterlife." He leaned forward over the podium, his voice less pedantic, almost accusatory. "Without those things they feel rudderless, unclear about what the purpose of life is. Wouldn't you agree?"

There was something in his tone that scratched an itch Abby had felt for the last forty minutes or so. She stood up. "Well, what if John Lennon was right about the fact that without countries and religion and all that other stuff, the world wouldn't be in a constant state of war—that there would be nothing for people to have to kill or die for?" The look on her face made it clear she wasn't done. She had just thrown down the gauntlet; she waited for his response.

Wertz shifted into another gear. He was being challenged and, though he smiled condescendingly, Abby could sense him bearing down. "Well, you're muddying the waters here a bit, aren't you, young lady? No countries? No religion? Not quite the same thing, are they? I mean—"

She jumped in. "Perhaps not, Dr. Wertz. Or maybe they are *exactly* the same thing, a group of people tied together for something they perceive as a common good. Tied together by a border or a belief. Tied together to keep themselves separated from some other group of folks. And once they feel separated, really separated, then it's okay for them to try to gain advantage over that other group—and then to hate them—and then to kill them."

Her face felt flushed. "Isn't that what happens? Country against country, religion against religion? When did it start?" She pointed at the screen behind him. "I'll bet," she spit the words out, "it was long before 1090-1096." Her pointing finger morphed into open hands. And how long has it gone on? "Egyptians and Hebrews? Germans and Jews?" Her hands fell to her side; her voice dropped. "Christians and indigenous people?"

The heating system kicked in—the only sound in the room.

Abby could feel every eye glued to her. She could see Wertz rocking back and forth, clearly agitated yet grasping the intensity of the situation—the deep-seated anger which had been pricked in the black-haired students, male and female, who sat in front of him.

Without another word, Abby scooped up her belongings and worked her way down the line of seats toward the aisle and the escape it offered. She felt bad for the two young women she had to crawl over—sorry for the inconvenience, sorry for the attention she was bringing to them. Finally, dragging her scarf along the ground, her books and coat clutched against her chest, she made it to the aisle, then out of the lecture hall and through the doors into the bone-chilling cold of January in northwest New Mexico. What she didn't realize was that she was being followed.

4

"Hey! Hey," someone shouted. "You! The one without a coat! Hold up!"

Abby stopped and turned around, shivering. Running toward her under a bright blue sky was a young man—dark hair, solid build, probably twenty-something. Wearing jeans, an unbuttoned sheepskin jacket, and a big grin, he fit in perfectly with all the other students on the campus. The only thing he was carrying was a steno pad. She braced herself.

Finally catching up with her, his heavy breathing creating puffs of mist in the freezing air, he struggled to speak. "Sorry, sorry. I didn't mean to yell at you." He caught a quick, recuperative breath. "I just wanted to ask you a few questions."

Before she replied, Abby wiped tears off her face with the back of her hand. "Why?" There was an edge in her voice. "Am I in trouble?"

"No, not at all. It's just that I was in the lecture hall with you a few minutes ago and . . . ." His breathing appeared to settle down. "Listen, I'm sorry you're so upset."

"I'm not upset." The words had a bite. "It's this friggin' cold. It makes my eyes water."

His expression implied he might or might not believe her. He extended a hand. "Here, give me those books. Why don't you put your coat on?"

Abby didn't quite know what to make of the guy, but he was right. She was freezing. She handed over the notebook and clunky comparative religion text, then slipped into her eggplant-colored down jacket. While he waited, she ran a hand behind her ear and tipped her head, pulling her hair out of the top of the coat. She wound a maroon and white scarf tight around her neck. A brief shiver wracked her, and she wrapped her arms around her body. She gave him a quick smile. "Thanks."

"Listen, my name's Cliff, Cliff Davis. And you're right. It's freezing out here. Can I buy you a cup of coffee or something?"

Abby was instantly on guard again. "Oh, I don't know. I've got another class."

Cliff glanced at his watch. "Look," he shrugged, "given the fact you walked out of your last lecture early and there's still forty minutes before the next class sessions start, I'm thinking you have time for a quick cup of something that will take the chill out of your body. What do you say?"

Abby looked around, pondering. Remembering all the advice young women were constantly being given about not putting themselves in tricky situations, she took a quick breath. "Okay," she pointed, "but in the student snack bar. The coffee sucks, but it's warm and pretty cheap." She squinted an eye. "And just one cup, right?"

He gave her a big smile. "Sure." He bowed slightly and waved an arm forward, inviting her to lead the way.

They walked together in the bright sun, unconsciously keeping their heads down, neither saying a word. In less than two minutes, they stepped into a brown brick building, through a tiny lobby, and into a room filled with small tables and a few couches and arm chairs. She was grateful for the warmth. Cliff moved in front of her. "Let me get you that coffee. You find us a table, okay?"

Abby watched him walk away. She found a shaky table by a window and somewhat isolated from the handful of students that were already eating or drinking, talking or reading. She slipped off her coat and checked her phone while she waited.

Minutes later, Cliff returned, balancing his coffee and steno pad in one hand, a second cup in the other—two white packets lying on its lid. He put the second cup on the table in front of Abby. "Sorry, I didn't ask if you wanted cream or sugar."

She gave him another brief smile and a quick shrug. "No, black is fine. I'll use the sugar, but all they give you here are those little containers of artificial something that's white. The stuff is probably toxic," she grinned, "maybe even radioactive. We *are* in New Mexico, after all."

He cocked his head, apparently confused.

"The Alamogordo Test Range? The place where they did the first atomic testing ever?"

He ran his fingers through his hair, seemingly still lost.

She flicked a hand. "Never mind." Another tiny smile. "Anyway, thanks for the coffee." She took a careful sip and put the cup back down. "Questions?"

"Huh?

"Questions. You said you had some questions you wanted to ask me. Is this a survey of some kind?"

Cliff chuckled. "No, nothing like that. It's just that I was sitting in on that lecture and watched you stick it to that pompous jerk." A big smile crossed his face as he nodded his approval. "Well done."

"Maybe. It'll probably cost me. I'll most likely wind up flunking the class." She twisted her lips. "Not that I had much chance of passing anyway." She took another sip. "The regular professor is a pretty cool guy, but I guess it turns out that I'm not as interested in all that religious stuff as I thought I might be."

"Got it."

Abby paused, then leaned in. "Now, before I answer any questions, why don't you answer a few yourself?"

Cliff's face brightened. "Sure, shoot."

She took a deep breath. "Okay. First, who are you and what are you doing on campus? I've never seen you here before."

Cliff lifted his cardboard cup to his lips but put it back down before answering, a big smile on his face. "Like I said, my name is Cliff Davis. I'm a reporter with the *Farmington Daily Times*. It covers all the news in the Four-Corners region—Arizona, New Mexico, Utah, Colorado."

Abby furrowed her brows. "You *personally* cover all four states? Isn't that a bit much for one person?"

"Well, no." He grinned. "First, it's not just me, I'm not the only reporter. Second, I didn't say we cover all four states," he created a square with his fingers, "only the little area where they all come together, you know, the four corners. And given that it's out in the middle of nowhere, honestly, it doesn't take all that much covering."

She pushed her hair away from her face. "Are you messing with me?"

Cliff sat back in his chair. "Well, yeah, I guess I am. We do cover this whole region—Farmington, Shiprock, all the way east to Bloomfield."

"And why are you here today?"

"So, you probably heard the college recently received a 1.3 million-dollar grant to build an agricultural multi-purpose center. I was sent up here to do a background story. Honestly, I was just killing time before my next scheduled interview and I saw the notice that there was a guest speaker in your class. I thought he or she might be interesting, so I just dropped in."

Abby took a longer sip, pondering her next question. "And this is your life's dream—being a reporter for The *Farmington Daily Times*?"

A boyish grin slipped across his face. "Actually, no. See, I just graduated from Syracuse University—the Newhouse School of Communication. I studied journalism there, and I wanted to start at the beginning—print news, small city. I want to learn the trade from the bottom up, but there's not a lot of places left to get that kind of experience anymore."

"And that's what brought you to New Mexico?"

"Well," he shrugged, "yeah, I guess."

Abby rocked back and crossed her arms. "And how's that going for you?"

His smile broadened. "Great. I've only been on the job two weeks and I'm sitting at a table ready to ask a true rabble-rouser some important questions—if she'll ever let me get to them."

She considered the man in the seat across from her. On the one hand, he reminded her of Jimmy Olsen, the photographer who worked with Clark Kent at the *Daily Planet*—enthusiastic, idealistic, a little out of his depth. On the other hand, he didn't look like Jimmy Olsen. He looked more like a young George Clooney—dark hair, rugged face, sexy brown eyes, a really nice smile. "Okay. Give me your best shot. What is it you want to ask me?"

5

Cliff Davis opened his steno pad. "First, I guess I should get your name." There was no response for a moment. "Your name?"

"Abby."

"And your age?"

"Twenty."

"Now, Abby, is that short for Abigail?"

She paused before answering. "Abalone."

Cliff looked up from his notes, a question on his face.

She pursed her lips. "It's based on Navajo culture."

He started writing again. "So, Abalone is a Navajo name?"

"In a way." She began tapping quietly on the table with her fingertip. "According to Navajo tradition, the First Man was created out of white corn and minerals of turquoise. The First Woman was created out of yellow corn and minerals of abalone." Her hand relaxed. "My parents are both Navajo, but my dad never wanted to stay on the reservation. When I was born, I guess there was a big battle over my name. In the end, they compromised and named me Abalone after the First Woman, but my mom agreed she wouldn't fight him on calling me Abby."

He kept writing. "And your last name?"

"Duncan."

He looked up again. "Good-old American, right?"

She grimaced silently, disappointed in how tone-deaf the question was. Her voice fell away. "I guess."

Cliff was writing furiously. "So, your folks. Are they still together?" His eyes rose expectantly.

Abby chuckled. "No. They split up when I was six. Mostly, I grew up with my mom, first on the reservation, then here in Shiprock. My dad hung around until I was eighteen." She swirled the coffee in her cup and shrugged. "I saw him a lot. It wasn't terrible. A couple of years ago he moved to Texas to work in the oil and gas fields. That's what he's done all his life. And after I graduated from high school, my mom moved back onto the reservation—said she'd had enough and wanted to be with her people."

"And then—"

"Hey," her voice sharpened, "are these the questions you brought me here to ask?"

"Uh, no, not really." He gathered his thoughts. "So, which one do you consider yourself, agnostic or atheist?"

She looked straight at him. "Christian."

He stopped, pen held motionless above the pad. "Christian? So, all that John Lennon stuff you said in class, you don't honestly believe it?"

Abby pushed her hair out of her face again and let out a long sigh. "No, not really. Look, maybe you're not getting this. It's just that the guy was making me mad, boring me to death. And think about it. Doesn't it sound a little ridiculous to you that a couple thousand men would walk that far, willing to kill people they never knew, who didn't even live near them, all in the name of God?"

He pressed. "True. But I'm more interested in what *you* believe. He made air quotes. "'No countries, no religion,' yet you call yourself a Christian. I mean, are you what some folks refer to as a true believer?"

"Heck, I don't know. I guess. My dad couldn't care less about organized religion, though I've heard him talk about God in a general way. On the other hand, a lot of Navajo people are Christians, maybe twenty percent of those who live on the reservation, and my mom is one of them." She paused, taking a long sip. "Look, at first, Christianity was forced upon the Navajo and other Native Americans," her eyes tightened, "it was a terrible thing—forcing people to abandon not only their cultural heritage but the belief system upon which they based their whole approach to life. But that's not how it is today. My mom's folks, and others back before that, they went to church because they chose to. There are all kinds of Christian churches on the reservation, ten or more at least. My mom dragged me with her to church as a kid and I guess I just always felt like I was supposed to be a Christian."

Cliff hadn't written anything for a while, clearly fascinated. "So, you believe all that stuff, Jesus is the Son of God and all that?"

Abby rocked back in her chair, frustrated, her words rapid-fire: "All I know is that I believe there is a god, some kind of god. Christians say Jesus is the Son of God, that he came to save the world. The Jews just call him a prophet of some sort. The Muslims," she paused, searching the ceiling with her eyes, then grinned sheepishly. "Actually, I have no idea what Muslims believe," she chuckled, "we haven't gotten that far in class yet."

Cliff smiled, and it was clear he was enjoying the conversation, but he remained determined. "Come on now. You call yourself a Christian, but it sounds like you're not really sure about the whole Jesus thing. True?"

Abby shrugged, twisting her lips. "I don't know."

Cliff sat up taller, his eyes focused on her. "You must know what you think. In the end, doesn't everyone have to know what they believe, who they are?"

"Look," she leaned forward, squinting ever so slightly, "does it matter what I think? I told you, I believe in God. What makes me angry is what people *do* in the name of God, tramping across the world to kill folks who do or don't believe in God, or believe in a different God, or whatever."

"Right, but—"

Abby lifted her cup, pushing it toward his face. She turned it upside-down, showing him it was empty. "Time's up. I told you I'd give you one cup of coffee's worth and I did." She grinned. "You're on your own now, paperboy." She put the cup down, stood, and slipped her jacket back on. Scooping up her books with one hand, she wrapped the scarf around her neck with the other and winked. "Thanks for the coffee, and good luck with everything."

Cliff half-rose as she walked away, following her with his eyes. While she was still close, he called out. "Hey, one more question, and it's not about religion."

She turned and looked at him, a confident smile on her face. "What?"

Though it was not visible from their vantage point, he pointed over his shoulder at the giant formation that loomed over the city. "The big rock out there, the one they call Shiprock. Why do they call it that?"

She slowly shook her head and raised the corner of her lip. "I have no idea why *they* call it anything. My people have always called it Tsé Bit' a'i. It means rock with wings."

6

Tempe, Arizona - Wednesday, March 3rd

Ed Jarvis balled a fist in front of his mouth as a bubble of hot gas rolled up from his stomach and silently past his lips. He shook his head; this was the price he paid for those extra jalapeño peppers he had eaten for lunch.

Taking a last sip of the Diet Coke he'd brought back to his desk, he picked up a small stack of newspaper articles paper-clipped together. The note on top of it read: *You might find these interesting.* Pushing on the armrests, he lifted his 230-pound girth out of the chair and tossed the soda cup into an already-over-flowing wastebasket.

The sounds of computer keyboards, conversations, and the occasional ringing phone filled the quasi-modern newsroom of the *Arizona Clarion.* He lumbered toward the office of Marta Escobar, Editor-in-Chief, pausing along the way to quell another, smaller, attack from his stomach.

Ed knocked on the open glass door as he stepped through, not waiting for a response. "Got a sec?" His voice was low and gravely and resonated in his large body.

Marta, an attractive woman in her late forties, dark-haired with just a few stray filaments of gray, glanced up from her desk and gave him a sardonic grin. "I like the splash of color on your tie. Ketchup?"

Confused for an instant, he looked down. "Yeah, I'm really into avant-garde stuff when it comes to sartorial decisions."

She leaned forward, immaculate in her tailored—and spotless—suit. Her next smile was warmer. "What can I do for you, Ed?"

He waved the small stack of clippings. "One of the interns left these for me. I guess she knows I handle religion as well as city and state." He reached across the desk, handing her the top article. "This caught her attention and mine too. Could you look it over when you get a chance?"

Marta's charm bracelet tinkled softly at her wrist as she took the flimsy piece of paper. She rocked back into her chair. "Let me read it now. If I don't," she motioned to the pile of papers and books on her desk, "it'll get lost in the rubble and I'll never get to it."

Ed waited patiently as she scanned the article. One hand in his pants pocket, he shuffled to the wall on her right, glancing over the awards and framed articles that documented the paper's ninety-plus-year history. He turned at her first words.

"Well, that's quite a piece, beautifully written." She grinned at him slyly. "And it seems the reporter was seriously taken with the interviewee." She raised her chin as she read in a sultry voice. "Beautiful, bourbon-toned skin, dark pools for eyes, surrounded by an aura of authentic truth." She stopped. "This Cliff Davis guy can write."

"Oh," Ed checked his tie again, "he can really shovel it all right. But what do you think about the article itself?"

Marta rocked her head and shoulders back and forth. "Not Pulitzer Prize stuff, of course, but somewhat interesting. You thinking of re-running it?"

"Listen, you know I'm always scrambling to find stuff to fill that hole. I made a call and checked the guy out. He's right out of Syracuse, only been in Farmington a month or so. But it is kind of an unusual angle—young girl takes on a professor by referencing John Lennon. Then there's the indigenous peoples' angle on things. I don't know. I think it could fly in a paper with larger circulation, like ours. What's your opinion?"

Marta sat pondering, bright red nails clicking against her lipstick-smudged ceramic cup. Finally, she shrugged. "It's your beat, Ed. If you have nothing better to run and you want to give it a try, I'm okay with that. Can't be any less interesting than some other things you have to go with."

Shiprock, New Mexico – Thursday, April 1ˢᵗ

Abby climbed out of her old Chevy. With the temperature in the low seventies, the day was a pleasant change from the much colder weather she'd faced most of the winter. Walking up to the shoddy two-story apartment building in which she lived, she could hear heavy-metal rock music blasting from the open window in one of the other apartments. She shook her head. *College life. What are you going to do?*

Stepping inside her tiny two-bedroom apartment, Abby greeted her roommate, Kai. In the Navajo culture, her name meant willow, and it fit perfectly the lithe, waif of a girl with flowing black hair and a quick smile. Abby tossed a question at her. "Well, Ms. Nez, any mail for us today?"

Kai was standing in the apartment's cramped kitchenette and appeared to have a grilled cheese sandwich in a pan. Abby was relatively certain she was waiting for the moment when the cheese would be delectably melted, yet not too hot to eat. Kai looked up. "There are a couple of things for you over there."

Abby turned. Surrounded by gray walls upon which several

posters covered a multitude of housing sins, a sad maroon sofa and matching armchair sat on a tile floor. In front of the couch sat an equally despondent coffee table. On it, Abby found a TV remote, an empty, crumb-filled plate, uncountable rings from wet glasses, and three envelopes. She picked up the mail.

"Anything interesting?" Kai asked.

"Something from the college, probably a bill. And one from some charity I sent five dollars to once. The last one is from the University of Arizona." She threw all three back on the table unopened.

Kai's eyes remained focused on her sandwich. "What's that one about?"

"Which one?"

"The one from Arizona."

"Probably just the university recruiting folks, trying to get more students—maybe more native students."

Kai lifted her masterpiece out of the pan. "Open it. Maybe they're offering some kind of scholarship you could apply for. You never know."

"Right," Abby's voice dripped with sarcasm, "I am, after all, on the dean's list."

Kai looked at her, surprise in her eyes. "You are?"

"Yeah, the list of students who won't be allowed to return next semester if their grades don't improve."

Kai shook her head. "Go ahead. Open it. What the heck."

Abby plopped down on the couch. The battered cushions sank under her slight weight. She tore the envelope, retrieved a single sheet of paper, and read in silence. After a long moment, one word slipped from her lips. "Unreal."

Still standing in the kitchen, Kai licked a yellow glob of melted cheese off her fingertip. "What?"

"You won't believe this, but I've been invited to come to Tucson."

"To go to school?"

"No, to take part in some dumb conference. They're going to pay for all my expenses, including room and food."

Kai wiped her lips with a dish towel. "No kidding."

"And," Abby's face lit up, "they say they'll give me an honorarium of two hundred and fifty dollars."

Kai's eyes widened. "Get out."

Abby waved the piece of paper at her. "Read 'em and weep, girl. Two hundred and fifty bucks." Her gaze returned to the letter.

Kai walked over and sat in the lopsided maroon chair. "So, what's the conference about?"

Abby was silent for a moment while she read. "Uh, gross." She looked up. "You ready for this?" She slipped into her best professorial voice. "Are Modern Religious Frameworks Sufficient for Today's Challenge?"

"Huh?"

"You heard me. It's one of those fancy symposiums in which a bunch of smart folks get together and talk about nothing but make it sound important."

Kai waited a moment then asked, "And why would they invite you?"

"No idea, lady. No idea. And I'm not going, either. I don't need anything to do with that. I'd just embarrass myself."

Kai sat up. "Really, you're going to pass up a trip to Tucson, all expenses paid, and two hundred and fifty dollars just for being part of some boring conversation? It can't be any worse than sitting through those comparative religion classes you're in."

Abby thought for a moment. "Oh, yeah. I have been taking that class all semester," she dropped her chin and looked directly at Kai, "not that I actually study any of it." She huffed. "And now I'm supposed to sit with all those professors and straighten out any misconceptions they may have about today's religious," she glanced at the paper in hand, "frameworks?"

Kai placed the last piece of grilled cheese sandwich in her

mouth and headed for the refrigerator. Opening the door, she took out a can of soda and popped it open. "Still. Sounds to me like it's too good to pass up."

7

Tucson, Arizona - Saturday, June 5
The air conditioner kicked on, waking Abby from a restless sleep. Rolling over, away from the blanketed body on the other side of the king-sized bed, her bleary eyes tried to focus on the red numerals that taunted her. 5:15 AM. *Crap.*

She wanted desperately to sleep longer, but her stomach was roiling and it felt like every nerve in her frame was doing some sort of spooky Halloween dance. Her body demanded she move.

Sliding out of bed, she almost tripped over clothing strewn haphazardly on the floor as she stumbled through the darkness to the room's large picture window. She pulled the long rod which hung from the wall-length curtains, drawing them slowly open. An incredible vista of reds and pinks rewarded her effort as billowy clouds completed the beauty of the Arizona sunrise.

She turned, taking in the spacious room at the Marriott Hotel on the edge of the University of Arizona campus. The gracious people who were running this year's "Conversations on Religion and Spirituality in Our Lives" event had paid for it. Huge bed, dresser, forty-six-inch TV, a bold and colorful pattern on the wall —it was not the type of lodging she was accustomed to. The room had a small couch to go along with the coffee and tea station which sat above the miniature refrigerator and below the tiny microwave. She noted there was even a mini-bar, though she wondered if the sponsors of the event had asked that it be emptied during her stay. She hadn't bothered to check.

She walked to the couch and sat. On the coffee table in front of her were two books, *The World's Religions*, by Huston Smith and *Comparative Religion for Dummies*. The first, purchased second-hand for her class, she had brought with her—as if a quick perusal of the book's 450 pages could prepare her for what she was about to face. The other she had picked up when she realized the futility of her initial plan.

The air conditioner kicked off, leaving her wishing she had some bad habits. A stiff drink sounded good, something to soothe her nerves, but the alcoholism which plagued so many Native American communities had long ago convinced her to avoid that trap. She closed her eyes and pictured herself sitting motionless on the couch, deeply inhaling a puff of white smoke from a calming cigarette. She could almost see its red ember glowing in the dim light of the room. Unfortunately, she didn't smoke—never had. Instead, she simply sat there, drifting in and out of consciousness. *How did I ever get myself into this mess?*

A few minutes before seven, the alarm on her phone pinged, startling her. The words slipped quietly across her lips. "What was I thinking?" She bolted off the couch and strode to the bed. "Kai, Kai. Wake up." She shook her friend. "We're getting out of here. Come on. Get up. We've got to get moving."

Propping herself up on an elbow, still groggy, Kai looked at her through squinted eyes. "What? We're leaving?"

Abby moved quickly through the room, snatching clothes off the floor, tossing them onto the bed in a wrinkled mound. "That's right. Now. Get up. We're going."

Kai sat up. "We can't do that. You'll get in trouble."

"Watch me."

Kai's gaze followed Abby as she flew around, grabbing things, throwing her battered suitcase onto the bed near her pile of clothing.

"But they already paid for the room and the big dinner you bought last night."

Abby's head whipped toward her. "And you ate half of."

Kai sat up, pulling her knees to her chest and locking her arms around them. "Abby, I'm telling you this is a bad idea. Just go through with the stupid thing and collect your money. So what if you embarrass yourself? We won't know any of these people. Just do it. Get it over with, then we'll get the heck out of here."

Abby was already in the bathroom gathering her toiletries. Her voice echoed off the tiled walls and floor. "No way. I'm not sitting on that podium with a bunch of stuck-up people who think they know all about God,"—she popped her head out of the tiny room and looked directly at Kai—"and then have them say," her voice dropped an octave, "'Ms. Duncan, what are your thoughts on the topic?'"

Kai slipped out of bed and walked into the bathroom. She stood behind her friend, both of their images appearing in the large mirror. She put her hands on Abby's shoulders and spoke gently. "Listen to me. You can do this. Please don't mess yourself up." Her tone turned edgier as they watched each other's reflection. "They asked you to come. They asked for your opinion. Give it to them. What do you have to lose? You have the right to believe whatever you want and if they don't like what you say, that's their problem."

"Are you not listening to—" The room phone rang; Abby stood motionless.

Kai nodded toward the sound. "You going to answer that?"

Abby shook her head.

It rang again. Kai huffed and walked out to the nightstand. She lifted the receiver as Abby stepped out of the bathroom as well. "Hello?" Kai listened for a moment, then held the phone out toward Abby.

Seconds passed before Abby took the receiver. She spoke, the word barely audible. "Hello?"

"*Ms. Duncan. Dr. Susan Sterling here, with the Religion and Spirituality Department.*" The voice was all light and sunshine. "*So glad you made it here safely last night. Everything okay with your room?*"

"Uh, yeah. Sure. Everything's fine."

"*Wonderful.*" The woman paused a moment, then continued. "*Listen, some of us made arrangements to get together for breakfast this morning, before the early session, and I wanted to invite you to join us. In fact, a few of us early birds are already down here in the lobby, ready for our first cup of coffee. We'd love the opportunity to meet you before the conference actually begins. Any chance you could be here in, say, half-an-hour or so?*"

Abby froze, realizing some woman she'd never met, never wanted to meet, had torpedoed her escape plan.

"*Ms. Duncan?*"

"Uh . . . sure. I guess I could be down there in thirty or forty minutes. How will I know who you are?"

"*Don't worry, dear. I'll recognize you by the photo you sent in with your acceptance of our invitation. All you have to do is step off the elevator and walk out onto the patio. We'll take care of the rest. See you in a few.*" The phone went dead.

Kai looked at Abby. "Trapped?"

"Like a mouse cornered by a cat—waitin' to get swatted around—then eaten."

8

I t was almost eight fifteen before Abby stepped out of the wood and chrome elevator, wearing indigo jeans, sandals, and a soft yellow top. She walked through the hotel lobby and onto the patio, where she found ten or twelve people sitting at small tables and couches surrounded by a high privacy fence and beautiful palm trees. Some had plates of food in front of them, others nothing more than a coffee cup.

A surprisingly tall, gray-haired woman in a tailored dress with swirls of blues and greens popped out of her seat and walked directly toward Abby. Slender, almost too thin, her bright blue eyes shone like high-beams on an automobile. Though she was clearly Anglo, her affinity for the turquoise jewelry that Navajo and other Native Americans often considered sacred was on full display. "Ms. Duncan," she extended her hand, "welcome to Tucson. I'm Dr. Susan Sterling."

Abby smiled as warmly as she could. "Thank you. It's a pleasure to be here."

Without asking, Dr. Sterling took her by the elbow and changed her direction. "Let's get you something to eat from the concierge lounge." She half-pulled Abby with her. "It's just the

classic hotel continental breakfast, but they do a marvelous job
with it. You can even make yourself a waffle or pancake if you'd
like." She let go of Abby's arm, turned, and winked at her. "I'm
more of an eggs benedict with a mimosa on the side kind of girl,
but this will do." A few steps into the building, she asked, "How
was your trip down?"

"Fine. It's a long drive, but easy and relatively pleasant. We," a
tiny shudder ran through her shoulders, "I mean *I* actually
enjoyed it."

Dr. Sterling gave her a quick, curious glance. "Good, good."

A minute or two later, they stood in a tiled area bordered on
each side by a cornucopia of breakfast foods. Dr. Sterling turned
to Abby. "Doesn't that enormous tray of fresh fruit look wonderful?" Without waiting for a response, she picked up a chilled
plate and dove in.

Abby followed, ambling along the counter, wanting to pile
fruit, and eggs, and sausage, and a sweet roll on her own plate.
Unfortunately, the nerves in her stomach told her she'd be lucky
to keep cold cereal and coffee down. She compromised, going
with the fruit and cereal and adding the largest cup of coffee the
hotel offered.

As she sat in the pleasant morning air eating breakfast, Abby
found herself explaining the details of her current life: school at
Diné College; work as a server at Pecos Bill's Bar-B-Que Shack.
Eventually, she found an opportunity to ask the question that had
been bugging her for over a month. "So, how is it you decided to
invite me to be part of this thing?" Her finger tapped on the table
as she waited for a response.

"Oh, Ms. Duncan," Dr. Sterling caught herself, "can I call you
Abby?"

"Sure."

She continued. "It was that article in the *Arizona Clarion*." Her
eyes drifted upward. "I think it might have been a reprint from
some smaller paper." Her gaze re-engaged with Abby's. "Whatev-

er." She shrugged gently. "Anyway, it was very refreshing. Apparently, you gave that visiting lecturer a serious talking to. And I just loved reading about how you used John Lennon's thoughts from the 1970s to challenge the religious thinking of the eleventh century." She winked at Abby again, leaning in. "I was quite the Beatles fan myself in the day." Her eyes rose again as she touched her chin with her finger. "Although, I guess that's not really a Beatles song, is it?"

Still confused about why she was at the conference, and unaware of what article Dr. Sterling was referring to, Abby shook her head. "I don't think so. I'm pretty sure my dad had the album with that same title. It was a solo album as far as I can remember."

"One way or the other," Dr. Sterling continued, "I can't wait to hear your prepared remarks on today's challenges, you know, from a different, young person's, perspective."

Abby's mind freaked. *Prepared remarks? They never asked for prepared remarks. Holy crap!* She felt her stomach cramp. *I don't have anything ready.* She tried her best to hide the panic that was bouncing through every square inch of her body. *Oh, crap, crap, crap!*

Dr. Sterling, who had already scarfed down her food, stood up abruptly. "Listen, I've got to go and check on things, make sure everything's just right for all you speakers." She gave Abby a warm smile, one full of obvious expectation. "You enjoy your breakfast, young lady. I'll meet you inside."

JUST BEFORE NINE O'CLOCK, Abby walked into the large event room. Taking in the beige walls and brown carpet with random squiggly lines of yellow and orange, she stopped in her tracks when she saw the space was filled with two or three hundred chairs. They faced a low portable stage with five stools and a podium on it. She squirmed when she admitted to herself one of those stools was for her. She took out her phone and sent Kai a text. PLS PACK OUR STUFF AND PUT IT IN THE CAR. I WANT TO GET OUT OF HERE AS SOON AS THIS THING IS OVER. C U AROUND 12.

~

PROMPTLY AT NINE, Dr. Sterling started the program. After welcoming the event participants, she began her introductions. "And now I'd like to introduce the members of our panel."

She worked her way down the platform. First, she introduced Reverend John Singleton, a pastor from Colorado and the author of several books on contemporary Christianity in post-modern America. His hip gray shirt, white tie, and black pants convinced Abby he was probably the leader of one of the new-style Christian churches with a worship band, gigantic video screens, and high-tech lighting.

She came next to Imam Asim Afzal, a bearded man who Dr. Sterling said had been on the panel several years in the past and was also a well-known author. Along with his khakis and flowing linen shirt, he wore a white crocheted kufi and a big smile.

Rabbi Rebecca Cohen was introduced third. Her white shirt, man's tie, and brown jacket gave Abby the impression that the woman might be pleasant but was most likely not a barrel of laughs. After an illustrious career with many Jewish service organizations, Rabbi Cohen now researched and wrote about the Jewish faith as practiced around the world.

Dr. Sterling smiled at Abby, then turned back to the audience. "Finally, our last guest is Abby Duncan." Even from behind, Abby could sense the woman's enthusiasm. "A student at Diné College in Shiprock, New Mexico, Ms. Duncan has recently been recognized as a fresh voice in the fields of religion and spirituality. I'm certain you will find her thoughts well-grounded in the artistic expressions of the younger generation and that she shares a refreshing perspective." She turned again, for no apparent reason, and grinned at Abby.

Abby tried her best to smile at the audience in the same way the other presenters had, but all she could think about was what a load of crap Dr. Sterling had just dumped on those people. *A new voice? A refreshing perspective? Who is she kidding? And is it a young person's perspective she's looking for or that of a* Navajo *young woman?* Abby's heart sank into her stomach.

"And without further ado," Dr. Sterling said, "let's begin."

The audience clapped politely, and Abby became distinctly aware of people opening notebooks and laptops, clearly ready to record the wisdom which would flow in torrents off the temporary stage upon which she sat, dying inside. Rev. Singleton started things off. Speaking of the times in which Jesus lived, he made point after point about the parallels between the challenges people and societies face now and the difficulties which threatened those who Jesus and his disciples had addressed.

Next came Rabbi Cohen. As austere as Abby had imagined, she spoke of the special covenant God had made with the Hebrew people and how that covenant, and the Hebrew's successes and failures in living up to it, were meant to be a model to all other cultures and communities in the world. Her closing remarks focused on how following the admonitions given to the Hebrews through God's scriptures and his prophets would have made life better not only for them but for everyone in today's world. It all struck Abby as pretty much right on target.

Pleasantly funny and light-hearted, Imam Afzal led his audience through a thumbnail sketch of Islamic thought, particularly the five pillars: a profession of faith in Allah, and accepting Muhammad as his prophet; daily prayer; fasting; charity; and a pilgrimage to Mecca once in a person's lifetime, if possible.

Abby enjoyed listening to the man until her brain could no longer block out the fact that when he finished, it would be her turn. As he moved beyond the five pillars, her mind drifted, lost in confusion and the fear of what she was about to face. She even startled herself when the voice in her head whispered words which suddenly seemed incredibly appropriate. *Oh, God, please help me.*

The wave of applause which greeted the completion of Imam Afzal's comments woke Abby from her reverie. It was followed by the instructions that tumbled out of Dr. Sterling's mouth. ". . . and after a break, we will reconvene in this same room for questions and answers. Later, after lunch, you'll be able to choose one of our break-out sessions in which we hope you might continue your discussions." She smiled at Abby once more. "And now, Ms. Abby Duncan."

9

It took every ounce of strength Abby could muster to get up and out of her chair. The podium seemed both a hundred yards away and right in her face. Without knowing how, she found herself standing behind it, reflexively tapping the microphone as if it might have stopped working in the thirty seconds since Dr. Sterling had used it to introduce her.

She swallowed. *Okay, girl. Let's do this.* She closed her eyes and slowly released her breath. She knew the words would come to her—in a moment.

She licked her lips. Another quick breath in. *Let it out. Not yet.*

Scanning the audience, she no longer saw a crowd of people. There were individual faces. They were waiting. Each one of them. Waiting and staring at her. It felt as if they were all leaning forward, toward her—at her.

The room had become silent—not quiet—silent. Only the low hum of the air conditioning and the tiny buzz of the overhead lights were audible. Abby's skin crawled.

Come on, lady. Say something. Oh, God. Say something.

A quick breath, another swallow, and the words slowly,

painfully worked their way up from her torso—into her mouth—past her lips—into the room. "God loves you."

Silence. Stillness. Hundreds of eyes staring at her. "God loves you. He loves you."

More silence. More stillness. Her hands shaking.

She wasn't sure why, but Abby turned and looked directly at Rev. Singleton, then Imam Afzal, then Rabbi Cohen. Finally, her eyes rested plaintively on Dr. Sterling. Each of them hung expectantly on her next words.

They came. "God loves you." It felt personal.

Frightened and overwhelmed, she looked back at the audience, then smiled at them.

She couldn't stand the pressure any longer. Leaving the podium, she walked quickly to her chair, grabbed her purse, then turned and hurried off the stage. The smallest ripple of sound buzzed in the room.

She strode up the aisle. Each row of listeners seemed to come to life as she passed them. They turned in their chairs and watched her. The audience became an ocean of curious faces. The sound of voices grew from a hushed whisper to a rumble of mumbled questions.

"Did you see that?"

"What was that about?"

"Who is that?"

As she approached the exit, a man opened the door and held it so she might pass hurriedly by.

She was in the lobby now, running—running for her life.

"Abby, Abby. Abby, it's me." Kai's voice was strained, confused, worried. She was running behind Abby. "Where are you going?"

Abby spun around. "Home, Kai. We're going home." She started running again, panicked. "Come on. Please. Please. Come on. Let's get out of here." She kept running—out of the building, across the parking lot, trying to remember where her car was parked—not sure if Kai was behind her or not.

As they drove out of town, Kai at the wheel of Abby's car, they headed up AZ-77 North. After a long silence, Abby was the first to speak. "Why were you there?"

Kai looked at her, then back at the road. "Where?"

"In the lobby, exactly when I needed you to be. What were you doing there?"

"Duh, I was there because you were there. You didn't think I'd miss the chance to watch you on that stage, did you—find out what you were going to say?"

Abby turned to the passing desert; browns, grays, and oranges flew past her eyes. Fist clenched in front of her mouth, she chewed lightly on her finger. A full minute passed before she spoke again. "Thanks for being there. No telling where I would have wound up if you hadn't been."

"Sure. I saw the whole thing, you know. I caught part of that imam speaking. That was cool. But when it was your turn, dang, I was dying for you."

"I was stupid, wasn't I?"

The next response was immediate. "No, you weren't stupid. You were just somewhere you shouldn't have been, somewhere you never wanted to be, and I'm sorry."

Abby looked at her roommate, her friend. "For what?"

Kai kept her eyes on the road. "For talking you into accepting the invitation in the first place. You didn't want to go, but I made a big deal out of your getting two hundred and fifty dollars and all the other free stuff." She shook her head. "Wasn't worth it—never was."

Abby let out a long breath. "No, it was my own decision. Nobody—" Her phone rang with the sound of an old fashioned telephone. She glanced at the screen.

Before Abby could say anything, Kai asked, "Tucson?"

Abby pushed her hair out of her face. "Yeah."

"You're not going to answer it?"

"No." Abby canceled the call.

Kai checked her mirror. "What if they're mad at you for leaving? What if they come after you for the money?"

Abby shrugged. "They paid for the room and food, but they can't cut a check until you do what you're supposed to do." She looked out the side window. "Guess that's one check that's not going to be," she made air quotes, "in the mail."

"Guess not."

Neither woman spoke again for a while. Finally, Kai broke the silence. "So, what now? Will you get back to that Dr. Sterling? Apologize—tell them you were feeling sick or something?"

Abby shook her head gently. "Nope. Just going back home and forgetting the whole thing."

"Really?" Kai gave her a quick glance. "Like it never happened?"

"That's right. Look, we're on summer break. I'm just—" Her phone rang again. She canceled the call and continued. "I'm going to ask Gus if I can pick up some more hours at Bill's. If he gives them to me, I'll just put in my time, save up for next semester, and hope that you and I have a little fun every once in a while—maybe do some camping."

The sounds of the road filled the silence between them. Eventually, Kai asked, "So, what you said up there on that stage, do you believe that?"

Abby thought before she answered. "I guess."

"You believe that God loves you?"

"Yeah, I guess most folks do, don't they?"

Kai checked her rearview mirror. "And all that stuff about Jesus—you believe that too?"

Abby wagged her head, frustrated. "Why does everyone want to know what I believe? Can't I simply float along here doing the best I can? Do I have to act like those people on stage today, all puffed up and dead certain that they have all the answers? Do I —" Her phone rang again. She spit the words out. "Enough of that." She turned the device off and shoved it into her pocket. What she couldn't turn off were the questions in her mind.

10

Shiprock, New Mexico - Sunday, June 6th

"Abby?" Kai knocked softly on her roommate's bedroom door. "Abby? You awake?"

Having slept-in after an eight-hour car trip and a restless night, Abby rolled over in her still-darkened room. "Yeah, I'm awake. Come on in."

Kai walked in holding out her phone. "Hey, you've got to see this. It's on YouTube." She hopped onto her friend's bed. "Check this out."

Abby's eyes struggled to focus at first, but it didn't take long for her to figure out what she was looking at. "Give me that." She grabbed the device out of Kai's hand.

What she saw was a phone video taken from the rear of the event room in Tucson. The rumble of the air conditioning and the buzz of the overhead lights were the only sounds that supported the image of Abby standing silently at the podium, looking desperately ill-at-ease. Finally, barely audible words came out of her mouth. "God loves you." The picture jiggled. "God loves you. He loves you." The last syllables rattled out of the tiny speaker as she turned to the other speakers. "God loves you."

The camera then began tracking Abby as she walked across the stage, hurried up the aisle, and ran out of the room. Mumbled questions arose from the audience as they twisted in their seats. The video ended abruptly.

She stared at the frozen image. "Who took this? Where'd it come from?"

Kai tilted her head. "Really? You don't know that anything that ever happens anywhere is on somebody's phone? Obviously, it was a person sitting in the audience, someone who expected you to say something smart and interesting. Once you got going," she grinned, "he or she realized what they had was way cooler than that."

Abby took in a deep breath and let it out. "Right. A person making a fool of herself." She slipped out of bed, opened the window blinds, then walked to the mirror sitting on top of her second-hand dresser. Examining the circles under her eyes, she spoke. "And now there's probably a couple hundred people getting their jollies watching me do just that."

"Oh, yeah? Think again." Kai smiled sadly. "Do you know how many views this video has gotten already?"

Abby turned to Kai, her brows squeezed together.

"Over six thousand and growing. Looks like you've become a YouTube star, lady. You're going viral."

A sigh slipped past Abby's lips as her chin dropped to her chest. "That is not a good thing." She grabbed a brush off the top of the dresser and began brushing her hair, frustration powering every stroke.

Kai rose and stood behind her. "Don't worry about it. Videos like this come and go." She shook her head. "Remember, at any given moment, there are millions of people watching millions of things on YouTube. Could be not a single person you know will ever see it." She turned and walked out of the room, speaking over her shoulder. "Come on, let's get something to eat."

Abby hung back, trying to release the knot in her stomach.

Why is this happening to me? I'm no religious do-gooder, and I certainly wasn't trying to create problems for anyone. She let out a deep sigh. *I just wish everyone would let this be.*"

Kai called from the kitchen. "You coming?"

"I'll be there in a sec." She glanced in the mirror and whispered, "I'm doing the best I can."

ABBY HAD HUNG around her apartment until two thirty that afternoon, reading, thinking, and ignoring phone calls from Tucson. By then, she'd had enough of beating herself up over her performance on Saturday and was ready to get out of the apartment and head off to work.

Working the four-to-closing shift, she was glad the Sunday evening crowd was all Gus had hoped for. The busier she stayed, the less chance she would have time to think about Saturday's events.

Though the place shut down at eleven, Abby knew she would have to stay at least an additional forty-five minutes to clean and prep for the next day. As usual, Gus turned up the volume on the TV and let the local news play while the crew worked alongside him. Abby didn't mind. She rarely paid much attention to current events, and she figured it was good for her to catch up on things every once in a while. What reached her ears while she was cleaning tables, however, caught her off guard.

Gus had tuned the TV to a local affiliate coming out of Roswell. As was always the case, near the end of the half-hour show, the weekend anchor teased a human-interest piece. "Over in Tucson this week, some participants in a religion and spirituality conference at the university had a *spiritual* experience of their own. Stay with us. We'll be right back with the story."

Abby froze. Desperately hoping the newsman meant something else, she realized there was every chance he was referring to her debacle. Mindlessly wiping tables, the three minutes of commercials she had to endure seemed to take an eternity.

The anchor returned, a brown-haired young man in a pink sports jacket that looked too large for him. "The Department of Religion and Spirituality at the University of Arizona held its annual conference Saturday, and many of those who attended got quite a surprise. Joanna Cortez, from our sister station in Tucson, has the story."

Abby stopped wiping and stared as a bright-eyed young reporter with a bouncy, professional hairstyle followed. "This past weekend, participants came from all over to listen to and chat with noted authors from several religious traditions: Hebrew, Muslim, Christian. They were also hoping to hear from a New Mexico college student named Abby Duncan—and hear from her they did. It might have been short and sweet, but some believe what she said was inspired."

An image of a tall woman wearing lots of turquoise jewelry appeared on the screen. At the bottom, the graphic read: Dr. Susan Sterling, University of Arizona. She spoke into the microphone a reporter held up to her. "It was the most amazing thing. We had invited some renowned experts from the three largest Abrahamic traditions, respected authors in their fields. The information they brought was important and insightful. But when that young lady, that Abby Duncan, began to speak, something wonderful, almost mystical, took place."

The image changed, showing Abby at the podium in Tucson. It was not video from someone's phone. This was high-quality, close-up video apparently shot by a professional, one most likely hired by the university.

As Abby watched herself standing silently in front of two or three hundred people, Dr. Sterling's voice continued. "It was as if some incredible spirit filled the room, drawing every heart and mind to what she was saying. And for all the articulate ideas and important information the other presenters brought to the table, her words," she sighed, "her words cut to the core of what we were trying to grapple with at the event—the very essence of why we care about religion and spirituality in the first place."

Abby's recorded voice displaced Susan's. "God loves you. God loves you. He loves you." Abby saw herself turn to the others on the podium. "God loves you." Then she watched as she grabbed her things, left the stage, and quickly left the room.

The face of the young reporter popped back onto the screen. "As you can imagine, reactions in the audience varied, but for some," she nodded and smiled, "the experience was more than anything they had ever hoped for out of the conference. Joanna Cortez, reporting for Eyewitness News."

As the reporter's face gave way to the pink-jacketed anchor, Abby's mind crashed back into the present. Spinning around, she was relieved when it appeared no one else on the floor had been paying the slightest bit of attention to the television.

Abby kept her head down as she hurriedly wiped down the last few tables, then walked to the kitchen. Steam from the dishwasher and the smell of disinfectant filled the air around her as she tossed her cleaning rags into the appropriate pile, clocked out, grabbed her purse, and headed for the restaurant's rear door. Convinced she would make it out of the building before anyone could ask any questions, she stopped mid-step when her eyes landed on Gus.

Standing near the exit, a large meat cleaver in his hand, he was staring at her. Frozen, she waited for his words to impale her. When he made no effort to speak, Abby girded herself, then walked silently past him and into the night.

11

A s Abby walked into her apartment, she hoped to leave the TV news story behind her—desperately wishing no one who knew her had seen it. Kai and her boyfriend, Jamie, were sitting on the couch, and from the looks on their faces she knew her wish had not come true. She stopped just inside the doorway. "You saw it?"

Kai nodded. Jamie, blonde-haired, blue-eyed, and big enough to play on any college football team, ran a hand through his shoulder-length mane. "Sure did. Man," he shook his head, "that was one weird scene."

Abby walked over to the armchair, dropped her purse on the floor, and sank into the sagging seat. "Yeah, you could say that."

Kai sat up taller. "You okay? Can I get you something?"

"I'm fine. It's just that . . . ."

Kai waited a couple of beats then asked, "It's just that what?"

Abby's eyes reached out for understanding. "It's just that the whole thing is such a mess." Her pace picked up. "I never wanted to go there. I never meant to get people riled up. And now, this Dr. Sterling, she's turning it all into a big deal. She's making it sound as though I'm some religious expert or something. I'm not. I never said I was." She slumped further into the chair. "I never said anything like that."

Jamie sipped the drink he was holding. "Bummer."

A painful silence filled the room as Kai stood and walked to the refrigerator. She retrieved a can of soda, popped open the top, and brought it to her roommate without a word.

"Thanks." Abby took a long drink.

Kai sat back down next to Jamie. "Can I ask you a question, a serious question?"

"Sure."

"That Dr. Sterling, she said a lot of the folks in the room thought it was some kind of spiritual experience, that something special happened when you were up there on stage. Did it?" She hesitated. "Did it feel that way to you?"

Abby looked at her for a long time before she answered. "I don't know. I mean, at first, I was just scared, afraid I didn't have anything important to say—afraid I was going to make a fool out of myself."

Kai twisted the ends of her hair. "Then?"

"Well, it was strange. I can't describe it. It's like the words just came to me—as though I hadn't thought of them myself." She shook her head. "I don't know if I said them because I thought they were important or because I couldn't think of anything else to say. I mean, I heard them in my mind, in my own voice, but it was almost like they weren't my words—that they were coming from someone else." Again, her eyes reached out for solace. "Does that make any sense to you?"

"I guess so." Kai looked to Jamie as if hoping for some support, then turned back to Abby. "I mean, sometimes I hear myself say things I don't expect—like I surprise myself by what I'm saying." She pondered for a moment. "I guess what's important is this: do you believe what you said? Do you believe God loves all the people in that room, each one of them?"

Abby flashed her response. "No, that's not the question. It's not a matter of what *I* believe. Who cares what *I* believe? The question is, where did those words come from? Why were those the words that came out of my mouth? Why did some of those people, Dr. Sterling and the others, why did they believe it was such a big deal?" Tears slipped from her eyes and down her cheeks. "And why is this happening to me? I never wanted any of this to happen. And what the heck is tomorrow going to bring? I've been dodging Sterling for two days now, and with the story on the TV . . . ." She let out a deep sigh. "God knows what's going to happen next."

Drink in hand, Abby stood and headed for her bedroom. As she passed Kai, her dearest friend reached out, squeezing Abby's elbow. "Whatever it brings, I'll be here for you. I'll help you through it."

To Abby's surprise, the next words came from Jamie. "Me too, Abby. Anybody gives you any trouble, you give me the word. I'll take care of it."

Abby was pretty certain this brawny young man had no idea what she was going through, but she appreciated the support. She smiled at him. "Thanks, Jamie. I know I can count on you."

A FEW MINUTES LATER, Abby lay on her bed, looking at the ceiling. One hand held the half-consumed can of soda; the other held the phone she had turned to for distraction. But no amount of scrolling through TickToc and Instagram had turned her mind away from the question clawing at her. Finally, in a hushed voice, she did something she hadn't done in a long time.

"God, if you exist, could you help me understand what happened this weekend? Was that something special, or am I just someone who's so dumb the only thing she could think to say was, 'God loves you?' Please, if you're really there, if you do love

me, could you help me out—could you help me understand—
could you make all of this just go away?"

A lbuquerque, *New Mexico – Monday, June 7th*
        Alan Emmons, News Director at KAQE-TV in Albu-
querque, reached across the desk and picked up his phone. He
punched in three numbers. A voice chirped a single syllable out
of the handset and he responded. "Hey, Lydia. Listen, I saw a
piece on the eleven o'clock out of Roswell last night. It was about
a young woman from Shiprock who made a big splash at some
religion and spirituality conference." He paused, listening, then
went on. "Do me a favor. Look into that and see what you can find
out." He listened again. "Good. Try to get back to me sometime
this morning if possible."

～

LYDIA DOLE WALKED down the hall in her tailored blue pinstripe
skirt, white blouse, and dark blue pumps. A former mentor had
told her to dress for the job she wanted, and she wanted the job
currently held by the man she was on her way to see. She stepped
into his office. "Got something for you, Al."

Apparently, the same mentor had not tutored Alan Emmons.

His wrinkled white shirt clung to his thin body, as did the smell of his cheap cologne. A sports jacket and tie were casually draped over a wooden hanger that hung from the bookshelf near his enormous desk. Several gold figurines and framed documents representing awards for excellence in journalism were scattered around the spacious office.

Lydia would have preferred to lay the notes she had written on Al's desk, but she couldn't find a single inch of unoccupied space. Instead, she leaned forward and reached all the way across it, putting them in his hand. "I rustled up that Roswell piece, originally out of Tucson, and watched it. Then I found an article from a newspaper in Farmington. Some guy named Davis wrote it earlier this year. The girl's name is Abalone Duncan. Everyone calls her Abby. She's Navajo. Goes to Diné College in Shiprock and got invited to that conference because of what she said to a visiting professor in some comparative religion class."

Al smiled. "I like it. She checks all the boxes. She's Navajo, good-looking, and she managed to pull off some kind of divine miracle at the university. What do you say? Do we get her on Barbara's show?"

Lydia subtly bit her lip. Al's comments would normally have put her off, but she'd heard crap like that from him a million times already. She plowed on. "Here's the thing. I'm not so sure about the *miracle*. If you listen carefully to what she said, the only words that came out of her mouth were, 'God loves you.'" She half-closed one eye. "Not exactly Sermon on the Mount stuff."

Al ran his fingers through the scraggly goatee that distorted his visage. "All right, but why not? Barbara's show could use a lot of help. She's stuck on Sunday afternoon, competing with sports and old movies. Let's get her somebody other than the local religious crew talking about their latest fund-raising gambit." He sat up taller. "Let's get her a guest that might actually catch somebody's interest. If nothing else, a face worth looking at." He grinned at her.

Lydia swallowed her indignation. "Budget?"

"You're the producer. It's only a three-and-a-half-hour drive. Tell the girl we'll put her up in a nice hotel and we'll even pay her scale for showing up." He paused. "But not too nice a hotel. Barbara's show doesn't make us a penny."

"You're the boss. I'll get right on it. Then I'll call Barbara and give her a heads up." She turned and headed for the door.

"One other thing." Al looked up from the computer upon which he had already started working. "Tell Barbara not to go easy on this girl. Sometimes Barbara's show sounds more like a bunch of old biddies sitting around gossiping over a cup of tea than an interview show. Tell her to make believe she's on *real* television and actually ask some stiff questions." He turned his attention back to the screen.

"Right." Lydia walked out of the office, contemplating what color she would have it painted after she got Al's job—and had the place fumigated.

Shiprock, New Mexico - Monday, June 7th

Abby came out of her bedroom, still dressed in dark red pajamas. She plopped on the couch next to Kai, phone in her hand.

Kai looked sideways at her. "Who was that?"

Abby rubbed her nose. "Nobody."

"A scam call or a real nobody?"

"A real nobody. A TV producer from Albuquerque. She asked me to be a guest on some show this Sunday afternoon. I told her to forget it."

Kai shifted in her seat. "Really? Why?"

"Why?" Abby tightened her fists and sat bolt upright. "Because I'm never getting involved in anything like that again. I don't care how much money they offer me."

Kai replied gently. "They offered you money?"

"Yeah, it's something they call, 'scale.' I think it's a union thing."

Neither woman spoke for a long time. Eventually, Kai ventured a question. "So, they want you to talk about what happened in Tucson? Is that it?"

Abby settled back into the cushions. "Right, but I told her I really didn't have much to say about it."

Kai stood and walked to the tiny kitchen. She filled a coffee cup with water, then put it into the microwave. The small machine rumbled while she spoke. "I hope you realize that this is going to keep happening—that this won't be the last person who'll want you to talk about Tucson. I'm afraid that between the YouTube video and that story on the news, people are going to keep asking you about it—trying to make something out of it."

Abby stood as the rumbling turned to beeping. "That's my point. They're *making* something out of it—more than what it really was. And I'm tired of them," she stiffened a finger, "poking at me. I just want to be left alone."

Taking a tea bag out of a low, metal container, Kai dropped it into her cup. "So, there's one way you might get them to stop."

Abby had walked to the kitchen as well. She took a mug out of the cupboard. "And exactly how could I do that?"

"By doing what they want you to do. Go on the stupid show. Tell people just how you feel—that you're not even sure anything special happened." Kai smiled. "It will make you one of the worst TV guests in history, but it'll probably stop anyone else who's thinking of tracking you down."

"No way." Abby shook her head forcefully. "I'm not doing that. Why should I let them turn me into a sacrificial lamb?"

Kai grinned. "Honey, you can be the lamb, or you can be the cook, but you're going to the barbeque one way or the other. Now if you'd like to be the person who gets what they want, you call that woman back and tell her you changed your mind. You'll be there for the show on Sunday."

Abby ran her fingers through her hair. "You think so?"

Kai shrugged. "I think so. And guess what, I'll bet they're going to put you up at another cool hotel and pay for food and gas."

"Put *both* of us up in a cool hotel, and pay for food and gas."

"What?"

"I'm not doing this without you." Abby wagged her empty cup at Kai. "You think it's such a good idea, then we'll go through this whole thing together, right? And I'll *tell* her I'm bringing a guest who's eating as well."

Kai thought for a moment. "How far to Albuquerque?"

"Three-and-a-half hours."

"This Saturday?"

"Show is on Sunday. We travel on Saturday. And guess what?"

"What?"

"This time we're going to have some fun. Screw 'em. If I'm bowing out of public life, let's do it on their dime and have a little fun while we're at it."

13

Ibuquerque, New Mexico - Sunday, June 13th
Abby and Kai woke up in a pleasant Hampton Inn room in Albuquerque—two queen beds this time and food for both of them paid for by the TV station. They'd gone dancing the night before and even had the opportunity to take a dip and lie out by the pool before eating lunch and heading to the studio. It was the most fun Abby had had in a long while.

As they left Abby's car and walked toward the station's entrance—big, colorful KAQE-TV letters shining over the doorway—Abby was relaxed. She knew why she was there and what she had to do. Without seeming combative or unappreciative, she wanted to put this thing to bed and be done with it.

After being greeted by the receptionist and buzzed through the locked doors, they followed a young female intern into the dark and chilly studio—to the set of The Barbara Ellis Rice Show. Declining the pleasant offer of bottled water, Abby was seated in a dark green canvas director's chair while Kai was shown to a wooden stool just out of camera range. A low table with an attractive display of succulent plants sat between Abby's seat and a matching chair. The only thing missing was Barbara Ellis Rice herself.

As she waited, Abby began to question the wisdom of being there. *Even if Kai's right, and this is what it takes to get people to leave me alone, who am I to even think about being on a show like this? All those religious people watching. And what do I have to say? Nothing. Nothing important, other than the fact that I'm not even sure what happened in Tucson.*

Abby's thoughts were cut short when the show's crew entered the studio. The set lights came up as a young man with hair flopping in his face clipped a microphone onto Abby's floral top and carefully ran the thin cable down her back to a battery pack.

A few minutes later, a large woman in her late fifties entered the studio. Abby took in the woman's dark blue, knee-length dress and well-coiffed hairdo, pretty certain the imposing figure was her host. Just before the young man finished connecting Abby's mic, he whispered, "Be careful. She seems to be on the warpath about something today." Stepping back, he gave her a big smile and said loudly, "You'll do fine. Have a great show." He disappeared behind a camera and slipped on a headset.

As Barbara Ellis Rice walked onto the set and took her seat, she gave Abby a perfunctory smile. Rice had already clipped on her mic and run it through her clothing. A different crew member turned on her battery pack and slipped away.

Rice adjusted herself in her chair. "Welcome, Ms. Duncan. Glad you're here. Is it all right if I call you Abby?"

Abby smiled as warmly as she could, though the sense of trepidation crawling through her body was growing by the moment. "Sure, no problem."

"Did you have a nice trip down?"

"Just fine."

"And the accommodations, they were okay?"

"Excellent."

Though it was highly unlikely, given the amount of hair spray she had apparently used, Rice touched her coiffe as if a wisp might be out of place. "So, listen, I won't ask you anything before the show starts." Her lips spread, creating a faux smile. "Your answers will be much more authentic if it's the first time you hear the questions."

The floor manager, a sandy-haired young woman in jeans and a KAQE T-shirt, stopped in her tracks, obviously listening to a message coming to her through a headset. "Five minutes to air." She turned to the host. "Mic check please, Barbara."

Rice responded. "Testing. One, two, three, testing."

"That's got it." The floor manager turned to Abby. "Would you mind checking your mic as well?"

It felt weird to Abby to hear herself say, "Testing. One, two, three, testing."

The next few minutes crawled by. Abby had expected her host to be at least minimally chatty until they went on air. Instead, the woman looked over her notes, barely acknowledging Abby's presence. There had been many times in Abby's life when she had felt shunned because of her heritage, because she was Navajo. She couldn't help but wonder if this was yet another one of those times. Finally, the floor manager called out, "One minute," and Abby started to regret having turned down the bottled water.

"Thirty seconds."

"In five, four, three . . . . We're live. Standard open is running. Ten seconds."

Abby could hear muffled theme music leaking through the floor manager's headset as the woman stared at Rice, her hand raised. Eight seconds later, the hand fell, pointing at the host, and a giant smile exploded on Rice's face.

"Hello. I'm Barbara Ellis Rice and welcome to the show. My first guest today is Ms. Abby Duncan, a student at Diné College in Shiprock, New Mexico." She turned to Abby. "Greetings, Ms. Duncan. Is it okay if I call you Abby?"

The question threw Abby off balance for a moment. Finally, she realized it was for the sake of the audience. "Oh, yes, certainly."

Rice turned back to the camera. "Abby was recently a speaker at the 'Conversations on Religion and Spirituality in Our Lives' conference held at the University of Arizona in Tucson. While there, she was part of what seemed to be an extraordinary spiritual event. We'll talk more about that after we learn a little bit of Abby's background."

Rice asked Abby some simple questions designed to let the audience know about Abby's Native American heritage and that her field of study was environmental issues. Rice then told her viewers about the article written by Cliff Davis and picked up by The *Arizona Clarion*. She turned her attention back to Abby. "So, let me ask you this, how long have you held negative feelings toward organized religion?"

Abby eyes popped open. That was not the question she had expected. "Uh, I, uh, don't necessarily have negative feelings toward organized religion per se. I don't know that I ever said that."

Rice gave her a motherly smile. "Come on now, Abby, all those John Lennon thoughts about imagining there was no heaven, no countries, no religion. Those aren't exactly expressions of support, now, are they?"

Abby was still trying to get her bearings. "Uh, first of all," she swallowed, "those are John Lennon's ideas, not mine. Second, when I referred to them, I was responding to a visiting professor who . . ." she caught herself, "who was talking about the first crusade to Jerusalem. I think my point at the time was that it seemed strange that men would walk thousands of miles across the world to kill people they'd never met and do it in the name of God."

Rice put on her *I'm trying to understand what you're saying* face. "So, the attempt by those Christian warriors to free Jerusalem from the grips of invaders appeared somehow disingenuous to you? Is that what you're saying?"

Still flustered, Abby wished she had paid more attention to the actual information in Dr. Wertz's lecture. "I'm not actually saying that."

Rice was right on her. "Well, dear, exactly what are you saying? What were you saying at the time?"

Abby took a deep breath and spoke forcefully. "My point is that, from my modern-day perspective, it's hard for me to justify the slaughter of innocent people on religious grounds."

"Okay," Rice cut in. "Now, let's move on."

Surprised, Abby dropped her chin for a moment, letting out a quick breath. She was confident the next question would be about the conference in Tucson and she was ready for it.

"I understand that your desire to study environmental issues comes out of your father's lifelong work experience in the gas and oil fields around Shiprock. Given your Native American heritage, do you see any conflict of interest there between the Navajo belief system concerning the use of the earth's natural resources and America's need for cheap, abundant sources of energy?"

Blindsided, Abby was stunned. *What is this woman talking about?* After ten seconds of total silence, the best Abby could come up with was, "Could you please rephrase the question?"

Barbara Ellis Rice rose up in her chair, a condescending smile on her face. "As I understand it, the Navajo have a totally different concept of the earth and its bounty than western cultures. Isn't it true that if you live on the Navajo reservation, you can't even build a house on your own land?"

Abby sat up taller as well. "No, that's not true." She hitched. "Well, it *is* true, but not in the way you mean." She saw Rice give her that patronizing look again. "You see, you have to ask the tribal elders for permission to build a house somewhere, and that comes with certain limitations."

"What kind of limitations, dear?"

Abby could feel her blood start to boil. "You can ask permission to build a house, and it's often given. However, you don't own the land, you're only given permission to use it for a certain period, say twenty-five years."

Rice rocked back in her canvas chair, a look of incredulity on her face. "Why, then, would a person invest in building a home on land they don't even own?"

Abby clenched her teeth, trying to keep calm. "They don't own the land because they *can't* own the land. According to our culture, the land is not *ownable*, it's just part of the Navajo cultural world. It's for all the people, the Diné."

Rice pressed. "And your father's work, taking oil and gas out of the earth, owning it, selling it, that didn't conflict with your Navajo belief system—doesn't it still?"

Tears welled up behind Abby's eyelids. "You don't understand. Two cultures. I grew up in two cultures. Cultures with different beliefs about things like that. It was hard. It was—"

"I'm sure it was, and we can come back to that in a moment if you'd like." Rice turned to the camera, smiling broadly. "But now, I'm afraid we need to take a break. We'll be back for more interesting discussion with Abby Duncan right after these messages."

14

Abby sat through the three-minute commercial break steaming, her fingers tapping on her leg. While Rice asked the floor manager to bring her a mirror, thoughts of murdering the woman bounced around in Abby's head. *Who is this lady? My dad? She had to bring up my dad? And saying people on the res couldn't build homes? What bull.*

The floor manager's voice rang out. "Thirty seconds."

Rice puffed up in her chair while Abby felt herself brace for the next segment.

"We're live in five, four, three, . . ." The floor manager cued Rice.

"Welcome back to the Barbara Ellis Rice show. My guest is Abby Duncan, and she's here to let us know about a very special spiritual moment which occurred at the 'Conversations on Religion and Spirituality in Our Lives' conference held at the University of Arizona in Tucson last weekend." She turned back to Abby. "Abby, why don't you tell our audience all about it."

Abby started carefully. "First, let me say that not everyone there considered it a spiritual experience. All I said was, 'God loves you.' I didn't mean it to be an earth-shattering statement. I just—"

"I'm sorry to interrupt, dear, but I've seen the video. When you spoke those words, many of the people who were there seemed stunned, as if it was a message from on high. Wouldn't you agree?"

Abby struggled to find the words. "Listen," she pushed her hair out of her face, "haven't you ever experienced a moment when you surprised yourself with something you said? Like you weren't really sure where the words came from, but you did believe they were true?"

Rice scrunched her eyebrows. "I'm not so certain about that. But if those weren't your words," she rose up again in her chair, "are you saying those words came from someone else—perhaps from God himself?"

"Look," Abby felt her entire body tense, "I don't know where those words came from." She leaned in. "But it's not like they were crazy or anything. Haven't you heard other people, pastors and preachers, say that very thing? Go into any church, and even on some street corner, and you can find someone standing there saying, 'God loves you,' right?"

Rice leaned in almost menacingly. "But Abby, that's not at all what we're talking about here, is it? Those people in the audience, and even those on the stage with you, they certainly seemed to sense something special, something mystical happening." Her intensity increased. "Are you certain that those were *your* words? No, you're not. You said so yourself. So, are you now implying God was speaking through you? Is that it? You're some representative of God?"

Abby worked to hold back her anger—and her tears. "No, stop. Please stop. I'm not saying that."

Rice's words landed on top of Abby's. "But you do believe God loves all those people."

The answer flew out of Abby's mouth. "Yes. I do believe that."

"And you just admitted the message you shared with them wasn't yours, correct?"

"Well—"

"And if those weren't your words, then I guess we can safely assume they *did* come from some other source. That you *are* some sort of messenger from God, or at least you *say* you are."

"Wait a minute." Abby's face was flushed with frustration. "Don't put words in my mouth. I *never* said I was a messenger sent from God." Her anger blossomed. "And I'm tired of people saying I said this or said that—meant this or meant that."

It was Abby's turn to lean forward. "And another thing. That stuff you brought up earlier about Navajo culture and the earth." Face flushed, eyes tightened, she bore down. "You don't know anything about those people, *my* people. And as for taking oil and gas out of the earth, my father always said that the oil and gas were put there for humans to use for a season. But so were the sun and the wind and the waves. And maybe the season for some of those is coming to an end, and it's time for others to take their place." Abby realized she was now sitting at the very edge of her seat. "And how dare you criticize the Navajo or my dad without taking the time to understand who they are and how they see the world?"

Just as Abby was considering storming off the set, she noticed the floor manager signal Rice it was time to wrap up the conversation. The woman sat regally back in her seat. "Well, be that as it may, Abby, it appears our time is up." She grinned dismissively as if she were the one who had struck the final blow in their verbal joust. "Thank you so much for sharing your views." She turned to the camera. "We'll be right back with another interesting guest."

Not waiting for anyone to assist her, Abby stood. "Come on, Kai, we're done here." She grabbed her purse and stepped out of the studio and into the hallway. The floor manager ran after her. "I'll get that mic for you, Ms. Duncan. Here, let me help."

As she reached gently up the back of Abby's top, pulling the mic and its cable down and removing the battery pack from her belt, she whispered, "Good for you. You gave that witch what for and it was well deserved."

While the mic was being removed, Abby looked through the small window in the studio door. As far as she could tell, Barbara Ellis Rice seemed extremely pleased with herself.

15

A tlanta, Georgia - Sunday, June 13th
    That evening, in the EPN studios, located in down-town Atlanta, a stunning woman with coffee-colored skin and blazing green eyes wrapped up her split-screen interview. "Thank you, Senator McCaffery, for taking the time to speak to us on a Sunday evening." She directed her attention to the audience. "We'll return with some expert predictions on second-quarter results from our economic team in just a minute."

"Clear." The floor manager walked to the anchor's desk with notes in his hand. "This just came in. They'll tell you about it in a moment." He turned to walk away. "Back in two minutes, thirty."

The anchor looked vacantly upward as a producer's voice filled her ear. *"Okay, Stephanie, we've got a live one for you. Some woman just called in from Albuquerque. Said she hosts a community and religious affairs show on Sunday afternoons and that today's guest told her she was some sort of emissary from God."*

"On air? The woman said it on air?"

"Well, not quite in those words, but something like that. The woman, a Barbara Ellis Rice, sent the video. We've looked it over. It's

been edited, but I'm pretty sure we're okay running it. We've also tracked down a second source."

"Really?" Frustration came through in Stephanie Richardson's tone. "Some fruitcake says something on local Sunday afternoon TV and we run it on national television?"

"Steph," there was a wry note in the producer's voice, *"it's Sunday evening for us as well. We've been running the same stories for twelve hours. You work the weekend desk; you get to handle stuff like this. Don't worry, I'll walk you through it. We're back in a minute thirty."*

The floor manager took his position between two cameras and pointed to the one on his right. "Back in five, four, three . . ." The theme music played. The floor manager cued her.

The woman read from the teleprompter. "Welcome back. I'm Stephanie Richardson and this is EPN Weekend News. This just in: we've received reporting from an affiliate in Albuquerque, New Mexico, about a young lady who says she has a special relationship with God." A pair of images appeared next to hers on the monitor in front of Richardson. "Our guests are two women who have worked with the young lady in question and are here to share their stories: Ms. Barbara Ellis Rice, host of *The Barbara Ellis Rice Show* on KAQE-TV in Albuquerque, and Dr. Susan Sterling, from the Religion and Spirituality Department at the University of Arizona at Tucson. Good evening, ladies."

Both women smiled and nodded.

"Dr. Sterling, let me start with you. Now, I haven't had much time to catch up on this story, but I understand the woman in question, Ms. Abby Duncan, was a guest at a recent event you held."

"Good evening, and thanks for having me on." Dr. Sterling took a quick breath. "Yes, it was our annual 'Conversations on Religion and Spirituality in Our Lives' conference, and Ms. Duncan was one of our speakers."

"And did she have anything particularly unusual to say?"

Dr. Sterling beamed. "Oh, yes. I believe you could say that. Strangely, the words she used are words we hear all the time. All she said was, 'God loves you.' But there was something very special about the way she said it. And many of the people who were in the room that morning seemed to feel there was, I don't know, perhaps a special anointing of some sort on what she said."

The perfect professional, Stephanie Richardson simply repeated, "God loves you?"

"Yes, yes, God loves you." Dr. Sterling looked a bit sheepish. "I guess you had to be there, but believe me, something highly unusual happened on the stage that morning."

"And you, Ms. Ellis Rice, will you please tell us about what happened on your program this afternoon?"

Rice's experience on camera came through. "Yes, good evening, Stephanie. Well, my experience was equally as compelling as Dr. Sterling's, though perhaps in a different way. Ms. Duncan was a guest on my show, and I had asked her about her participation in Dr. Sterling's event when she said some extraordinary things."

"Like?"

"I asked her where those words had come from, that phrase, 'God loves you.' Was she just expressing her own thoughts? Strangely, she seemed reluctant to be specific, while at the same time admitting those were not her own words."

"Can you tell us more?"

"You see, when I asked her plain as day if those were her own words, she indicated they weren't, but she wasn't forthright in ascribing them to some other person, or being, or power. Honestly, I really felt she was hiding something."

While Rice was speaking, Richardson's producer said something in her earpiece. She took the cue. "Okay, then. I'm being told we have some video from your show this afternoon. Let's go right to that."

The video began, and Rice's face appeared. *"I'm sorry to inter-*

rupt, dear, but I've seen the video. When you said those words, many of the people who were there seemed stunned, as if it was a message from on high. Wouldn't you agree?"

Next came a response from Abby. "Could you please rephrase the question?"

"Well, dear, exactly what are you saying? What were you saying at the time?"

"Look, I don't know where those words came from."

"And if those weren't your words, then I guess we can safely assume they did come from some other source—that perhaps you are some sort of messenger from God, or at least you say you are."

"Yes. I do believe that."

The video ended and Richardson picked up the ball. "Now, in all fairness, we must tell our audience this video has been edited and we haven't had a chance to see the whole conversation in context, but Ms. Ellis Rice, would you say that interchange honestly represents what happened this afternoon on your show?"

Rice turned suddenly demure. "Well, Stephanie, as a professional broadcaster, I must always withhold my personal opinions, but you did hear those words come directly out of Ms. Duncan's mouth."

"So—"

Rice interrupted. "And if I could add something."

"Certainly."

"In an earlier segment of the show, I had the opportunity to speak to Ms. Duncan about her Navajo background, her studies in environmental issues, and her views on oil and gas drilling. I'll quote her as directly as I can. She said, 'My father always said that the oil and gas were put there for humans to use for a season. But so were the sun and the wind and the waves. And maybe the season for some of those is coming to an end, and it's time for others to take their place.' I believe those were her exact words."

Richardson pressed. "And you think . . . ?"

"Well, one could certainly make the case Ms. Duncan feels she has a unique relationship with someone special," Rice's eyes rose to the ceiling, "someone who might have had something to do with providing those things since the very beginning and planning for their use over time. I mean, who's to say?"

"And," Richardson's demeanor changed just slightly, "I promise we'll be looking into exactly that. For now, I'll have to leave it there, ladies. Thank you so much for joining me this evening." The other two faces on the screen disappeared. "We'll be back in just a moment with the latest predictions from our expert economic team."

S *hiprock, New Mexico - Monday morning, June 14th*
Abby sat silently at the kitchen table, coffee mug in hand, an empty cereal bowl in front of her. Kai had finished her breakfast as well and was getting ready to head out. "I'm going to meet Jamie at his place." She slipped on her sunglasses and picked up her keys. "We're thinking of taking in a movie this afternoon. You want to come?"

Abby kept her eyes on the coffee mug. "No thanks. I guess I'll just stay here today. Know what I mean? Plus, I've got a call into Gus. There's a chance he might let me come in and work a few hours tonight."

Kai's voice was upbeat, and Abby sensed she was trying her best to lift Abby's spirits after the debacle at the TV station in Albuquerque. "Okay. Well, if you change your . . . ."

Abby looked up. "What?" Kai had pushed aside a curtain and was peeking out the window. "What is it?"

"I'm not sure. There's some woman I've never seen before out in the parking lot. She's leaning on her car, and some guy is sitting inside it. Looks like they're waiting for something."

Abby rose and moved to the window, standing next to Kai,

and peered out as well. She saw the woman—short hair, khaki pants, blue oxford shirt——obviously trying her best to seem inconspicuous. "Who do you think that is?"

Kai shrugged. A moment later, her expression changed. "You don't think . . . ."

Abby took a deep breath, "That they're here for me? I sure hope not." Agitated, she looked around the room then back at Kai. "Look. You go out there. Just ignore them. But if they ask anything about me, you say I'm not here. Got it? Don't tell them you don't know me. They'll know you're lying. Just tell them I'm not here, I didn't come back from Albuquerque with you."

Kai's concern crept across her face. "Are you sure? I could just stay here. I'll call Jamie and—"

"No. I've got to figure out what's going on. You go out there. Let's hope they don't pay any attention to you and we're just wrong about everything." She put her hand on Kai's back, nudging her toward the door. "Go on. It'll be all right. Say, 'Hi,' to Jamie for me."

Kai nodded, turned the flimsy doorknob, and walked out the door. "See ya."

Abby's heart was pounding as she watched through the window, but Kai made it to the parking lot without any response from the woman and her half-hidden partner. Unfortunately, she halted a few steps later.

Abby couldn't hear what was said, but she could certainly tell what was going on. The woman had suddenly approached Kai, asking questions, pointing occasionally at their apartment. The man—thin, early thirties, ball cap and jeans—had stepped out of the car, opened the trunk, and pulled out a video camera and tripod. There was no question in Abby's mind. These two were there to speak to her.

As Abby watched, she could see Kai doing her best to put the female reporter off. The fact that the young woman kept looking at their apartment gave Abby the impression she didn't believe for a minute Abby wasn't inside. Unconsciously, Abby nervously rubbed her chin with the back of her hand. She hoped Kai would somehow get the woman and her partner to leave.

Without warning, the reporter nudged past Kai and started for the apartment. Shocked, Kai reached out and grabbed the woman's arm, spinning her around. The two struggled, as the videographer quickly put his equipment down and headed toward them.

Abby's mind was ablaze. The last thing in the world she wanted was to be confronted by these jerks from the local news, but watching Kai physically try to defend her was too much. She burst through the doorway and ran out, screaming. "Get away from her, you creeps!" She ran directly at the woman who had frozen, her hand still wrapped around Kai's arm.

"Ms. Duncan—"

"Don't give me Ms. Duncan. Get your hands off my friend. Get off her, and get the hell out of here."

The woman let go of Kai's arm as the man stepped between her and Kai, clearly hoping to defuse the situation. "But Ms. Duncan, all I want to do is ask you a few questions."

By then, Abby was only inches from the woman's face. "You want to talk to me, you talk, but you keep your hands off my friend. Now get out of here."

Abby turned back toward the apartment, grabbing Kai's arm and pulling her along.

While the videographer stayed silent and still, the reporter refused to retreat. Following Abby and Kai, she spoke breathlessly. "But don't you see, I'm here to help you. I'm here to give you a chance to defend yourself."

Abby stopped, still facing away from the woman. "Defend myself? From what?"

The reporter took a breath, clearly trying to settle herself down. "Certainly, you've heard, haven't you?"

Both Abby and Kai turned to face her. "Heard what?"

"Heard what Barbara Ellis Rice said about you on EPN last night."

Abby turned back and briskly started toward the apartment again, Kai barely keeping up. "I don't give a flying fig what Barbara Ellis Rice said about me on EPN or anywhere else."

The reporter pressed. "And you don't care that she played a video segment from the show?"

Abby kept walking while both Kai and the reporter followed. "Why should I care? I didn't say anything wrong, anything that wasn't the truth."

"You mean, you *do* think you might be a special emissary from God, that God speaks to people through you?"

Abby and Kai both stopped in their tracks, turning slowly toward the woman. "What?" Abby's face twisted. "I never said any such thing. I'm no special emissary from God. I'm nobody special at all. How in the world did she try to make that case?"

The reporter lifted her shoulders. "With your own words?"

"What the heck are you talking about?"

"Ms. Duncan—"

The name shot out of her mouth. "Abby."

"Abby, my name is Debbie Thompson. I'm with KFRM in Farmington, and I'm afraid you have no idea what's going on." Her eyes implored Abby. "Please, let me show you something, will you? Please, let me help you."

17

Abby glanced at Kai and received a look that implied she should give the woman a chance to speak. "How are you going to help me?"

Debbie Thompson lifted her phone. "Just let me show you something." She looked around. "Is there somewhere we can sit down?"

Abby looked around as well. "Right here," she pointed, "we can sit on the grass."

Abby and Kai marched the few steps to the grassy spot and sat down, their legs crossed. Debbie seemed reluctant, perhaps because of her nicer clothing, but took a deep breath and followed suit. She scrolled on her phone for a moment, then handed it to Abby. "Here, take a look at this. It's a clip from an interview Barbara Ellis Rice did on EPN last night."

Abby and Kai leaned together to watch. The first thing they saw was the face of the older woman. *"I'm sorry to interrupt, dear, but I've seen the video. When you said those words, many of the people who were there seemed stunned, as if it was a message from on high. Wouldn't you agree?"*

The clip continued. When it ended, Abby dropped the phone

as if it were a hot iron. "No . . . no, no, no. That's not right." She looked at Kai. "That's not how it went, is it?"

Kai lifted her hands and shoulders, seemingly baffled.

Abby turned back to Debbie Thompson. "I didn't say that, did I?"

The woman clasped her fingers around her phone. "Well, that's you on the screen, and those are *your* words coming out of *your* mouth."

Tears were forming in Abby's eyes. "But—"

"But," Debbie interrupted, a sly smile on her face, "with some good editing, we can pretty much make anyone say anything we want." She paused. "Now, if you would like to respond."

Kai grabbed Abby's arm and pointed. The videographer had quietly picked up his camera and put it up on his shoulder. He was slowly walking toward the three women, recording.

Abby's eyes widened and she flew off the ground, shouting. "No!" She ran toward the cameraman. "Turn it off! Turn it off!" Kai was up and running with her.

So was Debbie Thompson. "Abby, Abby, we're just trying to help you!"

A car screeched to a halt in the parking lot and Jamie exploded out of the vehicle, yelling. "What's going on?" In an instant, he was charging the cameraman as well. "What the hell are you doing?"

Moments later, all five were a tangled mess of arms and legs, grabbing and pulling, ducking and swinging. Finally, Kai managed to pull Abby away while Jamie drove his shoulder into the videographer, landing him on his butt—holding onto his camera for dear life. Debbie Thompson simply backed away, apparently unable to think of anything else to do at the moment.

As Kai led Abby back to their apartment, a puffed-up Jamie stood guard and watched Debbie Thompson and her partner gather themselves and retreat to their car.

INSIDE THE APARTMENT, Abby plopped down on the couch, tears running down her cheeks. Kai watched her for a moment, then headed toward the kitchen area. "Let me get you something to drink."

By the time Kai returned with a glass of water for each of them, Jamie was walking through the door. "What the heck was that all about?"

Kai turned to him. "That stupid TV show in Albuquerque. That crazy lady edited the words Abby said, mixing them all up, making her sound looney tunes."

Abby could see the concern on Jamie's face when he asked, "How so?"

Kai answered. "She made it look like Abby was saying she'd been sent by God to deliver a message to those people in Tucson."

"Oh," Jamie responded, "that sucks."

Kai took a seat next to Abby on the couch and a long silence filled the room. Eventually, she turned to Abby. "Can I ask you a question?"

Abby's voice showed the stress of the morning. "Sure."

"I never asked you this, but when we were in Tucson and you were up on that stage, what really did happen? Why did you say what you said?"

Abby looked at her. She could see Kai's honest desire to understand. "You know, it's really all a blur for me." She thought for a moment, then started again, more determined. "You were there. You knew I wasn't prepared to answer any difficult questions. Heck, we were just taking advantage of the opportunity to get away on a trip."

"Right." Kai hung on Abby's every word, as did Jamie.

"So, I walk up to the podium and nothing," she shook her head, "nothing—just an empty mind. And then, after a long time, here come those words. They're right in front of me, as if I could reach out and touch them. And I have no idea where they came from. It did seem different, though, like I *had* to say them." She took a deep breath in and let it out. "That's all I know. They were just there. I needed to say something. I said them."

Another long silence followed as each of the three pondered what Abby had just shared.

"So," Jamie's voice was tentative, "do you think maybe it's true —that maybe those words were sent to you by . . . by, you know . . . . God?"

Abby collapsed backward on the couch, another sigh escaping her lips. "How would I know?" She sat back up. "And guess what? I don't care. I don't *want* to know. All I *do* know is that I've had it with people like Barbara Ellis Rice and that Debbie Thompson. Screw 'em. I'm done with them."

Kai reached out and touched Abby's arm. "You're right. You don't need to mess with those folks anymore. Let them think what they want. You don't care." She looked at Jamie, then back to Abby. "And we don't care either. We know who you are, just a good person trying to do the best you can. We're just going to forget it and move on." She nodded. "Give it a day or two and I'll bet this will all blow over. You just—"

Abby's phone rang with its old-fashioned telephone sound.

18

Abby looked at the phone, letting it ring and ring until it finally stopped. A few moments later it began again. Kai turned to her. "You going to get that?"

With a sigh, Abby picked it up. "Hello . . . . Yes, this is Abby Duncan . . . . Who is this? . . . No, I'm not interested . . . . Seriously, I'm telling you, I don't have any interest in doing that . . . . Look, please leave me alone. Please don't call again." She hung up.

Jamie sat up in the armchair. "Who was that?"

Abby half-shuddered. "That was someone from The New Mexico Clean Earth Coalition. There's a big rally this weekend, and the girl said they wanted me to speak at it."

Jamie scrunched his face. "Why you?"

Kai huffed in exasperation. "Because, dummy, her field is environmental studies, and she knows more than a little bit about that kind of thing."

"And," added Abby unenthusiastically, "she'd seen the story on EPN—heard what I said about oil and gas having a season and it being time to move on."

Jamie rubbed his hands up and down his muscular legs. "You going to do it?"

It was Abby's turn to huff. "Are you kidding? After everything that's happened? Do you think I'm stupid or something?"

No one responded for a long moment. Finally, Kai spoke gently. "You know Abby, you and I both chose environmental studies as our majors because we thought we could make a difference somehow. You grew up here in Shiprock with your dad working in the oil and gas fields. I grew up on the res hearing my mom and dad complain about how the land was being raped by those companies. We both thought that understanding more about how things worked, how they needed to work, we might be able to move folks in the right direction."

Abby nodded. "True, but these people never heard of either one of us until this weekend. Now they want to trot me out at their rally simply because some of them know who I am, and they want me to say that I'm in total agreement with them. I have no idea what they stand for."

Kai responded quickly. "Maybe it doesn't matter."

"What?"

Kai's energy level was rising. "Look, one way or the other, you know they're for a cleaner earth. And maybe they've got a reasonable approach, maybe not. Maybe they're ready to pull the plug and we all go back to living in the dark. But you can go there and say whatever you want to say—all the things we've talked about here and at school. You can tell them there's a way to get there that's doable."

Abby stood up and walked to the window. "No. I'm not doing it." She peeked between the curtains. "I won't put myself in that position again." She turned to face Kai. "Listen, you know I agree with you. And any other time, either one of us would have jumped at the chance. But not now, not after what I've just gone through—what I'm going through." She shook her head.

Jamie seemed to sense it was time to break the tension in the room. He stood. "Hey, what do you say I go down to Gino's and pick up a pizza? I'll stop on the way back and get a six-pack of Coors too. Let's just chill this afternoon."

Kai seemed eager to move things along as well. "Sounds good. I'll go with you." She turned to Abby. "That work for you?"

"Sure. I'm staying here, though. You get that, right?"

Kai smiled. "Makes sense. You just get us set up and find a movie we can watch. Jamie and I will be back in a few minutes."

As Abby watched them walk out the door, she couldn't help but wonder if there might be another news crew waiting to ambush them. Whether there was or not, she was exhausted from the stress of the morning; pizza and a movie sounded like pretty good therapy.

WHEN JAMIE AND KAI RETURNED, they found Abby had cleared off the coffee table and washed the breakfast dishes.

Jamie spoke first. "Sorry it took so long. I forgot how early it was. We had to wait for them to make the first dough of the day." He grinned. "But we've got the freshest pizza you've ever had, that's for sure."

Kai looked at Abby. "You okay? Anything happen while we were gone?"

"Nothing good. My phone rang again. It was another news crew asking for an interview. I told them to forget it. After that, it went off every five minutes. There must have been seven or eight calls. I just stopped answering. But trust me, it was one news station after the other. It's driving me crazy."

Jamie plopped the pizza down on the coffee table. "I can't blame you. That would get me pretty riled up as well." He pulled two cans of beer out of their plastic netting, then popped each of them open. "Don't those folks get it?" He handed a can to Kai. "Can't they just leave you alone?"

Abby walked to the refrigerator to get herself a soda. "Doesn't appear so." She shook her head. "Looks like I'm not going to be answering my phone for the next month or two."

"C'mon." Kai took a seat on the couch. "Let's eat this thing before it gets cold."

Digging into the pizza and starting the movie, the three of them tried to settle in and enjoy a little time away from the world. Abby put her phone on silent. But every once in a while, it would buzz and dance its way across the coffee table.

Finally, Kai had had enough. When the phone buzzed, she picked it up and answered. "Listen," she half-shouted, "can't you people leave this poor girl alone? Can't you . . . ." She stopped and listened, then turned to Abby. "It's some guy. He says he's a friend of yours. His name is Cliff Davis."

19

Abby remembered the man with the Jimmy Olsen enthusiasm and the George Clooney looks. After chatting with him on the phone, she agreed to meet at a local pub called The New Mexican Standoff. The western-themed bar sported all kinds of saddles and spurs, pistols and rifles, sombreros and cowboy hats. Abby arrived around four o'clock and ordered herself an iced coffee.

A few minutes after four, Cliff Davis walked in. The twenty-something's dark brown eyes and solid build were exactly as she remembered. He had, however, traded in his jeans and sheepskin coat for khakis and an open sports jacket—shirt, no tie. Abby couldn't help but remember she had found him attractive five months ago; nothing she saw that afternoon changed her opinion.

Cliff walked over to the table. "Abby." He extended his hand to her. "Nice to see you. Thanks for agreeing to meet with me."

Abby took his hand momentarily and smiled. "It appears you've moved up in the world." She nodded. "It looks good on you."

"Yeah, well, things change, right?"

"Right." Her tone turned a bit sardonic. "Are you still writing for the *Farmington Daily Times*?"

He looked a little embarrassed. "Actually, no. I'm working in television now."

Abby's eyes opened wide. "What happened to learning your trade from the ground up—print news, in a small city?"

"Turns out that writing obits and covering city council meetings is not as romantic as it sounds." He raised his hand and called a server over. "Not romantic at all."

A sandy-haired young man with a bar towel tucked at his waist came to the table. When he spoke, it was with all the enthusiasm of an armadillo warming itself in the afternoon sun. "Hi. I'm Sean. I'll be your server. What can I get for you?"

Cliff glanced at Abby, silently asking if she wanted something besides her iced coffee. She shook her head. He looked up at the server. "What do you have on tap?"

Sean ran through several local brews and Cliff settled on a Marble Double White. As the young man walked away, Cliff turned back to Abby, "It's brewed on Marble Street in downtown Albuquerque."

Mention of the city sent a chill through Abby's soul. All she could muster in response was, "Oh."

Cliff leaned in, a sly look in his eye. "You're familiar with Albuquerque, aren't you? You've been there recently?"

Abby stiffened, ready for some sort of challenge.

His expression dissolved into a broad smile as he raised his hands in front of him. "Whoa, wait a minute. Just kidding, that's all. Not looking for trouble here."

Abby relaxed a tiny bit, but felt less than convinced that she had done the right thing by agreeing to meet with Cliff. She decided to get on with things. "Okay, you said it was important that we talk. So, talk."

Before Cliff could begin, Sean appeared with his drink—a

tall, twelve-ounce glass filled with a rust-colored brew, a slice of orange adorning the rim. "Here you go. Want to run a tab?"

Cliff nodded. "Sure. And put the lady's drink on it as well."

"Got it." The young man shuffled away.

Abby smiled her appreciation, then pressed. "You were about to say?"

"Listen, Abby, I'm here to help. I mean it. I know you've taken some pretty good hits since I wrote that article, and I feel bad about it."

She shrugged. "No big deal. I'm okay. It'll all fade away soon."

Cliff took a sip that left a tiny foam mustache on his lip. "I'm afraid that might not be the case." He stopped. "Why are you smiling?"

Abby dramatically drew the back of her hand across her lips.

Cliff mirrored the motion, then looked down at his hand. He grinned sheepishly. "Thanks."

"No problem."

Cliff straightened. "Listen, Abby. I'm not kidding. I spoke to Debbie Thompson this afternoon—"

She sat bolt upright in her chair. "Debbie Thompson? The one who came to see me this morning?"

He caught a quick breath. "Yes, that Debbie Thompson. We work together at KFRM."

She leaned across the table. "You're kidding, right? You work with her and that camera guy—the ones who tried to interview me and tape me when I didn't know what was going on?"

Cliff raised his hands again. "Whoa, stop. Debbie's an okay lady. She was just doing her job."

Abby could feel the heat in her face. "Just doing her job? And are you just doing *your* job now? Is that what this meeting is about?" The pace of the conversation accelerated quickly.

"No, no. Please, listen. No one from the station even knows I'm here. This is between you and me, Abby, I promise. I'm not here to do a story on you. I'm here to help if you'll let me."

Abby stopped, waiting to hear more. *Can I trust this guy? What's his angle? Why am I even giving him a chance?* Her finger began tapping on the table. "Go on. Tell me why you're here."

Cliff took another long drink, careful this time to check his lip with his fingertips. "Look, I saw what this Barbara Ellis Rice did to you and it sucked. She had no right. She cut up that interview like it was a fine piece of meat, then stuck it together all topsy turvy like a Frankenstein version of your conversation." He leaned in. "I know. I went back and watched the entire interview *and* the clip she brought to EPN. It was a disgrace."

Abby's lip curled. "I should sue her for what she did to me."

Cliff nodded. "You're right, you could sue her, and EPN as well, but you'll never win. More importantly, I don't think you understand how all this works."

"I don't understand how what works?"

"Listen, even if you won in court, which is not likely since you're a broke college student and both those stations have lawyers out the ying-yang, it wouldn't matter. It's not what the courts say that changes people's minds, it's what the media allows them, then makes them, then forces them to hear and see. That's what makes the difference. If you want to change what people think of you, you have to be out there letting them know what to believe."

Abby sat up taller. "What if I don't want to do that? What if I won't give them the satisfaction of saying anything?"

Cliff sighed. "Then I'm afraid they're going to toss you around like a stuffed doll until they get tired of playing with you. And trust me, some of these folks have a very long attention span."

Abby looked down at her now-warm iced coffee. Her finger was tapping again; her insides were shaking. She rolled her lip under before speaking. "So, how do I do that? How do I tell people what to believe about me without sounding like some crazy person?"

Cliff placed a hand on one of hers. "No, you don't *tell* them what to think of you, you show them. You do something, something that's authentic, something you believe in, and you let them see that." He self-consciously removed his hand.

Abby felt lost. "Like what? What do I do?"

"I don't know. You're into environmental studies, aren't you?"

Abby scrunched her face. "How do you know that?"

Cliff let his eyes drift to the side. "Uh, it's my job to follow up on stories. I guess I've kept up with you ever since my article got reprinted in the *Arizona Clarion*." He refocused on Abby. "Anyway, is there something you could do there? Some project you may be involved with that I could to do a piece on—anything but this religious stuff?"

Abby shrugged. "You're not going to believe this, but I was just invited to speak at some clean earth rally. I told them I wouldn't do it, but I guess I could call them back."

"That," Cliff looked excited, "sounds great."

Abby shook her head, "But it's not like they ever spoke to me before. They're just asking me because people are talking about me."

"Doesn't matter. They're giving you a platform. Take it. Go up there and say whatever you want, but go up there and say something. You need to do it."

Something in Cliff's words sent a chill through Abby. "What do you mean, I *need* to do it?"

Cliff braced himself. "Listen, Abby, you may not realize this, but there are people out there who are ready to attack you."

"Attack me?" Abby rocked back. "Why would they want to attack me?"

"Sadly, for saying what you said, even if you didn't really say it."

Abby's hands rolled into fists. "That's crazy. I didn't say anything wrong. And if I did, so what?"

"Listen, that's just how things go nowadays. They saw you on

TV. According to them, they watched you say some things which make them very angry."

"That's terrible."

"Yes, that's terrible. What's worse, is that you just might be exactly what they're afraid of."

S hiprock, *New Mexico - Saturday afternoon, June 19th*
   Just after one o'clock, Abby put the last mouthful of her tuna sandwich back on the plate. Her stomach was roiling, and the notion of eating had lost its appeal. Finishing her glass of milk, she washed down what she had eaten and pushed her chair back from the table.

She stood, walked into the bathroom, and began to brush her teeth. Taking in her reflection, toothpaste foaming around her lips, she stopped brushing in mid-stroke. *What the heck are you doing? Why are you putting yourself out there again? Haven't you had enough already?*

"C'mon, Abby," Kai's voice reverberated through the tiny apartment, "we'll be late. Jamie and Cliff Davis are outside waiting."

"Coming," Abby shouted, her mouth still full of toothpaste. She rinsed, pulled the bottom of her powder blue T-shirt down over the top of her jeans, stepped from the bathroom, and walked straight through the apartment and out into the sunlight of a beautiful, azure blue sky.

Abby, Kai, and Jamie piled into Cliff Davis' gray Jeep Wrangler. They headed off for the APS Four Corners Generating Station near the San Juan River, the site of the rally sponsored by The New Mexico Clean Earth Coalition. The initial small talk soon died down and was followed by a long pause in the conversation. Abby broke the silence. "At least it's not too hot today."

"Uh-huh," Cliff responded from behind the wheel.

A minute or so later she tried again. "After we're done, would you like to check out Pecos Bill's? It's kind of a cool place and I can get us an employee discount."

Cliff turned to look at her. "A little nervous?"

Abby scrunched her face. "No. Why?"

Cliff chortled, "Perhaps because you're talking about the weather and what we're going to do after the rally instead of what you're about to do this afternoon?"

"Oh."

"Listen," Cliff continued, "I get it. Even though EPN has issued an apology for airing that interview without having checked it beforehand, some folks on the internet and some radio and TV outlets don't seem eager to let all of that die down. You must be a little apprehensive about how today might go."

"Look, I'm just there to tell people what I've learned in school and what I believe about environmental issues. Besides," she shrugged, "it's a rally and not a protest. It'll be okay."

"I hope." A few moments later, Cliff spoke over his shoulder. "Jamie, nice to have you along. Are these things important to you as well?"

Jamie smiled at Kai, beside him in the back seat, then answered. "Not really. I mean, I agree with all this environmental change stuff, but the real reason I'm here is just to support Abby —protect her if she needs it."

"I see." He smiled. "And you think she might need protection?"

"Probably not, but after what happened on Monday, you never know."

It took another twenty minutes or so to reach their destination. The rally organizers had managed to secure permission to place an open flat-bed truck and a few speakers in the parking lot at the edge of the generating station's property. Twenty or thirty people milled about, waiting for the program to begin. Cliff took a camera and tripod out of his trunk, set up, and was ready to record when the event began.

Just after four o'clock, the head of the coalition, a fifty-something Navajo woman in subdued traditional garb, stepped up onto the flat-bed and began. "Friends, fellow lovers of our earth, we are here today not to protest, but rather to celebrate. This generating station sits on land leased from the Navajo Nation. And though the energy it has generated has provided a powerful economic engine for the region and created good-paying jobs, there have been problems. The pollution expelled by the burning of coal fouled the air with nitrous oxide and formed a haze that was detrimental to both tourism at the Grand Canyon and the canyon's ecosystem as well—not to mention our sacred land.

"But thanks to protests, court decisions, and the eventual cooperation from the folks at APS, as well as leadership from the Navajo Nation, great strides have been taken in resolving those problems. We're grateful for the efforts of everyone involved, and I'm glad to say that by 2031, this coal-fired generating station will be decommissioned." After spirited applause, the woman continued, speaking about the progress and cleaner air that had been achieved. She told the crowd the day's rally was an opportunity to let the rest of the world see what could be accomplished when people come together to face difficult environmental challenges.

Watching, waiting her turn, Abby's fingers tapped against her leg. The same thoughts ran through her mind over and over. *You're here to share what you know and think about how we can save this planet. This has nothing to do with religion. Just tell them what you know, let them see who you are. Maybe all those other people will finally leave you alone.*

When the speaker had finally finished, she introduced Abby. Though her stomach flipped at the mention of her name, Abby braced herself, walked up the makeshift steps, and took her place on the flatbed amid a smattering of applause.

A few puffs of billowy, white clouds danced in the sky as she began. "Thank you so much. It's a great honor to be here." As she spoke, Abby noticed several signs held up in the crowd of now seventy or eighty people. One read, *There is no Earth 2.0*, another, *There's no wealth on a dead planet*, and another, *There's no Planet B*.

Abby started by reiterating some of what the first speaker had said. Then she brought to bear some of the knowledge she had gained in her studies. "Did you know that if we were able to compress the earth's ozone layer, it would only be about 0.3 centimeters thick? And are you aware that eight kinds of ultraviolet rays from the sun bombard the earth every day, and the ozone layer filters out the longer, deadly rays but allows the shorter ones we need to get through? Yet, the people of the world don't seem to grasp the tremendous suffering that will occur on earth, the challenges brought on by climate change, if we are not willing to stop the destruction of that ozone layer." She went on for several minutes listing all kinds of other important information.

Abby stopped, pausing to gather her thoughts. "Let me speak, first, to my Navajo brothers and sisters, those who know of our four sacred mountains, who understand the concept of Hózhó— of living life in peace, balance, and beauty, and in harmony with the earth and each other. What do you believe our Dýin Diné, our divine spirits, would think of what has been accomplished here? I believe they would rejoice that with the changes accomplished here both the Navajo and others are moving in the direction of Hózhó. And I trust they would want that to be true across all the earth.

"And for those of you who are not Navajo—who believe only some higher power, some god, could have made a planet with all these subtle conditions in precisely perfect proportions to support life—what do you believe that higher power is thinking? Could it be that higher power would like to see the success the Navajo Nation and APS have achieved here replicated?" Enthusiastic applause rose from those in front of her.

She paused, looking over the crowd, then continued. "You know, my father is a fan of old rock 'n' roll, and one of his favorite groups from the '60s is The Byrds. They recorded a song written by a man many people here today may never have heard of, a folk singer named Pete Seeger. Seeger, in turn, had taken the idea from an even older source, the Bible. I'm sure you've heard this somewhere before: To everything, there is a season and a time for every purpose under heaven."

Her next words floated into Abby's mind. She knew what they were. She knew she was about to say them. But the sensation that passed through her psyche the instant before she did was a sense of rightness, a sense of authority. "My father says oil, and gas, and coal were here for humankind to use for a season, but that season is coming to an end."

A roar of clapping and hooting erupted in the audience. At the same moment, two things happened. First, a feeling of warmth and peace enveloped Abby's body. Second, several new signs appeared in the crowd. One read, *She speaks for Him*; another, *God is listening*.

As the applause died down, Abby felt the urge to continue. "And listen, there's something else I need to tell you about today." As she looked over the small sea of faces, she sensed their rapt attention. "Looking further back than my own lifetime, I know things have happened in the world—big things, little things, important things: America fought in two world wars; President Kennedy, his brother, and Dr. Martin Luther King were all assassinated; America put a man on the moon; and so on. And through all of that, we turned to trusted news media to tell us about those things, things that made up the fabric of a shared truth upon which we could all move forward. Maybe we agreed or disagreed with each other's opinions and ideas, but we shared the same facts.

"Today, I tell you, things have changed. With the coming of the internet and cable television, there are not only an unknown number of places to turn for the truth, there also seems to be an unknown number of versions of the truth." Words she had heard in some sermon came to her. "Now I can't quote it directly, but I remember that the Bible says something like, 'There will be men who will distort the truth.'" Her eyes searched the crowd. "Why would they do that? Now, it seems, people are more willing than ever before to distort the truth simply for their own benefit.

"And I know, because," she turned a thumb toward herself, "if someone hadn't distorted my truth, I wouldn't be standing here in front of you today." She pointed, drawing her finger across the whole crowd. "So, I warn you. As you share this message about saving our earth, beware of those who will take your words and turn them against you." She raised her arms in a gesture of inclusion. "Now, let's go forward, speaking *only* the truth, not exaggerations. And let's be the ones whose actions of love for the earth and for each other," her open hands turned to fists, "drown out the voices of those who would try to convince us of *their* truth, a truth based in greed, short-sightedness, and deception." As the crowd roared its approval, Abby's consciousness shifted, as if she had just awakened from a daydream or trance. She instantly felt overcome with the need to escape.

Abby flew down the steps and was greeted by Kai, Jamie, and Cliff, big smiles on their faces. Before they could congratulate her, she pushed past them and headed as quickly as she could toward Cliff's car.

As she made her way through the throng of people wanting to shake her hand or speak to her, a feeling of panic began to rise in Abby. Several of the sign-carrying members of the crowd did their best to get between her and her destination. Using his wide body, Jamie made space for her to move through the crowd. Only the lack of a suit, dark glasses, and an earpiece distinguished him from a member of the Secret Service. Kai followed close behind while Cliff hustled to pack up his gear.

After a few moments of scuffling, Abby, Kai, and Jamie finally reached Cliff's car and ducked inside. When Cliff caught up and jumped in, Jamie urged, "Get us out of here!"

"Going!" Cliff fired up the Jeep and drove forward, leaving the small group of Abby's most ardent listeners behind.

21

A s the foursome made the trip back to Shiprock, the mood in the car felt electric. Driving through the rugged desert landscape, Abby watched patches of land green with irrigation slip by, while, in the crystal-clear sky, late-afternoon storm clouds appeared on the horizon. Jamie reached over the front seat and squeezed Abby's shoulder. "That was incredible. I can't believe it. You rocked back there."

Kai chimed in. "Incredible is right. You owned those people. Did you see how they hung on your every word? And when you talked about Hózhó and our divine spirits, and God, and how they all would want the earth to be clean and protected, that was unbelievable."

"And then," Jamie continued, still stoked, "when I had to run interference to get you through the crowd because they were all dying to shake your hand and everything, that must have made you feel like a rock star."

Abby responded quietly. "I never wanted to be a star." She kept her eyes focused on the road ahead. "I just went there to help—to teach people some things."

Kai leaned forward, hanging on the back of Cliff's seat. "What did you think, Cliff? Wasn't she great?"

"Yup, she was great—shared some important ideas."

After a moment's silence, Kai asked, "So, Abby, why did you run off the stage so fast? Those people couldn't get enough of you. They wanted to hear more."

Abby shrugged. "I don't know. One minute I was just saying what I believed, the next minute it was like I hardly knew where I was. I mean, who am I to be telling all those folks anything?"

"You, young lady, will know when you see the video I shot today," said Cliff, "when you hear how real, how authentic you came off while you were speaking. Trust me, I may be pretty new to this TV news business, but I can tell you one thing: you've got something special."

The conversation bounced back and forth between Cliff and Kai and Jamie, each of them recounting how well things had gone that afternoon. Abby, on the other hand, remained silent, absently running her fingers through her hair, lost in thought— wondering about how much of what she said had come from her and how much from . . . *who knows?*

THE FLOOR MANAGER at KAQE-TV raised his hand and got the attention of Bob Standish, one of the two anchors on the Saturday evening local news program. "Thirty seconds, Bob." Then, "In five, four, three, ..."

Bob's voice was as big and muscular as his nattily dressed frame. "Well, she's at it again." Reading from the prompter, nary a hair out of place, Bob continued. "This afternoon, Abby Duncan, a recent guest of our own Barbara Ellis Rice, spoke to a crowd of protestors at the APS Four Corners Generating Station thirty minutes outside of Shiprock, New Mexico."

"That's right, Bob." Linda Haverston, his equally polished

colleague, tagged in. "After making quite a few odd statements on *The Barbara Ellis Rice Show* last weekend, it seems Ms. Duncan was determined to keep implying she has a special relationship with," she grinned coyly, "should we say . . . a higher power?"

Bob picked up the thread. "Early this evening, we received some iPhone video from the protest. Let's roll that right now."

Shot from a distance, Abby appeared on the screen, standing in front of a microphone and speaking to the crowd at the rally. "My father says oil, and gas, and coal were here for humankind to use for a season, but that season is coming to an end." The video cut to another moment. "There will be men who will distort the truth." The video jumped again, her arms now suddenly raised. ". . . drown out the voices of those who would try to convince us of *their* truth." The video ended with the roar of approval that had followed Abby's speech that afternoon.

"So, you can see, Bob, it seems pretty clear Ms. Duncan has some sort of agenda and an obvious disdain for those who spend their days and nights bringing the people of our great state the news they need and deserve."

Bob cocked his head, "And this notion about what her *father* says. Is she talking about Mr. Duncan or are we supposedly looking at the next incarnation of Jesus?" He grinned. "We'll certainly keep an eye on this story for all of you."

Big smile from Linda. "And now let's find out what George has for us at the weather desk."

~

Sitting at a table inside the rugged interior of Pecos Bill's, with its plethora of nods to its western namesake she'd become accustomed to, Abby felt at home. Her two closest friends, Kai and Jamie sat across from her. Cliff, sitting next to her, was a man she had decided to trust, though she wasn't entirely sure about his motivation in helping her. She put her questions aside and allowed the pleasures of a simple pulled-pork dinner with baked beans, coleslaw, and a cold sweet tea to bring her a sense of peace and well-being.

Although Abby did her best to steer clear of the topic, Kai and Jamie seemed determined to continually revisit the rally—reveling in the way Abby had mesmerized and moved the crowd.

Cliff was just finishing a cold draft beer when his phone rang. "Hello. Yeah, hi, John . . . . Oh, I see . . . . Yeah, I've got video of my own . . . . Listen, thanks for letting me know." He hung up.

A sense of dread tightened Abby's stomach as she became convinced the call was about her. She asked Cliff with her eyes.

"That was my buddy John at the station. We're just a little outlet, so we try to keep up with what the bigger guys are doing around the state." He looked away for a moment before turning to Abby with a sigh. "It appears the folks at KAQE in Albuquerque got hold of some iPhone footage from today's rally."

"And?" Abby asked, the pit in her stomach growing.

"Looks as though they sliced and diced your words again, making you look pretty much like you should be wearing an aluminum foil hat."

Abby's eyes closed and her chin dropped. "Crap."

Jamie's voice was so loud several other diners turned in their direction, "Can they get away with that?"

Cliff nodded. "She's a public figure now. No one would expect them to air everything she said. Therefore, what they choose to air is kind of up to them, especially if they don't take things out of order." He rocked his empty glass back and forth. "John recorded their feed; I'll compare it with what Abby actually said. Chances are, though, they'll be okay as long as they haven't done anything too outrageous with their editing."

As disheartening as Cliff's words were, something inside Abby started to smolder—something even she didn't recognize.

22

After dinner, Cliff drove the others back to the women's apartment. As they piled out of the car, Cliff asked, "Abby, can we talk for a minute, maybe take a walk?"

"Sure."

They set off at a leisurely pace, strolling along a path that ran near the edge of a grassy field. It was only a few days before the summer solstice, and the sun had sunk into the pink and red of the western sky. As they walked, Abby felt the warm breeze on her bare arms.

Cliff began. "I hope you're not mad at me."

"For what?"

"For encouraging you to take part in that rally today."

"Why would I be? I had a great experience."

"True," Cliff grimaced slightly, "but it looks like your friends at KAQE are still intent on giving you grief—grief they couldn't have generated without you being on that flatbed this afternoon."

Abby shook her head. "No problem. First, looking back, I feel like I was supposed to be there. Second, I experienced something really special while I was up there speaking. I wouldn't want to have missed any of that."

They walked in silence for a while before Cliff spoke again. "You know, if you don't keep your head down, things are only going to get tougher. This blend of social media, radio, and cable TV can turn out some pretty toxic stuff, know what I mean?"

"Well, they're going to have to do that without my help for the next few days."

Cliff stopped and gently took her by the elbow. "What does that mean?"

Abby turned to face him. "It means that on our way back to Shiprock this afternoon, I decided it was time for me to go visit my mother on the reservation. I'll be gone about a week."

"Aren't we," his eyes narrowed, "already on the reservation?"

She smiled. "Technically, yes. Shiprock is on Navajo Reservation land. But I'm talking about the real reservation, where the Diné, the people, live a different life—where they're surrounded by Navajo culture and thinking."

"Oh." He pondered for a while. "Do you think maybe I could come visit you there, even just for just a couple of hours?"

She shook her head again, still smiling. "No. I'm sorry, but this is a trip I have to make on my own. You can go back to the bustling metropolis of Farmington and pursue your new TV career," her tone turned a little snarky, "maybe make some progress toward getting a job on one of the big networks. You're good-looking enough."

Abby regretted those words the instant they left her mouth. She was, after all, standing a mere arm's length away from the man, with his sturdy build and good looks, quick, insightful mind, and big, caring heart. A flush of warmth washed over her body.

She saw him stiffen and nervously lick his lips. "I, uh, guess I should thank you for the compliment."

Her own breath thickened. "No problem." She turned away. "I'm sure that's not the first time you were told something like that."

"Well..."

She pivoted sharply back to him. "Don't play coy with me, Cliff. I don't doubt that you've broken a heart or two in your time." She had trouble resisting his dark brown eyes. "Anyway," she turned away again, "I need to get back. Let's go, okay?"

"Sure, sure. I need to head back to Farmington, as well. I want to check out the video I shot and compare it to what came out of Albuquerque."

Resigned to her new reality, Abby started back toward her apartment, a few steps ahead of him. "Don't fret too much about it. I'm not all that worried about what they did, and, based on what you said, I'm not sure I could do anything about it, anyway."

SHIPROCK, New Mexico – Wednesday, June 23rd

Abby was in the kitchen making ramen for dinner when Kai walked into the apartment. Kai's eyes widened with her smile. "Abby, you're home. I didn't expect you." She plopped her purse on the coffee table. "I thought you were going to be gone all week."

Abby shrugged and smiled, spinning a wooden spoon in her fingers. "I guess it felt like I accomplished what I needed to get done and it was time to come home." She dropped a square of dry noodles into boiling water. "And three nights of sleeping on the ground was about all my body could take. I'm not a little kid anymore."

Kai cocked her head. "Sleeping on the ground? I thought you were staying with your mom."

Abby sighed. "Yeah, well, turns out what I really needed was some time alone, you know? So, I called my mom and told her I'd come see her some other time ... soon."

"And?"

"So, remember that spot where my dad used to take me camping—where you and I went senior year?"

"Yeah."

"Well, I called your cousin Johnny, borrowed some gear, and stayed there for a couple of days, just to think."

Kai had taken a seat on the couch and was going through the few pieces of mail she had pulled out of their mailbox on her way into the apartment. "Sounds cool."

"Right . . . pretty much."

Kai looked up, curious. "What does that mean?"

Abby poured the noodles into a bowl, then walked to the armchair. "It went well, it's just that something strange happened."

Kai's eyebrows went up.

Abby set her bowl on the coffee table and sat. "So, my third evening out there, I was scrounging around for kindling for my fire, and I pulled on what I thought was just the remnants of some dead bush. But instead of coming right up, it turned out the thing was really well-rooted. When I finally yanked the darn thing out of the ground, a large clump of earth came with the roots. I looked down in the hole that created and saw something."

"What?"

Abby shook her head. "A whole abalone shell."

"That's a little weird, isn't it? I mean out there?"

"Right. I guess it could have been dropped there by someone a long time ago."

"Or, maybe, it might have been there for thousands of years, from when this land was under seawater."

Abby nodded. "True, but here's the thing. You know how we say abalone brings a sense of peace?"

"Yeah."

"Well, when I poured some water in it and cleaned it up, I could hardly believe my eyes. All the blue, and purple, and green swirls, the luminescent white on the inside, they came together to make this incredible design, more distinct than you usually see."

"What kind of design?"

"I can't explain it, but the more I stared at it, the more this deep sense of peace came over me."

"Peace?"

"Yeah, peace. Not relief, it was more like the gnarled and bumpy parts, touching my palms, represented something I'm going through or *will* go through. But the part I was looking at, those beautiful swirls of color, filled me with this overwhelming sensation of well-being."

"Wow."

"Yeah, and even when I finally put the shell down and got back to starting the fire, I still had the same lingering sensation."

Kai sat up taller. "Let me see it. Is it in your bedroom?"

Abby shook her head. "You're not going to believe this, but somehow I got this powerful feeling I wasn't supposed to bring it out of the desert. That, in some bizarre way, if I did, it would lose its power."

Kai's face scrunched up. "So, what did you do with it?"

"I," Abby shrugged, "put it right back into that hole. I covered the shell up and walked away. I don't think I could find it again if I tried." She sat for a moment, then reached down and picked up her bowl.

Kai nodded slowly, almost reverently. "Back to Dinétah, back to the earth."

23

Monday morning, Abby was getting ready to do a noon-to-close shift at Pecos Bill's when her phone rang. "Hello?"

"Abby, it's me, Cliff. Are you okay?"

"Oh, hi, Cliff. Sure I'm okay. Why wouldn't I be?"

"Well, we haven't spoken in over a week. I've tried calling several times and haven't been able to get in touch with you. I was getting worried."

"Yeah," she sighed into the phone, "sorry about that. I just needed some time. I didn't mean to make you worry." She had to admit she didn't hate hearing that he had been concerned.

"So . . . did you have a pleasant visit with your mom?"

Abby braced herself. "Actually, I changed my mind. I didn't go to see my mom."

Cliff's words came quickly. *"You didn't go out on the reservation?"*

"I *did* go out on the reservation. I just didn't go visit my mom."

Cliff paused before asking the next question. *"So, who did you see?"*

"Nobody, mostly nobody."

"Oh, okay." He sounded confused and concerned.

"I went camping."

"Camping?"

"Yeah, there's a spot my dad used to take me to. I borrowed a tent from one of my friends and just went out there and camped."

"By yourself?" There was concern in his voice.

"Yeah, by myself. Listen, I was born on the reservation and lived there until I was twelve. I'm perfectly capable of camping out there by myself."

His apprehension was growing. *"And you were out there for a whole week?"*

Abby was hesitant to admit she'd come home early and hadn't let him know, but she didn't want to lie. "No, just four days."

"I see. Well," disappointment tinged Cliff's voice, *"I'm glad you're okay."* He paused for a moment. *"So,"* he asked softly, *"what did you do out there for all that time?"*

She answered slowly. "Thought. I mostly just thought. I spent some time with an old friend one afternoon, and I brought a book with me, but, pretty much, I just thought."

He pondered for a long while. *"Any chance you'll tell me what you were thinking about?"*

"Not right now. I've got to get to work. I had a friend cover my shifts while I was gone, so I'm kind of doing double duty. I'm off all morning tomorrow, though." Her voice turned playful. "Would you like to come to Shiprock and buy me breakfast?"

The smile in his voice was unmistakable. *"I'll have to check the schedule at the station, but if we do it early enough, I might be able to get there and be back in time to pick up an assignment in the afternoon."*

"Okay, but not too early. Even a Navajo woman needs her beauty sleep."

∽

A T EIGHT O'CLOCK SHARP on Tuesday morning, Cliff knocked on Abby's door. His huge grin greeted her when she opened it. "Ready for some breakfast?"

"That I am." She picked up her purse and stepped out into the sunshine of a beautiful New Mexico day—a few pillowy clouds, and a sun that was already climbing into the crystalline sky. They were heading for La Cocina, a cute little Mexican restaurant with brightly colored walls and painted tables that sat on the earthen-tinged tiled floor. According to Abby, it served the best huevos rancheros in town.

After ordering their meals and starting with cups of coffee, Cliff attempted some small talk, but Abby had other ideas. "Listen. You had some questions last night and I've been considering my answers, so let's get to it." Her smile neutralized any tension her words might have implied.

"Okay, if you're sure you want to get down to things before we eat."

Her smile broadened. "I'm sure. Now, what's your first question?"

"All right, then why did you tell me you were going to visit your mom and then do something completely different?"

"Hmm," she looked at him severely, her eyebrows furrowed. "A girl could take offense at that question—like I was responsible to you about where I go and when." Her smile returned. "But I'm not going to hold it against you this time. The answer is simple. I just changed my mind. Once I got out there in the open spaces, I realized what I needed more than comfort and advice was time to get my own thoughts together—you know, commune with myself.

"Anyway, I called my mom and told her there was a change in plans and I'd try my best to catch up with her some other time."

"All right." Cliff picked up his heavy, cream-colored coffee mug. "Thanks for the forbearance. Now, more importantly, what were you thinking about?"

Abby took a long sip of her coffee and sat up straighter. "Okay, look. I spent the first years of my life on the reservation. I was surrounded by, and part of, a culture that was entirely different from anything you ever experienced. When my mom and I moved to Shiprock, we started attending Sunrise Community Church, a full-on Christian church. It was a whole new experience. During those four days I spent in the desert, pretty much alone, I passed a lot of time thinking about each of those experiences: being part of the Navajo culture; being part of a Christian church. Trust me, it was quite a journey."

He put his mug down. "Go on."

"See, each of those spiritual traditions has their own mystical origin stories. For the Navajo, there are the four worlds. The first world was the dark world. That's where First Man and First Woman came into existence. They have supernatural powers. Then there was the second or blue world with all kinds of blue animals. In the third world, the yellow world, there were two rivers that formed a cross and the four sacred mountains, but there was still no sun. Finally, in the fourth world, First Man and First Woman created the sun, the moon, the stars, and the seasons. That's where the first humans were born.

She took another sip of coffee. "Of course, most people know about the origin stories from the Christian faith—that God created the universe in six days and rested on the seventh. He formed Adam out of clay and blew breath into him. Then he created Eve as a companion for Adam. They lived in paradise until the serpent came into the Garden of Eden and after that, there was sin in the world." Her eyebrows lifted, and she smiled. "And—I learned this in that class I took—that's pretty much the same origin story for Jews and Muslims too, all the way up to the story of Abraham, the guy who was promised as many descendants as there are stars in the sky. And when Jesus is born, he's a Jew. He says he's the Son of God, sent to earth to show people a new path to a personal relationship with God and a way to go to heaven. Christians and Jews call God Yahweh, though the Christians believe he is part of the Holy Trinity—Father, Son and Holy Ghost—while the Jews don't. Later, the prophet Muhammad comes along, and that's the beginning of Islam. Muslims call God Allah. Some people think Yahweh and Allah are the same God.

"But there are differences in what some believe about the nature of that God." She rolled her eyes. "I had to look it up in my textbook again." She took a quick sip and continued. "Muslims believe Allah is too holy to have a personal relationship with humans, but he revealed a covenant and a way of living that would be to their benefit if they chose to accept it. Christians, Jews, and Muslims all see Yahweh, or Allah, as a loving god who is concerned about our personal well-being."

The server, a middle-aged woman with gray-streaked black hair, arrived with two large plates, each covered with a large grilled flour tortilla, topped with refried beans, cheese, two fried eggs, and salsa. Just seeing the dish made Abby's mouth water. She looked up at Cliff. "Tell you what. Let's eat these while they're still hot. We can talk over coffee."

Cliff agreed, and they proceeded to devour their meal in near silence. When they had both finished and pushed away their plates, Cliff asked, "Can we get back to things now?"

"Sure, go ahead."

"So, you went out into the desert and you wound up thinking about your comparative religion class?"

"And Dr. Wertz, the guy who made me so mad in class?" She threw her head back and laughed. "No, I looked that stuff up after I got back." Her tone became more serious. "What I was thinking about was what I said to you the first time we met."

"Which was?"

"You asked me if I was an agnostic or an atheist, and I told you I was a Christian. Later, I told you I wasn't sure what I believed in, but I did believe in God."

"I remember."

"So, one night, I'm sitting there alone in the dark under this sky filled with stars, and it comes to me."

"An answer?"

She smiled coyly. "No, silly, a question. *Why* do I believe in God?"

The server stopped by the table and asked if they wanted more coffee. They both nodded. She poured quickly, then left.

Cliff lifted his cup but spoke before he drank. "You were saying?"

Abby picked up her cup as well. "Right. I had to ask myself why I told you so easily I believe in God."

"And your answer?"

"I guess you could call it a personal miracle."

24

C liff's eyes widened. "A miracle?"

Abby took her first sip of the freshened cup. "I guess. See, when I was seventeen and I'd just had my full license for less than a year, they predicted a snowstorm. The department of highways, or whatever they call it, had gone out and put some stuff down, you know, to keep the roads clear if they could."

Abby licked her lips, remembering the feelings that accompanied the event she was about to describe. "So, I'm driving along on the inner lane of a four-lane road, Route 491, and the light turns red." She sat up taller. "Now, I'm an inexperienced driver, and when the light turns red, I jam on the brakes no matter what. Unfortunately, two things happen: First, my car starts to slide on the stuff they'd just put down on the road; second, the guy coming toward me in the opposite direction decides to run right through the light. And there I am," her words came faster, "in his lane, cranking the wheel as hard as I could, trying to get out of his way. Meanwhile, here he comes, having sped up to get through the light, and me just yards away, right in front of him." She stopped.

Cliff was leaning in, listening intently. "And?"

"And the strangest thing happened. I knew there was no way we could avoid a head-on crash. I'm turning the wheel as hard as I can, but I know it's not enough. I close my eyes, and it's like I could hear the crash, tortured metal screaming, glass flying. But when I open them, there's nothing like that. I'm back in my own lane. I'm okay. The car's okay. It's like the two vehicles just passed through each other, as if all the laws of physics didn't hold. The crash that *had* to happen *didn't*." She looked straight into his eyes. "It just didn't happen."

Cliff put down his cup. "And you thought it was an honest-to-goodness miracle?"

She shook her head. "Not at the time, no. Honestly, I guess I just felt lucky. But later, it kept gnawing at me. That shouldn't have happened. It couldn't have happened. It just wasn't possible that we didn't crash into each other."

"But now you think it was a miracle."

"Have you ever read, *Miracles*, by C. S. Lewis?"

"No, I haven't."

Abby rocked back in her chair. "Well, I took it out of the library over the weekend. I tried reading it, but the guy is way over my head. He talks about naturalists and supernaturalists. The first group thinks nature is everything—he calls it 'the whole show.' But the supernaturalists believe nature is only part of the whole show, that there's a god, and he's *more* than nature—*he's* the whole show.

She moved her hands as if she were juggling two balls. "So, there are laws of nature, and there's God. And those laws of nature, like if one billiard ball hits another, the amount of energy the new ball gets, is the same amount of energy that's lost by the first ball, those laws are always in play—that kind of thing." She rolled her eyes. "You can see why it was tough to follow this guy and all his examples."

She took a sip of coffee and sat up. "Anyway, this is what I sort of believe. A miracle occurs when God interferes with the very laws of nature he set up in the first place. In other words, there are those laws of nature, like if a cancerous tumor is there one morning and nothing happens, no surgery or medicines, the tumor will be there the next morning. But if, for some reason, God doesn't want it to be there, then he *can,* and on the rarest of occasions *does,* set that law of nature aside and the tumor *could* be gone.

"Now, this Lewis guy, his explanation is more complicated. He says there are the laws of nature that are always in effect. Then God, who is greater than nature, *inserts* something new into the equation and the rest of nature immediately absorbs the new reality and handles it according to the normal laws." She shook her head. "It's complicated—too thick for me to understand."

Cliff nodded. "So, you think God made it so the atoms of your car could somehow pass through the atoms of that other person's car without causing a crash?"

She nodded her head. "Yes, absolutely."

"Interesting." He took another sip of coffee.

She leaned in. "Look, I know if I tell that story to a bunch of people, many of them will say the two cars just barely missed each other, and I didn't see it because my eyes were closed. But it doesn't matter. What counts to me is what I believe. And now, looking back, I *believe* it was a miracle—that God did, for some unknown reason, suspend the laws of nature that night or insert some new temporary reality, whichever. I don't know, maybe it was because he needed me to stay alive so I could do something in the future. Maybe it wasn't me he was saving. Maybe it was the other driver who was about to do some important work, and he didn't want me and my lousy driving to screw that all up. But, one way or the other, I believe he stuck his hand in there and made an impossible thing possible."

Cliff thought for a while. "And you're telling me all of this because?"

"Because when I was out in the desert, the first question I asked myself was why I believe in God."

"And you believe in God because he does miracles?"

She shook her head. "No. I believe in God because I had a personal encounter with him . . . or her. My life changed because that accident never happened, and trust me, in my best, most logical, most rational appraisal, there was no way in the world that accident didn't happen unless there *is* a God, and he *did* make something happen that couldn't possibly happen."

Again, Cliff ruminated a while before he spoke. "So, that's what you accomplished out there on the reservation, thinking about why you believe in God?"

Abby tipped her head back and finished the coffee. "Yes and no. I originally went out there to try to understand this whole thing, what I did in Tucson when I said, 'God loves you,'—and then everything that's happened since then."

"And did you come to understand this," he made air quotes, "whole thing?"

"Well, as for my having spoken words God gave me, I have no idea if that's true or not. I certainly didn't think so that morning, and I don't think I'm anything special." She wagged her finger. "But let me tell you something. All those religious folks who are saying nasty things about me on the internet, they all read their Bibles and talk in church about God speaking *to* people and *through* people. But if someone like Dr. Sterling implies God might have spoken through *me*, then something's totally wrong— God would never do anything like that." She sat back, trying to calm herself. As she did, her phone pinged, alerting her to a new email message.

Cliff finished his coffee and pushed his cup toward the middle of the table. "Wow, I guess you *have* been doing some heavy thinking. And I'm afraid you're right. Ever since that rally at the generating station, the internet has been bubbling over with posts about you—some good, some bad. And I'm sorry to say, I don't think for a minute people are going to drop this, not unless you go back out on the reservation and stay there for a good long while."

Abby looked up from her phone with an impudent smile. "I'm pretty sure you're right, and we're going to find out soon."

"Why?"

"Because I just had another invitation, one I plan on accepting."

25

B *ranson, Missouri - Wednesday, July 7th*
    Two weeks later, just three days after the Fourth of July, Abby and Cliff walked into the studios of CCC, the Christian Communication Cooperative. A large organization with facilities and technical people who supported a host of Christian television, radio, and internet programming, it was located in Branson, Missouri. Every inch of the building was pristine, smooth to the touch, shiny. The colors were crisp, with a heavy reliance on white as the main chromatic theme.

Dressed in a neat white button-down blouse and modest blue skirt, Abby felt she presented a suitable image for the obviously conservative show and audience. Cliff wore a jacket and tie.

Over the last two weeks, Cliff had been gathering information and video for a special KFRM had agreed to let him produce. The station was far from convinced that Abby's story was significant, but he had persuaded them they would regret it if it turned out to be noteworthy and they had passed up a chance to be in on the ground level. Trusting Cliff as she did, Abby had seen no reason to object. Given the sixteen-hour drive from Shiprock to Branson, the station had even sprung for two airline tickets, a rental car, and two motel rooms.

Cliff had also assumed the unofficial role of Abby's manager. He had convinced her that, in his limited time in the broadcast industry, he had already seen some of the pitfalls Abby might encounter, and how helpful it could be to have a buffer between her and anyone who wanted to interview her or ask her to speak. After her experience with Barbara Ellis Rice, it hadn't taken much to convince her to agree.

Cliff had done his best to dissuade Abby from doing an interview at CCC, but ever since her time out on the reservation, Abby had taken on an entirely new attitude. She had been poked at and ridiculed enough. It was, in her opinion, the right occasion for her to begin asking a few questions of her own.

As Abby and Cliff walked up to the receptionist's desk, a large man with slicked-back black hair and an expensive pin-stripe suit approached them. His smile was broad, his eyes full of life. "Mr. Davis, it's a real pleasure to meet you, sir."

Cliff shook the man's hand. "A pleasure to meet you as well."

The man turned immediately to Abby. "And this must be Ms. Duncan. So nice to have you with us. Billy is looking forward to your time together. In fact, I understand some of our regular viewers are so interested in you, they've come to the station." He raised his shoulders. "Of course, they can't be on this side of the building—security, you know—but there's a viewing lounge on the other side and quite a few are in there already. Twenty or thirty folks, I would think." He took a quick breath. "Can I get either of you anything?"

A tight smile crossed Abby's lips. Remembering her experience on Barbara Ellis Rice's set, she said, "Water, please. Thank you." Cliff nodded in agreement.

"Okay, then." He turned them toward a long hallway. "Let's have one of our girls do a little freshening up on your hair and makeup. The show starts right at eleven and you're Billy's first guest."

Twenty-four minutes later, Abby was sitting on a plush red chair, across from one of the most striking men she had ever seen. Tall, maybe six foot three, and built like an ex-football player, Billy Comstock filled the matching red chair. The studio lights reflected off his perfectly combed hair—blonde-turned partially gray—and if he had any blemishes, his makeup concealed them. His gleaming white teeth were straight as the kernels in a prize-winning ear of corn at the county fair, and his suit was right out of Savile Row. He gave Abby a generous smile, and when he spoke, his baritone voice was deep, round, and resonant.

"Welcome, Ms. Duncan, it's a pleasure to have you here today. Is it all right if I call you Abby?"

The question sent a little chill through her. It seemed like she'd been here before, and she was no longer certain she wanted to be here again. "Thank you, and yes, that's fine."

Comstock checked his notes as bright red digits on the studio clock counted down the last two minutes. Finally, the floor manager said, "We're on the air in five, four, three . . . ." He pointed to the host and the man's smile and voice erupted.

"Good morning, and welcome to the day the Lord has made. I'm Billy Comstock, and I trust you're having a blessed day. For the next hour, we'll be sharing stories we hope will convince you Jesus Christ, our Lord, is in every moment of every day, whether it feels like heaven or feels like . . . ." He gave the camera a big, theatrical wink. "Well, we all know what I'm talking about. And speaking of heaven, I must say, I have a beautiful young woman with me today, Ms. Abby Duncan." Abby saw the red light on the camera facing her begin to glow. "Welcome, Abby. It's our pleasure to have you with us."

Comstock gave the audience a thumbnail sketch of Abby's background, with an emphasis on her Navajo heritage. Thoughts flashed through her mind. *Navajo, Navajo, Navajo. Yes, I'm Navajo and proud of it, but can't you just see me as a person, a human being? And when a Navajo woman is asked about her experiences as someone who believes in God, does the focus have to be on the fact that she's Navajo, rather than what she believes?*

Comstock asked her to explain her journey to the show, and Abby did her best to lay out as honestly and simply as possible her path from comparative religion class, to Tucson, and on to her speech at the generating station. She had already decided not to mention her experience with Barbara Ellis Rice.

When Abby finished, Comstock's questions started. They were simple, at first, and she started to feel at ease. However, it wasn't long before the gloves came off. "Now, Abby. I know this must be a difficult topic. But there has been a lot of conversation on radio and TV, and even on the internet, about you believing you are a special messenger from the Lord. What can you tell us about your experience and, simply, whether or not you believe that's true?"

Abby took a deep breath. "Billy," she cocked her head, "is it all right if I call you Billy?"

Flustered, he nodded.

"You would say you are a religious man, would you not?"

Comstock sat up taller and chuckled. "I most certainly would say so."

"And do you believe you have a relationship with God?"

The tiniest bit of discomfort showed on Comstock's face. "I just told you, yes."

A sense of peace came over Abby as she pushed forward. "No, you said you were a religious man. Now, being religious means doing something on a regular basis." She shrugged and smiled. "I mean, you could wash your hands religiously, or exercise religiously." She moved forward quickly. "And, of course, you could read the Bible religiously or pray religiously," she leaned in, "things I'm sure you do."

He nodded, confident. "Of course."

She continued, using words she'd recently read in one of her textbooks. "Now, when we use the term, 'religion,' more commonly, we think of it as a formalized pattern of behaviors—ways we worship God, ways we behave socially, things we do or don't do because we believe in God, right?" She didn't wait for an answer. "In fact, for some people, how we dress, what we eat, what we can or cannot drink, those are all things some folks consider part of their religion." She smiled warmly, "So, let me ask you again, do you believe you have a relationship with God?"

Abby could see the veins in Comstock's neck bulging. "I just told you, young lady. I most certainly have a relationship with the Lord."

She nodded and smiled again. "I'm sure you do. But, if I could ask another question, can you imagine yourself speaking directly to God?"

Comstock answered with a deep and hearty laugh. "Again, most certainly. Every morning and every night."

Abby gave him a moment. "So, you have conversations with God?"

"Oh, Ms. Duncan," his mood was still jovial, "you can trust that I speak to the Lord all the time, but I don't necessarily expect to hear back, if you know what I mean."

Abby turned more serious. "But don't so many Christians say that on occasion God speaks to them? Things like, 'I saw a homeless man on the corner and God spoke to me. He told me to stop and buy the man lunch,' or 'God spoke to me and told me to call my friend. And when I did, it turned out her husband had just died?' People of faith say things like that, don't they?"

Comstock nodded cautiously. "Yes, they do. It's our assumption the Holy Spirit nudges us in certain ways to do his work here on earth." He pressed. "You're not challenging that, are you?"

"Absolutely not. But, if you don't mind, I'd like to ask yet another question. Do you think God is happy about how things are going on earth right now?"

Comstock turned serious. "Well, I'm quite sure there are many things that trouble his heart."

"And can you imagine asking him which things those are?"

"Again," his smile became fatherly, "I don't believe I would presume to ask the Lord anything like that and expect an answer. But I do believe he might be less than pleased about many things."

"Well, Mr. Comstock, I guess what I'm saying is that I don't believe it's all that hard to accept that God might want to put some words in the mouth of a young woman and use her to tell the world something. Do you find that hard to believe?"

Comstock's face began to redden as his large presence moved threateningly forward in his chair. "You mean, as if he were speaking directly through her. Come on now, Ms. Duncan, you wouldn't have us believe—"

"That God has the power to communicate to us in any way he chooses? I'm afraid, Mr. Comstock, that's exactly what I mean."

Abby could tell Comstock was at the end of his patience with her and about to respond aggressively when she noticed the floor manager waving his arms wildly. Comstock saw it, too, and shifted gears, an obviously faux smile crossing his lips. "Thank you, Ms. Duncan, for a fascinating conversation." He turned to the camera. "And we'll be right back with a song of faith from our own Allison Strong."

26

A bby unclipped her mic and popped out of her chair. With a quick handshake and a, "Thank you very much, Mr. Comstock," she turned and hurried toward the studio door. Cliff, who had been taping the interview on his phone, picked up her leather purse and followed. As soon as the heavy gray door closed behind them, he caught up to her and asked under his breath, "Did you have fun?"

Without stopping, Abby turned to him. "What do you mean?"

Cliff chuckled. "I mean, you just put a two-hundred-sixty-pound man with a half-million TV followers in his place, and did it with a smile on your face."

Abby didn't respond until they had passed through another door and into the lobby. "As far as I know, all I did was ask a few simple questions and raise a possibility which most of those followers talk about all the time anyway."

"Right."

As she passed by, Abby smiled at the receptionist. "Thank you for everything."

Cliff nodded as well and held the door for Abby.

They walked down the sidewalk and around the corner of the

building, to the parking lot where their rental car was waiting. Abby froze. Milling outside another entrance to the CCC facility was a group of nine or ten people—men and women, mostly in their fifties and older.

Cliff spoke sideways at her. "Fans?"

Abby kept her eyes on the small crowd. "They don't appear to be smiling. Maybe they're waiting for a shuttle bus or something?"

Cliff had his eyes on the group as well. "I doubt it. Let's just pray they're hoping to say something nice to you," he raised his eyebrows, "though it sure doesn't look like it."

They walked forward, slowly at first, and then with more determination. As the small crowd appeared to recognize Abby, Cliff whispered. "Brace yourself." They picked up the pace.

"Blasphemer!" The shouting started.

"Liar!"

"Who do you think you are?"

The crowd started in their direction. Abby and Cliff hustled toward their car.

"Fraud!"

"He wouldn't speak through you!"

"Go back to the reservation!"

The race was on. Abby and Cliff ran to their vehicle, Cliff fumbling with the unfamiliar fob, trying to unlock the doors. As they did, the crowd moved in their direction, deterred only by the fact that they didn't know which car the two of them were running toward.

Finally reaching their vehicle, Abby and Cliff grabbed the handles and yanked the doors open. Whap! As she tumbled into her seat, the corner of the door caught Abby's face, slicing the skin just below her eye.

Cliff turned, his eyes widening at the sight of blood. "Are you okay?"

"Drive! Drive!"

Cliff started the car, threw it into gear, and hit the gas as the first of the crowd reached the car. Abby could see the fury in their faces as they banged on the hood and the roof. The roar of the engine may have drowned out their words, but she had no problem understanding their message.

Once he had cleared the group, Cliff stomped on the gas, pushing the Ford to twenty, thirty, forty miles per hour.

SCREECH!! Cliff slammed on the brakes. Another driver, unaware of Cliff's speed, had backed out of her parking space and right into his path. His arms braced against the steering wheel, he managed to bring the car to a stop, avoiding a collision.

Abby wasn't so lucky. Throwing her hand out in front of her in the near-wreck, she wrenched her wrist on the dashboard. By the time Cliff looked at her, she was holding her wrist, grimacing, as a thin track of blood ran down her face.

With the crowd well behind them, Cliff motioned to the woman in the other car, indicating he was sorry and that she should continue. She took off. Cliff and Abby took a moment to buckle up, then he followed her out of the parking lot and onto the street.

A FEW MINUTES LATER, as Cliff calmly motored toward the main drag in Branson, he asked again, "Are you okay?"

Abby's heart had finally returned to a normal rhythm. She nodded, using a tissue from her purse to staunch the bleeding under her eye. "Yeah, I guess, but this cut below my eye hurts like crazy, and my wrist is killing me."

He scanned their surroundings as he drove. "I tell you what, let's find a place where we can get something to eat. Maybe the server will bring you a couple of cloth napkins and some ice to put on your face. I have a hunch you're going to have quite a shiner by tomorrow morning."

"What was that all about?" Abby's voice was subdued. "I didn't say anything wrong. I didn't accuse anyone of anything. I just—"

Cliff chuckled. "You just put their hero on the spot, asked him if he really did have a relationship with God, and then told them that God might have used you to speak to the world." He shrugged. "Nothing unusual at all."

Abby stiffened. "Sure, but what I said, that lots of Christians say God talks to them, that's all true and they know it." She pressed. "And I didn't say I actually believed God spoke to me or through me. All I said was that it shouldn't be so hard to believe God *might* do that. Was that so wrong?"

"Listen, young lady. I may be new to this business, but if I've learned anything so far, it's that people don't hear what you say. They hear what they expect to hear, what their prejudices allow them to hear, whether you said it or not." He took his eyes off the road and grinned at her. "And as for giving ol' Billy Comstock a hard time? I think you better realize you just poked the bear. His folks expected a sweet little girl like you, in your modest white blouse and your blue skirt, to speak a lot more respectfully to the man they send all that money to every month."

Abby thought for a moment, then asked seriously, "Do you think I did something wrong today?"

He looked at her again. "Not a thing—not a single thing."

CLIFF HAD LOGGED the afternoon as personal time, and Abby had nothing special to get home to, so they spent most of the rest of the day poking around Branson, a family-oriented tourist town. They weren't particularly interested in Silver Dollar City, an 1800s-themed amusement park, and Dolly Parton's Stampede Dinner Attraction was also a bit much for their current psychological state. Still, they enjoyed a walk down the main drag, checking out the theaters and people-watching. In the end, it was dinner at Mel's Hard Luck Diner, a 1950s style eating establishment with a blue-plate menu and singing servers, which fit their needs and brought the day to a close.

Exhausted, Abby asked if they could go back to the Holiday Inn Express where they were staying. Cliff obliged.

As she got out of the car, face still puffy and wrist aching, Abby was grateful to have Cliff by her side while they rode up the elevator and walked down the hall to her room. When they stopped at the door, she took out her plastic key card and slid it into the electronic latch.

The flash of the little green light and the click that accompanied it sent a tiny charge through Abby's body. All the energy and stress of the day poured into one instant—the moment at which their time together would end, or . . . .

She turned. His dark brown eyes were focused directly on her. She could sense him drinking her in. She could feel her heart pounding. Her tongue slipped across her lips while she inhaled deeply, unaware she was doing so. She let the breath out slowly.

Cliff lifted his hand. Wordlessly, he gently ran his fingertip along the cut on her face.

With a start, Abby took a quick breath. "Thanks so much for everything. You're a real good friend." She turned, pushed the door open, and was through it in an instant. As it closed, she leaned back against it and murmured to herself, "You're a real good friend? Really?"

27

Shiprock, New Mexico - Monday, July 19th

The following Monday, her black eye fading to green and purple, Abby looked up from her couch as the apartment's front door opened. "Hi."

Kai and Jamie walked in carrying groceries and seemed to be sharing some sort of inside joke.

"What?"

Kai raised her eyebrows. "What, what?"

"What are you two laughing at?"

Kai shrugged. "Nothing."

But Jamie motioned with his arm, waving it across the room which was littered with reading material. "Look at you. It's like you're turning this place into your own personal library. How many books do you have there?" He pointed as he counted. "One, two, three, four on the couch, three on the table," he stretched to look down by her feet, "and two more down there. What are you, some sort of genius now?"

Abby's hair was pulled back in a long ponytail. She flipped it over her shoulder. "Hey, I'm just trying to figure some stuff out."

Kai put the groceries down in the kitchen and returned to the living room, taking a seat in the armchair. "Like what?"

Abby reached for the coffee cup sitting precariously near the edge of the table. "Like how all these different religions fit together, you know?"

Kai gave Jamie a sly wink. "Go on."

"Well, ever since I got involved in all of this, I've wanted to know more about religion in general—more about why I call myself a Christian."

"That's why all the books?" Jamie sat on the arm of the chair, next to Kai,

"Yeah. But I've mostly been reading the Bible." She sipped her coffee. "It's so strange. I've read parts of it before because my mom made me do it for church, but now it's like a whole new book. I can't get enough of it. Seriously, I fall asleep at night reading it."

Jamie snorted. "A real snoozer, right?"

Abby waved him off. "Just the opposite. I can't make myself stop reading." She sighed. "Of course, I wouldn't say I understand all of it. Mostly it just makes sense to me when I read the New Testament, you know, the part after Jesus is born." She grinned, "Of course, you might like the Old Testament better, Jamie. There are lots of battles and killing and stuff, prostitutes at the temple, even God getting pissed and wiping out a whole city—real manly man material."

There was a knock at the door. Kai called out. "Who is it?"

"It's Cliff. Can I come in?"

Kai looked at Abby, who nodded, then responded. "Sure, come on in."

Abby had not seen Cliff since they returned from Branson. They had, however, spoken on the phone several times.

Cliff's gaze fell immediately on Abby when he walked in. "Hi." He turned to Kai and Jamie and waved. "Hey, guys."

"Hello yourself." Abby sat up straighter, an interesting jumble of feelings tossing around inside her. "How're you doing?"

Cliff nodded slowly and smiled. "Good. Everything's fine. Got some things to share with you, though, stuff you're not going to like."

Kai interjected, "You mean about what's been happening on social media?"

Cliff nodded again. "Yup. Seems like ever since Abby did that show with Billy Comstock, half the Christian world thinks she's something really special."

"And," Jamie asked, "the other half?"

Cliff grinned. "The daughter of Beelzebub."

Jamie scrunched his face. "Who?"

"Beelzebub." Cliff winked at him. "It's another name for Lucifer, the devil."

Jamie looked down at Kai. "Whoa."

"Great." Abby pointed to the only other chair in the room, a simple wooden affair. "Have a seat. Do you want a drink or something? Coffee?"

Cliff sat down, though the expression on his face told Abby he was less than pleased about sitting so far away from her. "Coffee sounds good, if it's not too much trouble."

Kai popped up. "Abby has a pot on in the kitchen. I'll get it for you. Cream? Sugar?"

Cliff smiled. "Black's fine. Thanks." He leaned back, crossing his legs, and addressed Abby. "So, you've been keeping up with all the social media stuff?"

She nodded. "Sure. I try not to get lost in it, but when people are writing about you, it's hard not to be curious about what they're saying." She took another sip of coffee. "Do you have something you wanted to tell me?"

Cliff leaned forward. "Actually, I do. Something we need to talk about, assuming you still want my advice."

Abby put her cup down on the table and leaned toward him. "Cliff, of course I do. What is it?"

"Well, I got a call today from someone who wants to do an interview with you."

"Who?" Abby asked.

"Someone from across the pond."

"What?"

"Someone from England, London to be exact."

Kai walked back in with Cliff's coffee. "Are you kidding?"

Cliff put his hands together in front of his chin as if he were praying and addressed Kai. "Hope to die. It's a TV show that deals with religious material from all around the world and they've picked up on our little Ms. Abby, here." He took the coffee from Kai. "The guy found out I was serving as your unofficial manager and called me. I drove over from Farmington as soon as I got off the phone."

"Cliff," Abby protested, "I can't afford to go to London, and I doubt your station is going to pick up the tab."

He shook his head. "Don't worry. We wouldn't be traveling to London. We'd do it via video chat. The show airs at nine in the evening. That's two PM for us."

Abby grinned. "Great, early afternoon. That's when I'm at my best."

Cliff pointed at her. "Well, you'll need to be. This guy is not another Barbara Ellis Rice or even a Billy Comstock. This is a professional journalist with a national broadcast in the UK, and you'd better be sharp if you're thinking of talking to him."

Abby got serious. "Do you think I should do it?"

Without a table nearby, Cliff bent down and placed his cup on the floor. "It depends. You agreed to talk to Billy Comstock because you thought you had something important to say. If you still feel that way, and you're ready and willing to prepare for it, then I say yes. If not, then it's time to bow out gracefully and hope this all blows over after a while."

Abby looked at Kai. "What do you think?"

Kai pointed to the pile of books around Abby. "Seems to me you've been getting ready for this interview before you even knew it was coming." She put her hands on her hips. "Listen, I don't think there's any question about it. Something's burning inside that brain of yours, and I think you've got to get it out. The issue is whether or not you can stay with the work of preparing."

Abby thought for a moment, then spoke slowly. "Well, first, the only other thing I'm doing is putting in my time at Pecos Bill's. Second, I've already got a place to get in a little practice."

Cliff tilted his head. "You do?"

"Yes, I do. I've been asked to speak this Sunday at the church my mom and I used to attend, and I've agreed to do it."

"Cool," Jamie said. "Can we come? I mean, we're not members or anything."

Abby grinned. "You don't have to worry about that. Everyone's welcome. In fact," she glanced at Cliff, then back to Jamie, "based on the way my last performance went, I might just be glad to have you there—you *and* Kai."

"All three of us," Cliff chimed in. "I wouldn't miss this for the world—not to mention that I'm getting paid to shoot all the video I can of the adventures of Abby Duncan."

Abby slowly pulled her ponytail through her hands, a touch of apprehension on her face. "You'd better have that camera locked and loaded. Who knows what's going to happen if I do what I'm thinking of doing?"

28

Shiprock, New Mexico - Sunday, July 25th

Sunday morning, Abby was up early, really early. By five fifty, there was light in the sky, and by six fifteen Abby could see the red ball of the sun just above the low mountains behind her apartment complex. It was not her habit to get up at the crack of dawn, especially when she had worked until closing the night before, but this was the day she was to speak at Sunrise Community Church, the church she had attended as a teen.

By eight o'clock, she had taken a quick shower, blown her hair dry, and eaten a sparse breakfast. Her stomach didn't seem all that eager to process more than coffee and two pieces of toast. There was a knock on the door. She walked across the room and opened it. "Morning, Cliff."

He stepped in, smiling. "That it is, a beautiful morning. You know, I went to school in cloudy Syracuse, New York. Moving out here to New Mexico, where the sun seems to shine so much, it's just kind of cool."

Without asking, Abby went to the tiny kitchen and poured him a cup of coffee. She handed it to him with an unenthusiastic smile, all she could muster at the moment. "I'll be ready in a couple of minutes."

"Great, but don't take too long. I want to get there early enough to set up my camera, and I've got to run all that by the pastor. What's his name?"

"Pastor James something." She grimaced. "I can't remember."

"Don't worry about it," Cliff said confidently. "I do this kind of thing all the time. I'll introduce myself. He'll introduce himself. Then you and I will both find out."

Ten minutes later, they walked out the door, leaving behind Kai, who was also up and doing something she'd never done before—preparing to go to church.

It was a short drive to the morning's event, and Abby and Cliff were in the building by eight thirty. Cliff spoke with Pastor James Horn—a young-looking man in his mid-thirties, blonde-haired, blue-eyed, tall, and slender—and arranged to set up his camera as inconspicuously as possible. Of course, the pastor would have to ask if anyone in the congregation minded Cliff taping the morning's service, but he didn't think it would be a problem.

Just before nine o'clock, Abby saw Kai and Jamie walk in. Two other young men were with them, one about Jamie's age, the other appeared a little younger. Both were tall and dark-haired with boyish faces.

Kai found Abby near the front of the church and wished her luck, commenting on how strange it felt for her to be in a church. Jamie then introduced the two other young men. "Abby, these are my friends, Peter and his brother Rob." He leaned forward and spoke softly into her ear. "After what happened in Branson, I got to thinking that maybe it wouldn't be a bad idea to have a couple of buddies with me."

Abby threw her head back and laughed. "Yeah, sure. Like just in case there's a brawl here and you have to carry me out over your shoulder."

Jamie dropped his chin sheepishly. "Well, you never know."

"Listen," she touched his arm, smiling broadly, "I appreciate the thought. And you know what, I'm pretty sure it *is* going to get a little weird in here this morning. So, it just might be a good thing you brought some friends." She was touched that he had been concerned about her and knew that Kai had gotten herself a good one in this guy.

Abby took a seat on the stage. For all the times she'd been in this church, she'd never seen the room from this perspective. It seemed strange to her. Sure, the folksy banners that used to hang on the walls were gone, but it was more than that. The sensation that she was there to be an integral part of the service changed her view of the place in a unique way. The faces in the pews, one of which had often been hers, were now looking at her, expecting something from her. Instead of feeling empowered by the position she had taken, she felt small—dwarfed by the responsibility that would soon fall upon her.

The service began with music from a praise band with drums, guitars, and a keyboard. Three singers—two women and a man with long black hair, all in their twenties—took turns leading the congregation, while the lyrics were projected on a screen at the front of the sanctuary. Abby knew a few of the songs and did her best to sing along. Mostly, however, she tried to calm herself and prepare for what she was about to do.

After the music, a greeting and a prayer, Pastor Horn introduced Abby. He mentioned that this was Abby's home church, and that she had recently become known for speaking about the Lord in a very personal way. Then, he turned and motioned to her. "Abby, it's great to have you here."

Abby took a deep breath and stood. She walked to the pulpit and looked out at the congregation, some native, others not. Something struck her as strange. The building was suited for at least two hundred or more congregants. But she knew this church. In her experience there were seldom more than seventy-five people sitting in the pews. She'd imagined the same number of people would be there that morning.

As she looked out over the crowd, however, she estimated there were at least a hundred people there, maybe more. She also noticed some seemed more comfortable than others, had sung the songs more readily, had smiled at and spoken to more people. It occurred to her that quite a few people in the room were not regular attendees of Sunrise Community Church. In fact, as she thought about it, the looks on the faces of a few of those folks didn't bode well for how this morning was going to go for her.

Looking toward the back of the sanctuary, she saw Cliff, his camera on a tripod. Though she had never been comfortable being recorded, and probably never would be, seeing his warm and supportive smile gave her a moment's solace.

A subtle cough from the pastor woke Abby from her reverie. She put her hands on the pulpit and started by thanking the congregation for the invitation to speak. She indicated it was an honor to return to the church she and her mother had attended while she was growing up, and about which she had fond memories. Then it was time to get down to business.

29

Abby shifted gears. "I know Pastor James invited me to speak here today because lots of people are talking about me and my recent experiences. Mostly, people are wondering whether the words I spoke that day in Tucson came from my own heart and mind, or if they were actually from the Lord." She stopped, smiled, and chuckled. "There, I've already said more words to you today than I said to those folks down there." It took a moment, but the audience got the joke and a comfortable laugh rippled through the whole congregation.

"But I'm not here today to say much about that. If you want to know exactly what I said on the matter to Pastor Billy Comstock, just poke around on the internet. It's all over the place. But to save you the trouble, what I said to him was: 'I don't believe it's all that hard to accept that God might want to put some words in the mouth of a young woman and use her to tell the world something.' Honestly, that's all I have to say about that—all I *can* say about that."

Abby's palms were sweating; she wiped them on her jeans before continuing. "It is also true that there are people who have tried to make something out of words I attributed to my father, words about environmental issues. They wonder, am I claiming to be the sister of Jesus?" She lifted the leather-bound book she had brought with her to the pulpit. "I'd like to read to you from the Bible—words from Jesus himself." She turned to a page she had already marked with a yellow Post-it note. "If you have your bibles and want to read along, I'm reading from Matthew, chapter twelve, verse fifty."

It amazed Abby to hear herself say those words, words which tumble so easily from the mouths of preachers every Sunday, words she never thought she would say herself. She pressed on, reading out loud. "Those who do the will of God, they are my brother and my sister and my mother." She closed the Bible. "That is all I have to say about that as well."

She paused a moment to breathe, her eyes scanning the congregation. "Now, I didn't run this by Pastor James, and probably should have," she glanced at the pastor, then returned her attention to the congregation, "but I'd like to ask you all to stand." The people complied, and another glance at Pastor James told her he was okay with the request.

"In a moment, I'm going to ask you to come up to this altar as a group and receive a blessing from Pastor James." Abby could sense the willingness of the people to do what she asked. "Before you do, however, I would like each of you to take your wallet from your pocket or purse and lay it on the pew where you're sitting."

There was a silent but electric response in the room. Questioning looks passed between family and friends; a pall of discomfort fell upon the room. She pressed. "Please, go on. Take your wallet, or whatever it is you carry your money in, and place it on the pew where you are sitting. Then please come to the altar to receive a blessing."

The congregation responded slowly. Almost no one moved at first. But after a moment, a few people slid out of their pews and into the aisles. Gradually, more and more people followed. Abby encouraged the others. "Come on, please. Please come and receive a blessing from Pastor James."

Abby turned to the pastor. She could tell he was as uncomfortable as his congregants, perhaps more so. She smiled. "Pastor, why don't you step up here and say a few words over these people."

After several torturously slow minutes, everyone present, including Kai, Jamie, Peter, and Rob, was moving toward the area in front of the altar. With so many people coming forward at once, the crowd flowed beyond the altar area, down the main and side aisles as well.

When they had gotten situated, Abby turned. "Pastor James?"

Pastor Horn stepped nervously into a place he inhabited every week, normally without any trepidation. He closed his eyes, took a long breath, and then raised his right hand. "Father in heaven, I come before you to ask your blessing on these people— people who have put aside other activities, work or pleasure, to come and worship you today. We know, Father, that you love us, you forgive us our sins; you want only the best for us and a personal relationship with us. Father, let this be a moment in which we feel your presence, not only in this room but in our hearts and minds." He sighed as if relieved of a great burden. "We pray this in the name of your Son, Christ Jesus, Amen."

While the preacher had been praying, John Lennon's lyrics about a world without possessions had drifted across Abby's mind. She turned to him. "What a wonderful prayer, Pastor James. Thank you for that." She turned to the people pressed together in front of her, speaking as if she were making a proclamation. "Now, before you return to your seats, I suggest you ask yourself this question: Where were your heart and mind as James was praying over you, asking a blessing for you—a blessing from God himself? This personal relationship you hope to have with God, is it interrupted when your money, your treasure, might be stolen? I would never dare to ask you to answer that question out loud. But if you know in your heart you were struggling to feel the blessing Pastor James brought to you because your treasure was at risk, then hear the words from our brother, Jesus Christ. 'No man can serve two masters. Either he will hate the one and love the other, or he will be devoted to one and despise the other. You cannot serve both God and money.'" She stopped, watching the faces before her for a response.

Not a single sound arose from the congregation, but the looks on the faces of some made quite clear their displeasure. She could almost hear the words running through those people's minds. *None of her business. Who is she to accuse us? What kind of nut does that?*

"You may return to your seats now, and thank you," Abby said. She turned to Pastor Horn. "Perhaps, you would like to say a few words about what just happened, or maybe let others share their thoughts?" Ready to return to her own seat, she suddenly realized most of the people were responding, but a handful had barely moved—those who didn't seem to be regular attendees—those who appeared to have come looking for trouble. Those folks had morphed into a small crowd—a crowd, she sensed, that was growing angrier by the moment.

Abby wasn't completely surprised. She braced herself, and instead of walking back to her seat, she grabbed her Bible and stepped into that knot of people. The first folks she encountered were slow to move out of her way, but she moved forward anyway. As she did, she could feel the anger pressing in on either side of her. Some of the negative thoughts turned to words, the nasty ones easier to hear. She kept putting one foot in front of the other.

It took twenty or thirty seconds, but eventually, Abby made it through. A chill ran through her body as she walked down the main aisle, clear sailing in front of her, but a few people already following her. She couldn't help but wonder if they were angry enough to hurt her.

"Let's all take our seats now," Pastor Horn called out, "and prepare for communion." But the small group following Abby failed to be dissuaded.

Just as one of the men got within an arm's length, Abby was thrilled to see Jamie, Peter, and Rob scoot through the pews just in front of her. Seconds later, they stood in the aisle, facing those behind her.

"Please, let's take our seats," Pastor Horn called out again. "Please."

Abby walked past her protectors, through the lobby, and out the front door. Her heart pounding, she stopped and looked back. With relief, she saw the three young men exiting the building, along with Kai. A sudden wave of worry rolled through her: what about Cliff? After a desperately long minute, Cliff emerged as well, tripod in one hand, camera in the other. She swallowed the lump in her throat.

Jamie shouted across the parking lot. "Abby! Jump in the Jeep with Cliff and get out of here! We'll leave as soon as you're gone!"

Abby had no intention of arguing. She hopped into Cliff's car while he tossed his equipment onto the backseat. Moments later, with Abby's eyes locked on the side-view mirror, they pulled out of the parking lot of Sunrise Community Church. She twisted her lips. "That went well."

30

As soon as Cliff pulled into the parking lot at Abby's complex, she leaped out of the car and hurried to her apartment. She marched directly into the bathroom.

Finally alone, Abby put the toilet lid down and sat. The fear and tension in her heart erupted; she wept. Tears flowed down her face, dripped onto her jeans. Sobbing silently, she shook. She had no choice but to let her body's reaction to the morning's events run its course. Even as she heard Kai and Jamie come into the apartment, she couldn't pull herself together.

"Abby?" Kai knocked on the bathroom door. "Are you okay?"

As she grabbed some tissue and wiped her nose, Abby tried to sound calm. "Yeah, I'm fine. I'll be out in a minute."

It took Abby another five minutes to throw cold water on her face, run a brush through her hair, and make some minimal repairs to her mascara. Putting on her happiest expression before opening the bathroom door, she stepped out into the living room.

"Well," Jamie said, "there's our girl—our hero." He gave her an enormous smile. "Man, Abby, you kicked butt this morning."

"Yeah, yeah," Abby waved him off. "No big deal."

Jamie had a six-pack of cold sodas in his hand. "C'mon

outside, Kai. It's too tight in here for everyone. We all deserve a little reward." He stopped, more serious and turned back to Abby. "Really, that was something."

Abby grabbed a bottle of sweet tea out of the refrigerator and followed him out the front door. Gathered on the lawn were Kai, Peter, Rob, and Cliff. Jamie walked among them, handing out cans of soda which were gladly accepted. Abby sat next to Cliff at the top of a small grassy incline.

Cliff lifted his drink. "To Abby."

"To Abby," the rest responded. She lowered her head regally in recognition.

"You know," Cliff said to her, "you kind of put Pastor James in a tough spot this morning. Could be some members of his congregation may not be too pleased with him right now."

Abby nodded. "I know. I was thinking that as we drove home. I should probably call him and apologize." She turned and looked sadly into his eyes. "It's just that I'm new at this." She leaned in. "I've never done anything like that before. I guess I should have known better, thought it through more."

Cliff put his hand on Abby's knee. "Don't worry. James is a big boy. And you raised a heck of a good issue with his folks. He should be grateful." He squeezed and let go. "Still, I'm thinking an apology would be nice."

Silence fell over the group as it appeared everyone took a drink at the same time. After a few moments, Peter, the older of the two brothers, spoke. "Abby? Can I ask you a question?"

"Sure."

"I've never been to church before, but it seemed to me those folks weren't expecting that. Things like that don't happen there all the time, do they?"

Abby shook her head. "Not that I know of. I attended church there for almost six years with my mom." She shrugged and smiled. "I never saw anyone else create that kind of ruckus."

Jamie asked, "So, what made you do that? Why did you talk about money and everything?"

Abby smiled at Kai, seated next to Jamie. "Well, as Kai can tell you, I've been a reading fool since Cliff and I returned from Branson. You've seen the books all over the place." She took a sip of tea. "Anyway, I got to thinking about what I said to Billy Comstock, that maybe it wouldn't be all that bizarre if God wanted to say something to folks and he put words in somebody's mouth. And though I know I'm not anything special, I came to that passage about serving two masters and it hit me—I'll bet God isn't exactly pleased about how people worry so much about money, how they cheat and steal sometimes."

Peter interjected, "So, you think God told you to say those things?"

Abby shook her head. "Listen, I didn't really say those things, did I? All I did was get people's attention and then read words from the Bible. That's what Jesus said."

"Still," a huge grin filled Jamie's face, "you sent those folks into a heck of a tizzy. I mean, the looks on some of their faces. I'd love to see that again."

Kai looked at Cliff. "We can, Cliff, right? You have video of the whole thing, don't you?"

An uncomfortable look crossed Cliff's face. "Well, yeah, I do."

She pressed. "Can we watch it?"

"Yeah," Rob joined in, excited. "Can we see the video you shot this morning?"

Cliff took a deep breath. "Okay, but it didn't come out the way I hoped it would."

Abby squinted at him. "What do you mean?"

Again, Cliff paused. "I don't think I can explain it very well. You'd have to see it, and all I have is a little viewing screen on my camera."

"It has an external output, doesn't it?" Jamie said eagerly. "I've got some cables inside. We use them to watch videos on the girl's TV. We could all watch it that way, couldn't we?"

Cliff hesitated. "Yeah, but . . . ."

"Hey, come on man," Jamie pressed, "we want to see it. Can we do that?"

Cliff sighed. "Okay, but like I say, I'm not sure you're going to see what you expect to see."

31

C liff and Jamie worked for almost twenty minutes before they figured out how to get the video to play on Abby and Kai's television. Finally, with Cliff in the armchair, Abby, Kai, and Jamie on the couch, and Peter and Rob standing behind them, Cliff started the video.

"As you can see, I set up in the back corner of the sanctuary and had a perfect view of the pastor as he spoke. I knew there was a window behind and above him, but by the time the service began, the clouds had rolled in so heavily I wasn't worried about the lighting—and I was getting decent audio as well."

The video continued, and everyone watched the pastor introduce Abby. As she walked toward the pulpit, Cliff said, "Here it comes." Every eye remained glued to the TV.

A collective gasp filled the room; a chill went down Abby's spine. Just as she had started speaking, light began to fill the space where she stood. In a matter of moments, the image on the screen blossomed, turning her body into a silhouette which burned with glowing light at its edges. Her every movement seemed ethereal, swirling the image as if it were liquid. Though her words were still audible, she looked like a spirit speaking from another plane. When the congregants approached the altar, some of them remained visible, but others, those closest to her, appeared to be drawn into her aura. Only as she finished speaking did the light slip away, leaving her to walk through the crowd appearing to be human once again.

Jamie was the first to speak. "Wow, that was totally freaky."

Kai, who had slipped under Jamie's arm as they watched, followed instantly. "Are you kidding? Freaky nothing, it was incredible."

Abby looked at Cliff, her face ashen. "Was that real? I mean . . . ."

Cliff spoke from the armchair. "Don't worry. It's just a technical thing. I set up the wrong way. The sun came out when I didn't expect it, and the amount of light overloaded the video input." He rubbed his forehead with his fingers, twisting his lips. "Trust me, it was just an electronic phenomenon. Nothing like that really happened. I promise."

Abby was shaken nonetheless. After all her denials of being some special messenger from God, the sight of her appearing to be a spirit-like being was more than her brain could easily process.

"Well," Kai said in an obvious attempt to break the tension in the room, "maybe we should let Cliff unhook all this stuff and the rest of us should go outside and enjoy this nice day." She smiled and pointed. "If anyone needs another drink, I think there are still a few left in the refrigerator. Help yourself."

Everyone except Abby and Cliff left the apartment. As they did, Cliff stood and crossed the room to Abby. Abby tried her best to keep herself together, but the stress of the day overwhelmed her again. She stood and fell into Cliff's arms.

"Hey, it's okay. Nothing special happened here, I promise. It was a video glitch, and it's all on me." He shook his head. "I should have known better than to take a chance the sun might come out again. Trust me, it's my fault."

Abby put a finger on his lips, silencing him. "It's not that, Cliff. I get it. I understand. But this whole day—choosing to challenge those folks. What was I thinking? Did I really believe that God was leading me to do that?" Tears slipped down her face. "Who am I to think that God even knows who I am?"

"Shhh." Cliff gently put his hands on her cheeks, focusing her eyes upon him. "Stop, Abby. I know this has been crazy hard on you, but you've got to trust yourself. I know you. You don't have an evil or vain bone in your body. You're just trying to do what you think is right. And if you can't trust your own instincts, then who can you trust?" He pulled her closer and whispered in her ear, "You *are* special, and I really do believe with all my heart that God not only knows you, he knows all about you. He knows your heart, where you've come from, who you're trying to be. He knows you, and he loves you."

It was the first time Abby got a glimpse of Cliff's faith, his belief in a personal God. She took a deep breath and allowed herself to melt into his arms. Here was a man who was offering such comfort while she struggled to understand herself and the world she was now living in—a world which had changed dramatically since she'd stood up in comparative religion class and challenged Dr. Wertz. Her moment's solace ended when the phone in his pocket erupted with the opening measures of Michael Jackson's *Thriller*.

"Sorry, sorry." He struggled to unwind himself from her arms and retrieve it as quickly as possible. Stepping away from her, he put the black rectangle to his ear. "Cliff Davis . . . . Oh, hi . . . . Yeah, in fact, I'm there right now. I'm actually with her. Why? . . . Really? They were there? . . . I see . . . All right. I'll tell her. And listen, thanks for the heads up."

Abby could tell it wasn't good news. Her face creased with anxiety while she waited for him to finish. When he did, she asked, "Who was that?"

"That was my station manager. She wanted to tell me there's a new video up on YouTube and it's getting a bunch of hits—probably on its way to going viral."

"And?"

"It's some woman who says she was in church with you this morning and she swears you called Jesus your brother, that you implied," he took a quick breath, "you are the sister of Jesus Christ."

32

A bby was stunned. She knew she had never said those words. All she had done was quote scripture about those who do God's will being the brothers and sisters of Jesus. But she also understood that it didn't matter. Things were going to get crazy. "Who would do something like that, Cliff? Who would say that when it wasn't true?"

Cliff returned to his seat in the armchair. "Apparently, she's not a regular attendee at that church. She'd come all the way from Santa Fe. I'm guessing she's a follower of Barbara Ellis Rice, maybe even Billy Comstock. One way or the other, I imagine she came looking to make trouble for you and you gave her just enough material to do it. She took the liberty to fudge a few words, and just like that, you're either a crazy person or . . . ."

Abby took a seat on the couch. She sat silently, thinking about what awaited her in the next days and weeks—wondering if she was up to the challenge. Eventually, she asked "How long before the interview with the folks in London?"

"August fifth. Almost two weeks. Why?"

A new determination began to grow in her. "Because we're going to use it as our chance to knock this story down." She stood and began pacing. "You make sure they know about the claims this woman is making," she stopped and looked at Cliff, "though I'm guessing they'll have heard all about it by then, and we'll take it on directly. In fact," she smiled at him, "we've got video proof." By the time the words had passed her lips, it hit her. She shook her head. "Never mind."

FARMINGTON, New Mexico – Thursday, August 5th

At one forty-five on August fifth, Abby took a seat on the news set at KFRM. It was early afternoon and the five o'clock show was still a few hours away.

Cliff had made arrangements for Abby to do her virtual interview there because he felt using her apartment as a backdrop would do little for her credibility. The station, of course, was already pleased about the kind of access Cliff was getting to the story of a young Navajo woman who was creating such a ruffle in the religious community. The London interview seemed even more likely to give the station a real national presence, and with that, a chance to raise their advertising rates when they finally broadcast Cliff's piece.

The Alex Bennis Show airs at nine PM in Great Britan, two o'clock in the afternoon, Shiprock time. As Abby waited patiently at the news desk for the interview to begin, she imagined herself the anchor of the local news—sitting under the lights, reading from the teleprompter, sounding like the voice of authority. Instead, she felt more like a modern-day prisoner, waiting to enter an electronic colosseum, ready to do battle with the emperor's best gladiator. She did, however, have a strategy, one she had not been willing to share with Cliff.

Running a simple one-on-one virtual interview required only a camera operator and an engineer on Abby's end. In addition, Cliff had agreed to serve as the floor manager for Abby. His only job would be to let her know when she was on-air and when she was clear.

The program began promptly at two Abby's time, but it was almost ten minutes before Alex Bennis turned to the interview. Abby spent much of that time doing something that had not come naturally to her until recently—praying.

Dapper and gray-haired, wearing a blue pin-striped suit and stylish light blue tie, he welcomed Abby to the show with a million-dollar smile. *"Good evening, Ms. Duncan. It's so good of you to join us here in Great Britain."*

Abby sat up tall. "Good evening, Mr. Bennis. Thank you for having me on."

Abby had heard Bennis' introduction and knew he had given the audience all the background information they needed. He got right to the heart of the matter. *"Ms. Duncan—*

"Abby," she interrupted, "please call me Abby."

"Yes, yes. I understand that's actually short for Abalone, a material the Navajo consider sacred. Is that true?"

Abby nodded. "Yes, it is."

"I see. Now, as I was saying, we were very glad to have booked this interview a few weeks ago, but it appears some significant events have transpired in the interim—events that make our time with you ever so much more important. So, let's get started. You recently spoke at your home church in Shiprock, New Mexico, and things got a little sticky," his tone became a bit wry, *"sort of a prophet-in-his-own-land moment. That is true, isn't it?"*

"Yes."

"And a young woman who attended that event has gone public, indicating you proclaimed yourself the sister of Jesus Christ. Would you like to comment?"

"Well, let me respond by saying all I did was quote scripture, Matthew, chapter twelve, verse fifty to be exact. 'Those who do the will of God, they are my brother and my sister and my mother.'" She stopped.

Bennis paused as if waiting for her to continue. When she didn't, he jumped in. *"So, you* did *mean to imply you are, in fact, the sister of Jesus?"*

Abby's tone made it clear she felt completely in control. "According to the scripture, are not all those who do the will of God brothers and sisters of Jesus?"

Bennis continued. *"And this woman, she's gone so far as to point out that Jesus came from a town which garnered no respect, Nazareth. 'Can anything good come out of Nazareth?' I believe the biblical quote goes. And you, I would assume, having been born on the Navajo reservation, have suffered similarly disparaging remarks?"*

Abby chuckled. "As for Jesus and I both growing up in places that, as you put it, garner no respect, I would point out that some scholars believe God specifically chose a woman from a town with little wealth or distinction to bear his son in order to show that he uses the weak and humble to do his work. 'God opposes the proud but gives grace to the humble,' is how I believe James puts it in the Bible. Perhaps those of my people who accept his existence should take it as a blessing that God sees us as worthy of his intervention." She grinned. "But as to whether that makes me and all the others who have been born on the reservation connected to Jesus in some special way, I refer you, again, to Mathew's words, 'Those who do the will of God, they are my brother and my sister and my mother.'"

Bennis smiled, clearly aware Abby had come prepared and would not be easy for him to manipulate—a worthy opponent, something he appeared to enjoy. *"Well said."*

Bennis took a deep breath. *"Okay, then, let us move on."* He glanced at his notes. *"Now, as I understand it, in your very first public statement, which I believe came at a conference of some sort in Tucson, Arizona, your message was very simple. I think your only words were, 'God loves you.' But it appears that in your later statements you seem to be more interested in something else, identifying the things you believe make God unhappy. Could you tell us more about that?"*

Abby was working hard to keep her outward appearance calm and under control. Her insides, however, were turning flips. She was about to take a very big step, and she hoped she was ready to handle the fallout. She pushed her hair out of her face. "I guess I would say that anyone who looks around would find it easy to identify at least some of those things."

He smiled. *"And what do you think might be bothering him the most?"*

"Oh, I don't know. I wouldn't want to venture a guess."

Bennis pressed. *"Just pick one."*

Abby paused for a moment. "Okay. The tensions between the Sunnis and the Shias. They are both followers of Muhammad."

"Correct."

"But in the name of religion, they attack each other, fueling a civil war in Syria, assassination squads in Iraq after the U.S. invasions, and ever-increasing hostilities among Muslim countries."

"Yes, that is sad, isn't it?"

"Do you think Allah is happy about that?"

"Well, I uh—"

"I believe the Quran says—"

Bennis' tone became defensive. *"Now wait a minute, Ms. Duncan. Are you saying you are a follower of Muhammad?"*

A look of innocence crossed Abby's face. "Oh, no, I'm a Christian. But what I am saying is that any logical person who is not biased by some political or tribal motive could easily see that people who profess to follow Muhammad—who, by the way, speaks of love and peace, patience and service—would certainly not be attacking each other in his name. Would you agree?"

A professionally sly smile traveled across his lips. *"I guess it might appear to be so. But it is also true that, as you point out, centuries of tribal hostility exist between those two groups. Thus, the*

*religious differences between those sects can often be colored by much of
what else goes on in that region of the world."*

"Yes, sir, in that part of the world as in yours."

Abby could see Bennis' reflexive reaction. *"Excuse me?"*

"As you recall, Mr. Bennis, starting in 1969, a thirty-six-year
period of strife referred to as 'The Troubles' brought pain and
suffering, and almost eighteen hundred deaths to *your* region of
the world. The Irish Republican Party fought for the independence of Northern Ireland from Great Britain while others in
Northern Ireland sought to remain part of the British Empire."
She scrunched her face. "And, if I'm correct, those two factions
were often identified as the Catholics and the Protestants," she
tilted her head in an aside, "though if they truly accepted what
they claimed to believe, I doubt eighteen hundred people would
have died in that conflict."

Bennis rocked back. *"Well, I see, Ms. Duncan, you have done
your homework. And not to correct you, but that was essentially a
political-cultural battle, not a religious one."*

"As are the struggles between the Shia and the Sunni, Mr.
Bennis—really reflections of the struggle for power between Iran
and Saudi Arabia. In fact, the Sunni and the Shia lived together
peacefully, often intermarrying, before their religious differences
were used to drive a wedge between them."

"Go on."

Abby leaned across the desk, intense. "So, we could say that
in both cases, Sunni and Shia, Catholic and Protestant, political
actors have wrapped themselves in religious cloaks—then used
the power generated by peoples' faith in their own religious
beliefs to attempt to achieve political goals. Would you not
agree?"

Smiling, Bennis tried to regain control of the conversation.
*"Perhaps we're getting a little far afield from my original questions, are
we not?"*

Abby appeared to relax. "If you recall, your original question was about the things I thought might bother God the most. You said, 'Just pick one,' and I did. I believe that it saddens God to see political actors, individuals as well as movements and countries, wrapping their arguments in religion. So, I'll ask you, do you think God might want to find a way to remind folks that watching people be driven to division and hate, even violence, in his name breaks his heart?"

Bennis took a quick breath. *"A good question indeed, Ms. Duncan, but I'm afraid I'll have to leave it there for the time being."* He shifted gears and addressed the audience. *"We'll be right back with our next guest."*

33

The red light went out on the camera that was focused on Abby, and Cliff reacted. "You're clear." As he walked over to her, the look on his face made it obvious that she had blown him away.

"Abby, where in the world did all that come from? That was incredible."

Abby smiled and shrugged. "What do you think I've been doing for the last month?"

"Listen, I know you've been reading a lot, but . . . ."

"Not just reading, Cliff, learning things: learning what's in the Bible; learning about how some folks abuse religion by using people's faith as a lever; learning how easy it is to convince people of something if you are in a position of religious importance and you tell them they're doing God's will if they follow your instructions—especially if your goal is to separate folks, to turn them against each other. Reading and learning, Cliff, that's what I've been doing."

Cliff stood across the anchor desk and watched the camera operator unclip Abby's microphone. As she rose to walk off the set, he stepped around the desk and took her hand. "You, Abby, are one special person. And whatever happens next, I want you to know I wouldn't be anywhere else but right by your side." He gently touched her cheek. "And trust me, it's going to be one heck of a ride."

THE NEXT MORNING, Abby's phone rang at eight o'clock. She was less than pleased. Rolling over, she picked it up and mumbled, "Hello?"

"*Abby, it's Cliff. You up?*"

"I am now. Did you have to call so early?"

"*Listen, I just found out something, and I thought you should know about it right away.*"

She propped herself up on her elbow. "What is it?"

"*I got a message from my station manager, Jill. She told me the network got wind of last night's interview and they made arrangements with Bennis' folks to air the whole thing next Friday night.*"

"The whole thing?"

"*Yeah, on* Insight, *their hour-long news magazine. It's the big time, Abby, millions of viewers.*"

Abby was silent.

"*Abby, are you there? Did you hear me?*"

She sat up. "Yes, I heard you. What do you think? Am I in trouble?"

"*Listen, Abby. Where you went the other night, taking on religious groups of all persuasions, implying that maybe they were confusing their faith with their politics, or worse, using their follower's faith as a tool for political purposes—that was dangerous stuff. And doing it on an interview across the ocean where nobody knows you is one thing. Saying those things on a network show here in America, that's another. Trust me, there's no hiding after that.*"

Her response was almost inaudible. "Oh."

"*So, listen, I doubt that I'll be able to do anything to stop this from happening, but I need to ask. Do you want me to try?*"

Abby stared out her bedroom window as she answered. "No, Cliff. I don't want you to try. I'm not sure why, but I just have this feeling that, somehow, I've been called to share this message with folks, to point out how people all over the world are using religion this way—using it to separate folks rather than to bring them closer to God. And I'm not saying I'm more important than anyone else, but it just feels like I'm supposed to do this." She ran her fingers through her matted hair. "Besides, it doesn't sound like there's anything you could do about it, anyway." She climbed out of bed and headed for the kitchen. "I guess that trip you were talking about yesterday has begun in earnest, and all I can do is buckle up and get ready."

"*And Abby?*"

"What?"

"*I want you to know I'll be there buckling up right beside you.*"

Wishing she could look him in the eye, she quietly said, "I know, Cliff. I do know."

Shiprock, New Mexico – Saturday, August 14th

Abby crawled out of bed around ten o'clock the next Saturday morning. After washing the sleep out of her eyes and running a brush through her hair, she headed for the kitchen. When she stepped into the tiny space, the expression on Kai's face told her something was up. "What?"

Kai reached for a chipped Pecos Bill's mug. "Here, let me pour you a cup of coffee. Then sit down. I've got something to tell you."

"What?" Abby pressed. "What do you need to tell me?"

Kai shook her head. "No. First, you sit and have some coffee. Then I'll tell you."

Abby bit her lip, but she could sense Kai wasn't going to budge. Anyway, the coffee smelled good, and she was definitely getting the feeling she was going to need it.

"Here," Kai put the mug down in front of her, "enjoy. It may be the last moment of peace you're going to get for a while."

Eyes focused on Kai's face, she took her first sip, then said, "Okay, what's happening?"

Kai pursed her lips. "It's that show last night. Ever since it aired, the internet is blowing up. It seems like half the people in the country want to strangle you, or at least, send you back to the reservation—never to be heard from again."

A weak smile crossed Abby's lips. "Only half of them?"

Kai held her own mug in both hands and took a tentative sip. "That's the funny thing. It appears the other half think you're a hero. You wouldn't believe how many folks are posting things on social media, saying it's about time somebody spoke out against all the stuff you were talking about."

Abby's response was still muted. "Oh."

Kai leaned in. "But listen. Don't focus on the people who think you're all that. It's the others you need to worry about." She shook her head. "I'm not kidding, Abby. You've got to be careful, really careful. One of those crazies might really try to hurt you."

Abby thought for a long moment. "Have you heard from Cliff?"

Kai nodded. "Yeah. He's the one who told me how big a thing this has already become. He said he wants to come over to talk to you, but I told him to let you sleep. It didn't seem like it would make much difference if you got some rest before everything hit the fan."

Abby smiled at her. "Yeah, good thinking. And Kai?"

"What?"

"Thanks."

"For what?"

"For caring about me. For being my friend."

"More than your friend, Abby, your sister. Don't forget. For all the stuff we think and do out here in the," she made air quotes, "'real world,' you're still my Navajo sister. I, and all the *people*, will never lose sight of that. We'll never leave you on your own."

34

There was a knock on the door, and Abby was sure it was Cliff. Part of her was eager to see this man who obviously cared for her, who was doing his best to walk her through this incredibly weird experience. The other part dreaded the conversation they were about to have—hearing him explain what might happen next, making decisions concerning things she knew little about. She called out. "Come in."

Cliff walked through the doorway with a Starbucks cup in each hand and a smile on his face—but it was more like the grin you give a buddy in the hospital after a skiing accident than the smile with which you greet your best friend. "How are you doing?"

Abby shrugged. "No idea. You tell me."

Cliff took a seat next to her on the couch and handed her one of the cups. "I figured you could use a little something special this morning. I know you're more of a black coffee kind of girl, but I thought you might enjoy a simple latte this morning. And as for how you're doing, well . . . ."

Abby nodded her appreciation for the coffee. "Come on, Cliff. Give it to me straight. Am I in big trouble?"

He lifted the lid off his cup. "I guess that all depends on how you look at it. After the network re-aired that interview last night, things really heated up. There's no question lots of folks are plenty angry about you implying their favorite politicians have been using religion as a tool, a weapon if you will, to move their agendas forward. Not to mention there are others who are mad at you for," he made air quotes, "saying you are the sister of Jesus Christ.

"On the other hand, there must be a lot of people out there who have been thinking along the same lines you have. You see lots of, 'It's about time,' and 'You go, girl,' comments on social media."

Abby sat up straighter and placed her drink on the coffee table. "But here's the thing. I never meant to get involved in politics. I wasn't trying to take sides one way or the other. The question that Bennis guy asked me was what do you believe makes God unhappy? It wasn't a political question; it was a God question. And my answer wasn't really about politicians, it was about God. It was about how I think he feels when all he wants is for people to accept that he loves them, to treat each other well, to love thy neighbor as thyself. Then people try to drag him into their battles and use his words to divide folks rather than to bring them closer to him."

Cliff took a sip of his latte, then subtly checked to make sure he didn't have a foam mustache. "I get that, but I'm afraid people hear things through their own filter. And right now, there are folks out there, Catholics, Protestants, Muslims, who think you went on national television to attack them where it hurts, right in the place their religion fuses with their political views."

Abby rocked back on the couch, pulling her knees up and wrapping her arms around them. "That sucks."

Cliff let a long moment go by. "Well, if you want, you may have a chance to try to set things straight."

Abby scrunched her face. "How?"

"I got a call from the network today. They want to book you on next Friday's *Insight* show. They've had such an incredible reaction to airing that interview they want to follow up with you in person."

Abby raised both hands, spread wide open. "No way. Every time I try to do something that has to do with television, I get my butt kicked." She shook her head. "I've had it with that."

Cliff scratched his ear. "Look, I know what you're thinking, and I don't blame you. But listen, this is network television, not the internet or some local yokel trying to make a name for herself. These are the real pros, people in the long line of Edward R. Murrow and Walter Cronkite. They're not characters who are going to take your words and twist them around. I mean, even Bennis, he may have been blindsided with that stuff about Northern Ireland, but the questions he asked you, they were straight-forward and fair. And when he was done, there was no commentary about your answers or editing of the tape. He let you have your say, and that was that."

Abby untangled herself and reached for her coffee. "Still, I don't know."

Cliff pressed. "Listen, if you don't want to do this, I understand. But if you want the opportunity to try to set things straight, to say that you're not making political statements, you're trying to communicate something you believe about God, then this is it."

Abby thought long and hard, then turned to him. "So, you think I should do this?"

"Honestly, yes I do."

"And we'd do it at the KFRM studios again?"

He took a deep breath. "Actually, no. They want you to fly to Los Angeles for the taping."

Her voice rose. "Los Angeles?

"Yeah, they believe they get a more honest and authentic conversation when they're face to face with the person they're interviewing."

"And they'd pay for the flight?"

"Sure."

Kai had slipped into the room. "Listen, I didn't mean to eavesdrop, but I've been looking over some of the stuff that's online. It's pretty scary. You're not going to send her out to Los Angeles on her own, are you?"

Cliff huffed. "No way. She doesn't go unless I get to travel with her."

"And Kai," Abby added quickly. "Kai goes with us, too."

Cliff looked back and forth between the women for a moment, then nodded. "And Kai gets to come with us as well."

"And security," Kai stepped closer, "she gets security right from the hotel to the studio."

Cliff cocked his head, thinking. "Yeah, I'll see what I can do."

Kai had walked over and taken a seat on the edge of the couch, putting her arm around her best friend. Abby looked up at her and smiled. "Thank you, sister."

35

F*armington, New Mexico - Thursday, August 19th*
The next Thursday, Abby, Kai, and Cliff took off from Four Corners Regional Airport in Farmington at 1:22. It was the third flight Abby had taken in her life, and she was still amazed by the fact that the runway perched on a little plateau at the top of a mountain. Taking off in an airplane which serviced only ten passengers, she could feel the turbulence the moment the plane left the runway, banked right, and was suddenly hundreds of feet off the ground—being tossed about by the swirling air. Seated beside her was an excited, yet fearful, Kai on her virgin flight. In the row behind them sat Cliff, nestled in a small, hard seat he partially shared with a very large man and his cowboy hat.

Two hours and ten minutes later, the plane touched down at LAX, the 3,500-acre airport which served Southern California and the world. For both Abby and Kai, walking along the concourses of this international melting pot, passing people of every type, hearing languages which were nothing but musical sounds in their ears, the experience was exhilarating. Cliff had been there several times before, and Abby and Kai were more than willing to simply walk behind him as he followed the signs to Ground Transport and the shuttle to the rental cars.

Although the network was footing the bill, Cliff had decided to book them into the Holiday Inn right on site. Being an employee of one of the affiliate stations, he didn't want to appear to be taking advantage of the network's hospitality. In addition, he thought it would be simpler, and perhaps safer, to stay close to the airport. Nonetheless, though it wasn't the Beverly Hills Hotel, Abby and Kai found the two rooms to be large, attractive, comfortable—and based on their experience, luxurious.

After settling in, the trio decided to head to a place one of Cliff's colleagues had recommended, Westfield Culver City, a mall on Sepulveda Boulevard. It was only a twenty-minute drive from the hotel, but what it offered was something these two young women from the Navajo reservation had never seen in person—a beautiful, three-level world of quasi-opulence.

The first thing Abby and Kai wanted to do was simply walk along every concourse in the place, their eyes drinking in all the visual treats professional window designers had created. When they'd finally had enough, they got down to business.

Before they left New Mexico, Cliff had told Abby the interview she was about to do would be nothing like anything she'd done before. This was the network, and every person they would meet would be at the top of their profession. More importantly, there would be millions of eyes upon her. She had to be dressed appropriately or appear somehow less than credible.

Abby had pointed out to Cliff that she didn't exactly bring home a king's ransom each payday. With rent, tuition, and expenses, there wasn't much left with which a girl could build her wardrobe.

Coming to the rescue, Cliff had offered to buy Abby something to wear. At first, Abby had told him she simply couldn't accept his generosity. She said she might try to borrow some money from her mom or dad. Cliff, however, had implied he would take the cost of the clothing out of the budget KFRM had given him to produce his documentary. Touched by his caring and willingness to fudge the truth, Abby had accepted. The trio spent their last hour at the mall buying an outfit which made Abby feel not only professional but more attractive than she usually felt in her jeans, sneakers, and T-shirts. By the look on the faces of Kai and Cliff, she could tell they heartily agreed.

After shopping, Cliff drove them to a local joint where they enjoyed a true California experience—eating sushi at an outdoor table and watching all manner of people pass by. Abby and Kai loved being in an environment so different from their normal existence, and it was almost nine o'clock before they made it back to the hotel. Aware that the next day was incredibly important, Abby and Kai said their goodnights and went to their room, leaving Cliff on his own. It was, however, midnight before the women talked themselves out and Abby was able to drift off to a fitful sleep.

ABBY, Kai, and Cliff met for breakfast the next morning, then spent the early part of the day taking in the sights of Los Angeles. By mid-afternoon, however, Abby was feeling the pressure of her upcoming interview and asked that they go back to their hotel.

Just before six that evening, Cliff called the network and asked that they send a security detail to escort Abby, Kai, and him to the production facility. Thirty minutes later, as Abby and Kai waited with Cliff in his room, there was a knock on the door. He opened it and found an enormous blond-haired man, perhaps six feet, five inches tall, and certainly weighing well over 250 pounds standing in the hallway. As large as his body was, his voice was soft, polite. "Mr. Davis? My name is Bruce Edelson. They sent me over to escort you to the studio."

Cliff nodded and extended his hand. "Nice to meet you,

Bruce. Thanks for coming." He turned and looked back at the Abby and Kai. "We're ready to go."

It being summer in Los Angeles, Abby wore a simple sleeveless navy dress and blue shoes, and carried a light-weight, white cardigan sweater. Around her neck was a thin necklace with a collection of small pieces of turquoise. Inexpensive, the jewelry still gave her a sense of honoring her Navajo culture. Kai was in jeans, sandals, and a colorful floral top. All three of them followed Bruce out of the building.

Abby was surprised to find that their escort had come to pick them up in a black Suburban with tinted windows. It all seemed a bit excessive to her, but Bruce told her it wasn't at all uncommon for the network to play it safe when a controversial guest was going to be on the show—especially if the controversy which surrounded them had to do with politics or religion. A little chill ran through Abby's body when she realized she was riding both those waves simultaneously.

The thirty-minute trip to the studios was uneventful and pleasant. During those thirty minutes, however, the web of twitching nerves which had been plaguing Abby's stomach all afternoon turned into a ball of tension that felt like it weighed ten pounds or more. She knew she was stepping into the main arena, and she had no idea whether the person she would meet there would be balanced and fair, or simply see her as someone to be toyed with then torn apart for the entertainment of the masses.

Bruce pulled the Suburban up to the front of the production facility. As he opened the door for them, Abby saw two small crowds, one assembled on either side of the entrance. Bruce spoke softly but firmly. "All of you just stay close to me, okay? This shouldn't be any problem."

While they were still thirty feet or more away from the building, however, the crowd on their right erupted in a volley of taunts and insults. Bruce's voice was suddenly commanding. He pointed. "Quick, through that door. Don't stop for anything."

With that, he headed directly for the crowd, his arms outstretched and voice bellowing. "Everybody back. You need to leave the property right now."

"Liar!" "Traitor!" The epithets flew at Abby.

Peeking as she ducked her head, she could see Bruce had some sort of walkie-talkie in his hand, calling, she hoped, for help.

Cliff threw his arms around Abby's and Kai's shoulders, trying to shield them as he pushed them toward the waiting door.

"You're no sister of Jesus!" The taunts kept coming, including the one she always expected: "Go back to the reservation!"

Looking to her right, Abby's fear exploded as she saw the group pushing back against their badly outnumbered guardian. The closer she, Kai, and Cliff got to the door, the closer they were to the crowd, now more of a small mob. Abby's heart pounded.

Without warning, the people on Abby's left, people she was equally fearful of and whom she would also have to get beyond, rushed up from behind Bruce. Instantly, Abby imagined the poor giant being overwhelmed—attacked from all sides. Cliff, Abby, and Kai froze as this second group rushed past Bruce, right into a confrontation with the angry protestors. Eyes wide, Abby was stunned by the pushing and shoving; her ears filled with shouts.

Suddenly, she was all but jerked off her feet as Cliff grabbed her and Kai by their wrists, pulling them toward the door and imagined safety. Just as they reached it, four uniformed security officers charged out of the building and threw themselves into the throng. Shouting, the officers moved the entire crowd back step by difficult step. As Cliff reached for the door handle, Abby felt something thump against her back. Paying it no attention, she and her friends flew through the entrance and into the silence and sanctity of the network studios.

36

S afe inside the building, the trio stopped to catch their breath. A woman in her mid-twenties—short black hair, buzz cut on one side, a butterfly tattoo on her left wrist—approached them. "Ms. Duncan? Mr. Davis?"

"Yes, that's us," Cliff answered for them all.

She smiled. "Hi. I'm a production assistant with *Insight*. Please come with me. We'll get you to hair and makeup, then on to the green room." She led them down a long hall, her heels clicking on the floor of polished black granite. Looking over her shoulder, she said, "I'm so sorry about what happened out there. We had no idea."

Cliff kept his arm around Abby as they walked. Pulling her close to him he whispered. "It'll be all right. Trust me."

They entered a room where two smiling people greeted them. "Hi, I'm Wil," a middle-aged man with a bleached blond goatee announced, extending a multi-ringed hand to Abby. "I do hair."

"And I'm Luzetta. I'll be doing your makeup." The dark-skinned woman with an afro put her hand behind Abby's back and directed her to a salon chair. Her friendly tone fractured.

"What's this?" She bent to examine the stain on the back of Abby's new dress. "Is that tomato?"

The tentative smile on Abby's face faded as Cliff spoke. "I'm afraid some bastard out there threw it at her. And that's a brand-new dress."

Luzetta's eyes widened and her toothy smile returned. "Well," she drawled warmly, "don't you worry about that, not one bit." She turned to her counterpart. "Willy Boy, call on down to wardrobe. Tell them we have a mess here they need to fix if they can and to bring something else for this beautiful young woman to wear if they can't." Her attention returned to Abby. "We won't have you going on national TV in soiled clothing, whether the camera sees it or not. And those folks in wardrobe," she grinned, trying to lighten the mood, "they're miracle workers. I'll bet they can take care of that with no problem, save that dress for you. If not, they can put you in any kind of clothes you want—make you a dancer, a doctor, a princess, or," she leaned in, "some hot-stuff super-spy if you'd prefer." A hearty laugh rattled in her body. "But let's get started on that makeup before Willy Boy over here starts complaining I'm not leaving him enough time for your hair."

FIFTY-FIVE MINUTES LATER, Abby walked out of the room with a sheepish grin, unable to believe how glamorous those two professionals had made her look. She hardly felt like herself. In addition, the woman from wardrobe had managed to completely eradicate the tomato stain, saving the nicest dress she'd ever owned. The experience only added to her sense that Hollywood really was the land of miracles—or at least the illusion of miracles.

A short walk down the hall took Abby, Cliff, and Kai to the green room. Noting its blue walls, Abby asked, "Is it true that they call it the green room because people who are about to go on air are so nervous they sometimes look green?"

Cliff chuckled. "That's what some folks say. Now, how are you doing? Any chance you're going to turn green on me?"

Abby shook her head, but her tone reflected her frustration. "No, I'm ready for tonight. I just hate how all of this started." She took a seat on the sand-colored couch, near a beautiful display of blue hydrangeas that rested on a nearby end table.

Kai sat next to her. "Don't let those fools bother you. Remember, if I'm not mistaken, that whole second group of people was here to support you. They jumped in there to make sure you could get into the building." She turned. "Right, Cliff?"

Cliff had pulled up a chair so he could be sitting near the women. "I think so. And Kai is right. You've just got to let that stuff go for now."

Abby looked directly into his eyes. "Don't worry, Cliff. It's not the crew outside that's on my mind right now, it's what I'm about to say in front of a couple of million people."

AT NINE O'CLOCK SHARP, the theme music and the standard introduction for *Insight* rolled into the homes of millions of television viewers. Some had specifically chosen to watch the show, many others had just flowed into it from the weekly sit-com that preceded it. However they had gotten there, the vast majority of them were about to lay their eyes on Abby for the very first time —a fact that set every nerve in her body jangling. Sitting opposite the host in a dark red upholstered chair, a thought filled her mind: *Father, I know that you are with me.* She took a deep breath and waited for the words she had become strangely accustomed to. "Coming to you in five, four, three . . . ."

37

The stunning blonde woman opened her mouth and round, melodious sounds rolled past her lips. "Good evening. My name is Cybil Harris and, this is *Insight,* our weekly news magazine. We're so glad you're with us tonight. My cohost, Hector Muñoz, will join us later with the story of a man who has served his country for over fifty years in a most unusual manner."

The woman in the stylish business suit and long, straight, perfectly combed hair directed her attention to a different camera. "My first guest tonight is Ms. Abby Duncan." She gave the audience a quick run-down of Abby's background and recent activities, including a short clip from the Alex Bennis interview they had re-aired the previous Friday.

Harris turned her attention away from the cameras toward Abby. "I understand you are most comfortable if I call you Abby. Is that true?"

Abby nodded. "Yes."

"Okay, then. We're so glad you could join us this evening." She quickly got down to business. "Abby, based on the conversation we just viewed, is it fair for me to say you believe you have a special relationship with God?"

Abby took a deep, calming breath. "Well, let me be clear. I do believe I have a special relationship with God. I think we all can." She was incredibly aware she was stepping into a very difficult place. "See, I believe in God, the God Christians and Jews call Yahweh, and I believe that Jesus Christ is his son, sent into the world so it might be reconciled to a loving God. And in the words of Jesus, as recorded in the Bible, those who do the will of God will be his brothers and sisters."

Harris jumped in. "And you believe that you," she made air quotes, "do the will of God?"

Abby smiled gently. "Certainly not always. But I believe that by my acceptance of Jesus and the grace he affords me, God sees me as trying to do his will. That's what I believe."

"And that's enough, just trying?"

Abby chuckled. "That's the best we can do, isn't it? I mean, the Bible tells us all have sinned and fallen short of the glory of God. But if we try to listen, open our hearts to what we think God is asking us to do, grace and the forgiveness of sins cover it all, they *have* to."

Harris pressed. "And you believe that's what you're doing right now, here tonight—doing what God has specifically asked of you?"

"Well," Abby smiled again, "it's not like I received a text message from him or anything. Actually, I'm here because you invited me. True?"

Harris paused for a moment, then smiled. "I guess I would have to say you're right about that. But do you ever receive specific messages from God, like the words you shared with the group in Tucson, 'God loves you?' Does he speak to you or through you directly?"

Abby took another deep breath, unsure of whether or not she should share the thoughts that were crashing around in her mind. Were they hers? Was she being urged by God to say them? Having come this far, through everything she'd experienced in the last few months, she decided to trust herself—or, she wondered, was she simply trusting God?

"As for the words I spoke in Tucson, I have to say I don't know. Could they have been the words of a frightened young woman who felt out of her depth addressing a conference on spirituality when she wasn't even sure what she believed herself? Could those words have popped out of my mouth because I'd heard them in church as a kid and couldn't think of anything else to say? Absolutely.

"On the other hand, could the Lord have put those words into my mind because that's exactly what he wanted to say to a group of people who were spinning their intellectual wheels trying to understand a bunch of complicated theories and practices when he felt that they might be losing sight of the most important thing in the world—that God loves them?" She took a quick breath. "I've come to believe that could be true as well."

She leaned forward in her seat, ready to take an even more challenging step. "See, if you don't mind, I'd like to share with you an experience I recently had."

Harris was clearly entranced. "Please, go ahead."

Abby focused, then began. "Well, recently, I spent some time alone in the desert."

Cybil rocked back in her chair. "You went out into the desert, like Jesus?"

"I went back," Abby said slowly, "to the reservation on which I was born. That land is mostly desert. And while I was there—"

"How long were you there?"

"Four days. I spent four days camping by myself, trying to come to grips with all I had been learning and experiencing." She took a deep breath. "Anyway, while I was out there, as I was looking for some firewood, I came upon an abalone shell buried in the sand."

"Abalone? Now, that's your real name, isn't it? Abby is short for Abalone?"

"Yes, but," she shook her head, "I don't believe that's particularly relevant. What I *do* know is that I had come upon one of the two most spiritually important objects for my people, the Navajo. Turquoise and abalone have a special place in our culture.

"Anyway, when I scraped the shell clean," she cupped her hands in front of her as if she were holding the shell, "I saw the most beautiful display of God's handiwork, an incredible swirl of iridescent colors and silver light. And, somehow, I experienced a tremendous sense of peace, a peace which I'm leaning on right now as I speak to you and your millions of viewers. So, I ask you, does that mean I have a special relationship with God? Was God speaking to me through that shell?"

Harris leaned back in her chair, smiling broadly. "I guess that's for you alone to discern, but right now we need to step away for a moment." She turned to the camera. "We'll be back with more from our fascinating guest, Ms. Abby Duncan. Stay with us."

38

"Welcome back to *Insight*. I'm Cybil Harris and with us is Abby Duncan. We're talking about her, her relationship with God, and some things she's said in the past that have certain people pretty upset."

She turned to her guest. "Abby, I understand one of the issues that has been front of mind for you has been the appropriation of religious beliefs to empower political agendas. Can you tell us more?"

Abby knew she was once again treading into dangerous territory. "First, let me make this clear: I am not interested in politics, I'm interested in people's relationships with God and with each other."

Harris raised a finger. "But you brought up some pretty touchy political issues with Alex Bennis."

"Look, I'm no expert on these things, but I've been reading and studying, speaking to people, and I believe I've come to understand some things I never realized were true. Now, as for what I said to Mr. Bennis, I didn't mean to offend any religious group nor take sides in any political argument. However, let me say this: there are times our religious beliefs are used by those in authority to drive their political agendas. The Sunni in the Middle East are taught to despise the Shia and vice versa; the Catholics in Northern Ireland were taught to despise the Protestants, and the reverse was true. As far back as the sixteenth century, there have been religious wars like the Thirty Years' War, which devastated Germany while pitting Catholics against Protestants. Even the great crusades, the thing that got me going on all of this in the first place, even those were more about taking over rich trade routes than about serving God. And why does this happen? Because people's faith in their religion can be used to blind them to the facts of the political and economic desires of those in power.

"And those are not the only examples. Even here in our own country, American flags stand proudly at the front of churches as if Jesus is some patriotic figure, the ultimate American—Rambo come down from the cross. Political rallies are held all over the country and people show up with signs saying, 'Jesus Saves,' or carrying 'Christian' flags. Preachers stand at pulpits and spout the latest political company line. It's called Christian Nationalism. And what does that imply?"

She continued without waiting for an answer. "To me it implies something like, 'Jesus is on our side.' Or, 'We must be the ones who are right because we follow Jesus.'" She shook her head. "But doesn't it also imply that since one faction contains followers of Jesus, the other doesn't—that God is not on *their* side?

"And who's to say whose side God is on? One group points to a particular part of the Bible as justification for their stance, but their opposition points to another. And just because one side is more likely to claim that justification, does that mean they're the ones who are right?"

Harris asked, "Does that mean you think Christian's shouldn't be involved in politics?"

"No, I don't believe that. They have as much right as anyone else to participate in our democracy. They *should* participate, and they can be led by their Christian beliefs. But problems can arise when a movement claims to be on God's side as concerns one particular issue. Somehow, in their minds, that association often seems to generalize to the group's stance on everything—as if God is supporting their position on whether we should raise taxes, or drill for oil on certain land, or allow immigrants access to citizenship."

Abby leaned forward in her upholstered chair. "But here's the most important thing." She spoke slowly. "God, is on everyone's side. Or maybe I should say he's on nobody's side—he's on his own side, working toward his own ends." She paused again, waiting for the words to sink in. "I believe that when God looks down at some confrontation between two politically charged groups, he doesn't see Republicans or Democrats. He sees individuals—sons and daughters—people he loves—men and women he hopes are trying their best to listen to and love not only the people they agree with but the people they disagree with. He doesn't want winners and losers, he wants folks who are trying to do their best to create a world full of love, acceptance, tolerance—who care for the earth and all the people who live on it—who are willing to balance their interests with the interests of others—and who try to love the world and everyone in it because they accept that God loves them, and his greatest desire is that they reflect that love to him and to each other."

Harris sat back in her chair and took in a long breath. "Please go on."

After a moment, Abby continued. "Now, I did have an interesting discussion with Mr. Bennis about that topic. However, if we could, I would like to focus on the question he asked me. In particular, what kinds of things I thought might sadden God about how people behave, how they treat each other.

"Clearly, I believe the use of religion that way is one thing that saddens God. But there are many others, and one of which is the way people separate themselves based on religious belief."

"For example?"

Abby let her eyes drift away from Harris for a moment as she collected her thoughts. "Okay, here's one. Some Christian denominations believe someone can only be saved if they are immersed, completely dunked in water to represent their death and rebirth in Christ. Others believe baptism is just an outward expression of an inward experience. For them, merely sprinkling water suffices, and even that is only a statement to the world about a decision the person has made in their heart and mind.

"My only point here is this: what people believe about baptism, or any of the many other points of theological dogma, shouldn't be the basis upon which they separate themselves—go to their own corners. Many people, especially young people, would love to have a god they can turn to for help, guidance, support—ways to see each other. But sometimes, it's the structure of religion itself, the things done in the name of God, that keep them away from God—and often away from each other.

"In fact, in a work called *The Message,* a modern translation of the Bible, the words Jesus speaks in Matthew, chapter eleven, are interpreted this way: 'Are you tired? Worn out? Burned out on religion? Come to me. Get away with me and you'll recover your life.'" She shook her head gently. "Now, other versions of the Bible don't use quite the same words, but you can see I'm not the only one who has had thoughts like these."

"Well," Harris said slowly, "I can see you've spent a lot of time considering all of this. But let me ask you, what is it you hope would happen now?"

Abby sat up taller. "Not an easy question to answer, Cybil, but let me try. I'm here tonight to say to the world, to anyone who will listen, it's time for us to stop running away from each other in the name of religion. What we should be doing is coming together in the name of God."

"And you think that's possible?"

"Listen, I know all the many religions, large and small, have differing views of God. Some believe, as I do, that God is loving and wants to be in a personal relationship with us. Others see God as more distant, perhaps more judgmental. But whatever people think of God, they always find him, or her, to be asking us to love each other, respect each other, take care of each other. Jesus tells us to love each other as we love ourselves. For the Jews, that same commandment, 'Love your neighbor as yourself,' is written in the third book of the Pentateuch or Torah, the beginning of what Christians call the Old Testament. Along with prayer, fasting, personal morality, and discipline, Muhammad calls for service to others. Even religions that don't focus on an individual deity share the same ethos."

"And," Harris asked, "you believe God has given you the task of making all of this come together?"

Abby smiled, relaxing. "Well, a Chinese thinker once said, 'A journey of a thousand miles begins with the first step,' and I believe that sometimes all those steps are not necessarily taken by the same person."

The pleasant smile on Harris' face seemed to indicate she was enjoying how the conversation was coming to a close. "And in your mind, what does that first step entail?"

"Asking ourselves if how we treated the person we met in the store, or at work, or on the highway fulfilled God's expectation of how we should live. It means thinking long and hard before allowing our religion to be used to promote some political movement, be it national, or even international. It means re-examining our personal relationship with God. Do we turn to God in times of stress? Do we thank God if we believe things have worked out well?" She hesitated for a moment. "Most importantly, do we trust that *however* things work out, God's hand is in it—that there's a purpose, a grander plan behind things, whether they go the way we hope or not?"

She continued. "Now, listen. I want to be clear about this. If a person's religious beliefs and practices do lead them to that kind of experience with the Lord, I think they should embrace them. My only point, here, is that I wish people would stop and ask themselves if that's true—that what they do in the name of their religion actually brings them into a closer relationship with their God and with each other. See, some people think of faith as the act of doing. I see it most essentially as the act of believing, of accepting the fact that there *is* a god, and that God loves you. All the doing, if it comes at all, must be based on the believing, the accepting."

Harris became more serious. "I love your enthusiasm, Abby, but you do realize you have touched some pretty raw nerves here tonight. In fact, I understand that you were already attacked on your way into the studio before tonight's show. Are you sure you're ready to face all those people who say you are challenging the very foundations of their lives—who may take it upon themselves to distort and reject everything you said this evening—who might, in fact, continue to accost you physically?"

Abby looked down at her hands. Shaping them as if she were holding the shell she found in the desert, she replied, "In the same way I held that abalone shell in my hand," she lifted her hands to chest height, "I believe the God I spoke of tonight will hold me in his."

Harris sat up taller, concern for Abby etched in her face. "Well, I'm afraid we're out of time. I would love to hear more about how you think we could start along that path. For now, I just want to thank you for your courage and your insight and wish you success and safety in your endeavor to bring a little more Godliness and humanity into this world." She turned to the camera. "We'll be right back."

39

Abby was ushered off the set during the commercial break. After a crew member removed her mic, she headed toward the open arms of Kai and Cliff. She stopped when she heard a voice call her name. She turned and saw Cybil Harris walking up behind her.

"Listen, I've only got a moment." Harris took Abby's hand. "I want to tell you how impressed I am with you." Her expression, however, was not one of joy and encouragement. "But look, take care of yourself and be careful. And if you ever need anything, please let me know if there's any way in which I can help."

The floor manager called out, "We're back in ninety seconds."

Harris squeezed Abby's hand tightly then released it. "Good luck, Abby." She smiled and looked at Kai and Cliff. "You guys take care of her, all right? She's something special, she really is."

With that, Harris turned and walked directly back to the set while both Kai and Cliff gave Abby a big hug.

Kai spoke first. "You rocked, lady. You absolutely rocked."

"That you did." Cliff was beaming. "I can't believe how well you handled yourself on national television." His gaze drifted over to Harris. "And it sure looks like you made a fan, a powerful one at that."

Abby gave them an "aw shucks" grin. "Was it really okay? I didn't make a fool of myself?"

Cliff shook his head. "Ms. Abby, you did not make a fool of yourself." He put his arm around her and led her out of the studio. "But what you did do was stir up a veritable hornet's nest. My phone has been blowing up ever since the first commercial break."

"How so?" Abby asked.

"Well, social media is exploding with folks accusing you of being some sort of religious charlatan. I'm afraid if we were in Salem, Massachusetts, right now, they'd be burning you as a witch." All three shared a nervous laugh.

"And in the second segment," Cliff continued, "when you took on the denominations, things got crazy in a lot of corners of Mainline Christianity Land." He shook his head again, "Trust me, you didn't make any friends there either."

Kai held up her phone. "But look at my Twitter feed. For every jerk who's tearing you down, there are ten others who think you're the greatest—as far as I can tell, mostly young folks. They say they wish they could experience God the way you do, or at least find a safe place to go looking for him—a place where they don't have to comply with all the rules and regs, implied or explicit, which have kept them away from even messing with religion."

Cliff checked his phone as well. "It seems there are all kinds of people who want to find a new way, a better way to connect to God." He gave her a big smile. "It's pretty darn impressive."

By then, they had left the studio proper and were heading for the exit. As they reached the lobby, Bruce was there, waiting for them. "Are you guys ready to get out of here?"

Cliff nodded. "Ready to go."

"We've taken some precautions, but you'd better prepare yourself. We managed to get those folks who were harassing Ms. Duncan pushed back an entire block, but we let some of her fans hang around." He turned to Abby. "Looks like they were watching your segment on their phones. We've got them behind a barricade as well, but I think they're pretty eager to see you."

Abby furrowed her brows. "Really?"

Bruce smiled. "Really. Now, stay close to me, okay?"

"Got it."

As Bruce led the three of them out to the parking lot, Abby couldn't believe her eyes. Fifteen or twenty people stood behind a wooden barricade some twenty yards or so away, waving and calling her name. She stood frozen until Cliff nudged her. "Come on. We've got to go."

But Abby couldn't resist. She started walking toward the small crowd, waving silently—overwhelmed by their reaction and unable to think of what to say. When she had taken four or five steps, Bruce took her by the elbow. "No, no. Into the car. After what happened before, we can't take any chances."

As Abby moved toward the suburban, the ripple of voices seemed to explode in a single word. "ABBY!" She turned. The hands of each person in the crowd were cupped in front of them as if they were holding something precious. It took a moment before it hit her: they were mimicking the motion she herself had made on the set when she talked about the abalone shell she had found in the desert. All at once, they lifted their hands higher, as if holding their shells up to heaven. An odd blend of excitement and peace swirled through her, touching her to the deepest part of her soul.

Cliff moved in behind Abby. "Come on, come on. We've got to go. Please, just wave and say thank you. Then, for goodness' sake, let's get you out of here."

Abby relented, and within moments, they were all in Bruce's

Suburban and on their way back to the hotel. As they left, Abby looked out the window and saw smiling faces and waving hands. In her mind, however, she also sensed a dark cloud hovering over those people—a cloud she feared might follow her in the days to come.

40

Bruce dropped the trio off at their hotel, wishing them a pleasant trip home and good luck in the future. Instead of heading for their rooms, Cliff insisted they make a stop in the hotel restaurant. Unfortunately, it was closed. They went, instead, to the bar and ordered some nachos to go along with a couple of beers for Cliff and Kai, and a sweet tea for Abby.

After almost an hour of reliving the evening, they left their table and Cliff led the way as they headed for their lodgings. When they reached the women's room, Kai slipped through the doorway so quickly it was as if she had simply disappeared. Abby found herself once again standing outside her room, alone with Cliff. Exhausted, yet still churning with excitement, confusion, and dread, she felt her insides shake as she resisted the one thing she really wanted to do at the moment—crawl into Cliff's arms and hold on for dear life.

Cliff looked intently into her eyes and moved a half-step closer. A moment later, however, with a quick breath and a boyish smile, he said, "Well, heck of a night. Now let's get some sleep. We've got a plane to catch tomorrow morning." He turned briskly and walked toward his room. Abby watched him go, both disappointed and relieved.

EARLY THE NEXT MORNING, Abby was brushing her teeth when she heard a knock on the door. Kai answered it, only to find Cliff standing in the hallway, balancing three Styrofoam cups. He hustled in, clearly eager to put the drinks down. "Morning, ladies. We don't have a lot of time before we have to leave for the airport, so I thought I'd bring you both some coffee. We can get something to eat once we're past airport security." He took the lid off one of the cups and asked, "Everyone have a good night?"

"A good night, but a heck of a morning," Kai replied

Concern crossed Cliff's face. "Is everything okay?"

Kai grinned. "I guess you could say that. Have you been watching what's happening on social media?"

"It's going wild, as far as I can tell. And I've already received three or four requests for Abby to speak at different places."

"But you haven't heard about the New Life Initiative?"

"The what?"

Kai picked up a cup of coffee. "Some couple in Oregon started a GoFundMe page called the New Life Initiative, and they're already collecting money."

"For what?"

Kai smiled in the direction of her best friend. "For Abby to use any way she wants as some sort of ambassador of spirituality and goodwill."

Cliff squinted. "You're kidding, right?"

Kai plopped down on the bed, coffee in hand. "And guess how much they're trying to raise?"

"I don't know," Cliff shrugged, "a couple thousand dollars?"

Abby stepped out of the bathroom. "A half-million dollars."

Cliff's jaw dropped. "Half a million bucks?"

Abby picked up the last coffee. "Of course, they've only raised about twelve thousand dollars so far. And I don't know if I could ever accept it."

Kai chuckled. "Oh, you'll accept it. Just think about what you can do with twelve thousand dollars."

Abby pondered for a moment, then looked to Cliff. "What's your opinion, Mr. Unofficial Manager?"

"I guess it depends." Still standing, Cliff leaned against the wall. "I mean, if you really wanted to take this on, trying to spread the message you shared last night, you're going to need lots of money."

"And time," Kai added. "You'd probably have to quit your job at Pecos Bill's—maybe even drop out of school for a semester."

Abby walked over and sat down on the other bed. "It just seems like a lot, you know? Quitting my job, dropping out of school—what if that money dries up or never even comes through?"

Kai pressed. "Oh, it's coming through. You can count on GoFundMe. They're the real deal when it comes to crowdsourcing. And as for the money running out, when was the last time you made twelve thousand dollars in one semester?"

Cliff dropped his empty cup in the trash. "Listen, we've got to get going. We can talk more about this on the plane. But if you're asking for my opinion, I'm thinking you're about to take the first step on that journey you were telling Cybil Harris about last night."

As the three of them stepped out of the elevator on the ground floor of the hotel, Abby faced something she had never encountered before, never imagined encountering—the real press. Videographers jockeyed for position while reporters from several national outlets thrust microphones in Abby's face.

"Ms. Duncan, can you tell us why you're so opposed to orga-nized religion?"

"Abby, is it true you were attacked on your way into the studios last night? Can you tell us about that?"

"Ms. Duncan, do you plan to launch a campaign against the politicization of religion?"

The questions came, one on top of the other, faster than she could make them out. Before she could even think of a way to answer, Cliff nudged her forward, his voice booming. "Not right now, folks, we've got a plane to catch. Thanks so much for your interest. I'm sure you can track me down if you want to set up a press conference sometime."

Holding Abby's hand, Cliff maneuvered Abby through the gaggle of reporters, lights, and cameras, with Kai close behind. They hadn't foreseen this development and had to fend off the press all the way to the parking lot and into the rental car. The last questions were shouted at them as they drove away.

Abby heaved a huge sigh. "Ho-ly moly." She shook her head. "That was incredible."

Cliff checked the rearview mirror. "Welcome to the big leagues. I told you that appearing on *Insight* would change every-thing." He glanced at her. "You okay?"

"I'm fine." She turned and looked at Kai in the back seat. "What about you? You all right?"

"I'm all right, but that was crazy. Is she going to have to face that from now on, Cliff?"

Cliff kept his eyes on the road. "There's no question that she's become a public figure, but maybe if we plan ahead, we can get control of that kind of thing. Let's hope so, anyway."

BY THE TIME their flight landed in Farmington, the world had changed for Abby and Kai. They had checked their GoFundMe page at every opportunity and it looked like Abby would have over forty thousand dollars at her disposal. Abby and Kai had decided that they would not be going back to school for the fall semester. Abby would spend her time reading, studying, and responding to as many requests for interviews and speaking engagements as she could. Kai would travel with her and help in any way possible. They would both, of course, take a leave of absence from their jobs.

Cliff, on the other hand, was pretty certain that KFRM would allow him to go nearly full time on this project, traveling with Abby and Kai whenever they were involved in some New Life Initiative activity. He would also help shepherd Abby through the maze of opportunities and perils that came along with this crazy idea. Every time he spoke to her, he was upbeat and encouraging, but Abby sensed there was a lot more trepidation in his heart than he was allowing to come to the surface.

Walking down the mobile stairs to the tarmac, Abby searched for signs of another onslaught of news reporters. She was relieved to find that Farmington was not as media-heavy as Los Angeles. Only two reporters were waiting to question her, people Cliff already knew. Pointing out that Abby had been under a lot of pressure in the last twenty-four hours, he was able to negotiate clear passage for her by promising a more formal news conference in the next day or two. Overhearing the conversation, Abby shuddered. *We're not in Kansas anymore*, she thought grimly.

41

S hiprock, New Mexico - Wednesday, August 25th
The following Wednesday morning, Abby looked out her apartment window and watched Cliff walk from the parking lot to her door. She saw him glancing at the young woman she had noticed hanging around the property. She suspected the woman was yet another reporter trying to catch her in a private moment.

Cliff knocked on the door, and Kai let him in. "Morning. I stopped in at City . . . . Oh, hello."

Abby pointed at the two twenty-somethings who were sitting on the couch, two sleeping bags lying near them on the living room floor. "Cliff, meet Jasmine Day," the girl with the big afro, tipped her head, "and Lisa Ryan." The redhead smiled. "They've come here from San Diego." She paused a half-beat. "To help."

Cliff nodded slowly. "Oh. Well, nice to meet you." He turned to Abby, "As I was saying, I stopped in at City Market and got a few muffins and a dozen eggs. I figured I'd whip up a little breakfast for you." He smiled at the new guests. "And, of course, for you as well."

Jasmine and Lisa looked at each other, then Lisa answered. "No, thanks. We'll get something later."

"Don't be silly," Abby took charge, "you're here now, and if we're eating, you're eating."

Kai stepped into the kitchen. "I'll put on some more coffee. Looks like we're going to need plenty."

While Abby helped Cliff with the eggs, she explained to him that Jasmine and Lisa had been so excited about the New Life Initiative, which they called NLI, they had taken a semester off from school to come and help Abby in any way they could.

Cliff looked down at Abby and spoke in hushed tones, "Where are they going to stay?"

She shrugged silently.

He leaned back, peeking at the women in the other room, then whispered again. "Listen, I need to do a pretty solid background check on these ladies. You never know, and we don't want to expose you to any problems. You all right with that?"

Abby nodded and whispered, "Sure."

Twenty minutes later, everyone was scattered around the tiny living room, well supplied with breakfast. Cliff polished off a muffin before he broke the amiable silence, a crumb still stuck to the corner of his mouth. "Well, since no one bothered to ask me why I dragged myself over here at nine o'clock in the morning, I guess I'll just have to spill it on my own."

"Can't wait to hear it." Abby smiled and subtly brushed the corner of her own mouth, hoping he would notice.

Cliff caught the signal and pulled the top of a finger past his lips. "Good. I've got two things to tell you and it appears," he looked around at the four women, "both may be very advantageous."

"Come on, Cliff," Kai interjected, "get to it."

"Okay. First, I received a call from a group running a big Christian music festival outside of Amarillo, Texas in three weeks. It's called Godspeed. That's about a seven-and-a-half-hour trip, but Abby would be speaking to over two thousand people." He looked around the room. "What do you think?"

Abby glanced at Kai, who nodded, then turned back to Cliff. "Sounds good. Any idea how long they want me to speak?"

He smiled, "As long as you want. It's a big outdoor event, folks camping there for two or three days. You can talk 'til the cows come home if you'd like. The question is, what do you want to say?"

"I'll have to think about it. Now, what's your other big news?"

"So, I got a call from a man who wants to stay anonymous. He and his wife have a cabin in the mountains outside Durango, Colorado, about an hour and a half away. He said they know what it's like to be in the public eye, and they wanted to offer you the use of the cabin at least until Christmas. That's when they usually bring their family up there for the holidays."

A huge smile crossed Abby's face. "A cabin all to ourselves, near Durango? Like I would ever say no to that. Kai comes too, right?"

"Absolutely."

"And maybe," Kai added, "Jasmine and Lisa could stay in this place while we're up there."

Abby was taken off guard for a moment, but then nodded. "Sounds good. But let's keep it on the down-low." She turned to the two women. "And you can't pay us anything. We're not allowed to sublet and we don't need to. If you want to stay here for free, that's fine with us."

Lisa spoke first, relief coloring her voice. "That would be great. Jas and I had no idea how this was going to work out. We just came here on faith. It kind of sounds like a God thing, doesn't it?"

Jasmine squeezed Lisa's hand. "Amen."

～

DURANGO, *Colorado – Saturday, August 28th*

Three days later, Kai, Abby, and Cliff pulled up to the mountain cabin in three separate cars. They were surprised at the size of the log structure: two and a half stories with a massive chimney and a covered porch that ran the entire length of the building. They were even more amazed when they went inside and saw the creek stone fireplace, modern kitchen, giant-screen TV, and the raised indoor balcony that looked out over the mountains through large picture windows.

Abby spoke, almost to herself. "So this is how the other half lives."

Kai strolled through the great room. "Will you look at this place? It's incredible."

"So it is," said Cliff. "And until you have to pack up and leave at Christmas time, it's all yours."

"Mine," said Abby, "and NLI's. Just think how great it would be to have meetings up here. To get folks together to talk and share—to make plans for how we move forward."

"Right," said Cliff solemnly, "but it has to stay very small, and anyone who comes here has to maintain total secrecy. The whole point of those people sharing this place with you was to keep you away from prying eyes."

"I get it, Cliff. I get it." And in her heart, Abby did get it. She remembered being chased outside of Billy Comstock's studio. She would never forget the small crowd that was waiting to harass her outside the TV studios in Los Angeles. She'd faced the press at the Holiday Inn the next morning. And she had no doubt there was plenty more of that in her future.

ABBY AND KAI spent the next three weeks settling into the cabin. Abby read and studied and prayed, working toward the very thing she kept talking about—being in a daily relationship with

God. Together they took long walks in the mornings and passed the early evenings sitting on the porch, taking in the incredible beauty of their surroundings. Jamie would drive up on the weekends to spend time with Kai. Once in a while, they would leave Abby alone and go into Durango just to hang out or take in dinner and a movie.

Jasmine and Lisa, who had taken on the task of building a social media presence for NLI, had generated more than forty thousand followers over several platforms. Jamie and his friends Peter and Rob were heavily involved as well. The brothers' father was a lawyer, and he helped set up a legal entity named the New Life Initiative which could collect the monies from the GoFundMe campaign, now well over $100,000 dollars. Jamie pitched in, helping in any way he could.

Every other week, the whole team met at the cabin. Abby shared what she had learned and led discussions. The time together was eye-opening for Peter and Rob, since they'd had no previous religious experience or instruction. They seemed particularly interested in seeing Jesus as a spiritual leader who called upon people to do good in the world—feed the hungry, house the poor, fight injustice. They struggled, however, with the notion of Jesus being the Son of God.

One day, Abby brought up the issue at a team meeting. "Rob, Peter, I've been thinking about the questions you've been asking, and I've found something that I thought might help. I was reading this book by C. S. Lewis." She held up a copy of *Mere Christianity*. "In it, he describes a paradigm called 'The Great Trilemma.'"

Rob looked at Peter, then back at Abby. "What's that?"

"Lewis says that the one thing we can't do is say Jesus is a great moral teacher but not accept his claim to be the Son of God." She scratched her nose. "Look, Jesus said he was the Son of God, and he either was or wasn't." She looked directly at them. "Right?"

Both brothers nodded.

"Now, Lewis points out that if Jesus were just a mortal man and made those claims, he would either be a lunatic," she giggled, "like a guy who says he's a poached egg, or he would be some kind of devil, simply not telling the truth." She tilted her head. "So, according to Lewis, Jesus was either a liar—a man who knew he wasn't the Son of God but said he was; a lunatic—a man who wasn't the Son of God but thought he was; or the Lord—the honest to goodness Son of God."

A lengthy discussion of all that Lewis had written followed, and Abby hoped that as they left and ruminated on what had been said, Rob and Peter would be able to clarify their own thinking as to what they really believed.

Whatever they decided, Abby was certain of one thing: she wasn't interested in telling people how important it was to do *good things*, she was interested in helping people know that there is a God who wants a personal relationship with them and who is trying to get people to understand and respond to that fact.

42

Amarillo, Texas - Friday, September 17th
Abby and her team arrived at the Godspeed Christian Music Festival in Amarillo, Texas, late in the afternoon. She was greeted enthusiastically by a several of the men and women who had organized the event, mostly in their late twenties and early thirties, but did her best to let Cliff work out the details of when and how she would address the attendees. She was glad they had made it in time to catch Friday night's headline act, a heavy metal Christian group named In HIS Name, and to hear the evening's featured speaker. Slipping away with Kai, she hid her face under a ball cap and hoodie and did her best to remain anonymous. All she wanted that evening was to fade quietly into a group of people who had come to worship and learn about God.

After camping overnight, Abby spent the next day walking around the gigantic field, interacting with Christians from all over that part of the country, mostly young. She could see from their faces that a handful were native, but most were not. Everywhere she went, excited campers surrounded her, begging for selfies. She did her best to oblige politely, though she was uneasy letting people make *her* the focus of their attention.

Abby took a break from the uncomfortable adulation at eight o'clock and sought peace and solitude to prepare herself for her ten o'clock address. The notion of standing in front of over two thousand people, sharing such important ideas, felt daunting to her. She spent the final fifteen minutes in silent prayer: *Father, I am only your servant. All I can do is give you my very best. Please give me strength and the words you want me to say.*

The last notes of Joshua's Descendants, another Christian rock group, were still echoing across the field when Abby took the stage. The crowd went wild, clapping and screaming— locking arms in a celebratory embrace. Had this been a political rally or a rock concert, one would have expected her to step to the mic, raise her arms, and yell, "Good evening, Godspeed!"

Instead, she stood silently before the microphone, waiting— waiting as the roar subsided—until the crowd was quiet—until the field was silent.

She spoke softly. "Hello, my name is Abby Duncan."

There was a ripple of noise in the audience, but nothing like the explosion a national personality might have normally received.

She paused again. "I'm honored to be here—honored to have the opportunity to speak to you about important things." She looked across the crowd. "By now, many of you know that less than a year ago I was just a student at a small college run by the Navajo Nation. You may even know something about my incredible trip from those days to this beautiful evening in Amarillo. Be assured, however, that I am not here to talk about me—that my story is not at all important. What is important is that we understand the difference between religion and having a relationship with God.

"Now, to be clear: I am not here to attack religion per se, nor any particular religious practices. The vast majority of you have come here under the auspices of the churches that have nurtured and trained you, who brought you the word of God. There are people in your lives who have generously given their time and treasure in an attempt to help you accept God's grace into your life, and for them, you should be grateful.

"But fulfilling religious practices *religiously*, marching through the daily steps which make someone appear to be in a relationship with God, should never be confused with actually having a relationship with God at the center of your life."

The crowd was silent as she spoke. "And so, tonight, as you have come together, you must ask yourself this question:" she paused, "Does the religion you follow bring you closer to God, or has it become a surrogate for God?"

Abby took a moment to let the question marinate in the minds of her listeners.

"Now, for some people, it seems the focus has shifted from having a relationship with God to fulfilling the demands of a religion. They try hard to do what they think they're supposed to do, believing that if they get enough things right, they'll be okay with God. But in the Bible, the writer Paul, who was once, by the way, a super believer in just that kind of thing, tells us no one can be *good enough*—that we're all human, and all of us screw up. We try to be good, but we can't always get things right, and then we're left with feelings of failure—disappointed in ourselves. We become convinced that God feels that way about us too.

"And though you're all here tonight at a Christian event, you know that many of your friends and their families want nothing to do with church—with religion. Now, it's not usually true, but when you listen carefully to what those people say, you hear words like hypocrisy and," she made air quotes, "'all those Christians are a bunch of phonies.' Why? Because there is this basic misunderstanding that believing in God is about how we behave —what we do.

"But that's not the way it has to be—that's not the way it is. God didn't create religion, people did. They did it as a way to reach up to God. Unfortunately, the basis of that thinking is the belief that somehow people are good enough to pull that off. More importantly, at least according to our Christian beliefs, it's not a matter of us reaching up to God, but rather, God reaching down to us—because he loves us—because he wants to be in relationship with us.

"Now, I know most of you here tonight are young, like me. You live in this world of instant communication, constant electronic contact, social media. And when you go to social media, what do you see? You see everyone's perfect expression of their perfect lives. Everyone just got something great, or did something *fabulous*, or is having the greatest time ever." She paused. "But, come on, you know that's not true. If it was, we wouldn't have over forty-seven thousand people a year commit suicide. Two years ago, that meant that fourteen out of every one hundred thousand young people aged fifteen to twenty-four gave up on life altogether." She paused again, lowered the energy in her voice. "No," she shook her head. "we're not all having the time of our lives.

"So, when you face the reality of your life, which for all of us is sometimes kind of dark, who can you turn to when you can no longer, in innocence, bare your soul to your parents—and when you're afraid to do so with your friends? Well, imagine if you could bare your soul to the God of the universe. Imagine if you could simply admit to God that you got something wrong, in the same way you wish you could tell your very best friend. And why? Because God wants to be your *very best* friend: the one who understands you at the deepest level; at a level so much deeper than any human could; who wants to be the friend who doesn't condemn you, but rather, helps you deal with your failures emotionally and spiritually—and who sometimes actually helps you with your problem.

"What I'm describing is not a matter of winning God's approval through going to church every Sunday, or tithing, or doing all the things you're told you're supposed to do. No, it's a matter of seeing God as your friend—the one who loves you more than you'll ever know—more than you'll ever be able to experience.

"Imagine what life would be like if no matter how well or poorly things went for you, no matter how much you screwed up, there was always someone who was with you, encouraging you to accept that he loves you, to accept yourself as he made you, and helping you to become all he meant for you to be."

Abby stood silent for a long moment, the crowd hushed and hanging on her next words. Just as she was about to begin again, however, Abby heard two large pops, one off to each side of her. Almost instantly, the huge stage lights aimed at her dimmed, then faded to darkness. Only a few small bulbs in front of her and the bright lamps above and behind her remained lit.

Rattled at first, she gathered herself and pressed on. "Now, some of you, many of you, perhaps all of you, are asking your-selves the same question I've asked for years: who am I that God would want to be in a relationship with me? Let me share some-thing with you."

She cupped her hands in front of her waist. "Just weeks ago, I stood alone in the desert, on my native Navajo land, and held in my hand the shell of an abalone, a sea snail. Though I cannot be certain, I believe it had been buried in the sand for thousands and thousands of years, since that land was covered by seawater, waiting for me to stumble upon it. Or maybe it was dropped by some ancient Navajo ancestor of mine more recently than that. It doesn't matter." She raised her cupped hands higher. "Having cleaned it out, I held it in my hands and gazed into the swirls of iridescent colors and silver light. I could feel the rough and battered, some might say ugly, exterior of the shell with my palms and fingertips at the same time my eyes were drinking in the incredible beauty of its interior.

"Though I didn't realize it at the time, I believe God has since spoken to my heart and helped me understand that is exactly how he thinks of me, of you, of all of us. When his eyes gaze upon us, he sees our gnarly, damaged exterior—the evil in our hearts, the failures in our relationships, the pain we inflict on others. But when he looks more deeply inside us, he sees only the beauty he put there at the beginning of time—the intelligence he gave us, the creativity that lives in us, the love we are capable of."

She looked down into her cupped hands. "That is the same beauty of the soul my Navajo brothers and sisters recognized as they experienced their creation story, for that is who we truly were at the beginning of time, all of us—beautiful creatures who were meant to live in perfect harmony with our creator and our environment. It wasn't until we gave in to our desire for independence that we broke the bond between us and God and began growing shells around ourselves, shells we would not have needed—shells which have become scarred and damaged and sometimes painful to touch.

"But God has loved us throughout. And now, I encourage you to believe, really believe, that God loves you even with all your flaws and failings. Ask God to be by your side all day long, ready to help you, ready to protect you—but most of all, ready to lead you closer and closer to becoming the person he wants you to be —the person he has always planned for you to be."

She lifted her hands, still cupped, as if making an offering to the Lord. As she did, she saw people in the crowd cupping their hands as well, then lifting them higher as she began to pray. "Father, please, by your grace, I ask you to take back my life, not because I am a wonderful person who has polished it and perfected it and who is now generously giving it to you, but because I have allowed that shell to grow around me in all its ugliness, and only you have the power to reveal the beauty that lies within—the beauty *you* put there."

She spread her arms out fully, her hands open wide. "Father, Yahweh, I open my heart to you and trust that you will welcome me back into the place in your heart which you have always kept for me alone."

Abby lowered her arms, and without another word, turned and walked off the stage, leaving the crowd reverently silent. Though the people she passed reached out, attempting to speak, to congratulate her, she moved silently and quickly past them. Descending the three steps to the ground, she turned immediately to her left and headed into the darkness and silence of the field behind the stage. She spent the next hour alone in that field, soaking in the peace that came from believing she had done her best to share God's message, his invitation, with the eager hearts and minds that had stood before her. Then, once again doing her best to go unnoticed, she walked back to her tent, slipped into her sleeping bag, and fell into a dreamless sleep.

43

At breakfast the next morning, cold cereal and hot coffee, Jasmine, Lisa, and Cliff pulled Abby aside. Jasmine took out her phone and showed Abby the video she had shot the night before. "Let me fast-forward to the last part, when some of the lights blew out."

Abby's face grew still as she watched; the words slipped quietly out of her mouth. "Really? Is that what it looked like when I was on stage?"

"I'm afraid so," Cliff said. "Once some of those lights went out, they left you dimly lit from the front, with bright light from above and behind. It made you look like you were glowing."

"And that," Lisa added, "happened right when you started speaking about finding the abalone shell in the desert."

Jasmine touched Abby's arm. "It was as if God had darkened the field around you, then shined some supernatural light down upon you."

"You looked," Lisa said, "like an angel, or maybe even something more amazing than that."

The women had compared the video to what Cliff had shot

the night before and shown it to the brothers earlier. Peter chimed in. "It's just like last time."

"No," Jamie shook his head, "last time it was a video glitch; she looked normal on stage. This time, she actually did seem," he scrunched his face, "ethereal."

"And another thing," Kai added, "last time we were the only ones who saw it. This time everyone here witnessed it."

Abby thought for a moment. "Have you posted the video?"

Jasmine and Lisa exchanged glances, then looked sheepishly at Abby. "Well, yes. That's what Cliff told us to do before you started speaking, and we didn't feel we could do any editing. We wanted people to see exactly what you said; we didn't want to be accused of manipulating anything."

Abby looked back at Cliff and sighed. "What do you think?"

"I think Lisa and Jas did what they were supposed to do. And it doesn't matter. I'm sure there'll be plenty of videos shot by people in the audience up there soon, if they're not already. I may have to put mine up there as well.

He put his hand on Abby's shoulder. "Listen, it's okay. You have thousands of followers out there, and they want to hear every word you have to say. I'm guessing you're going to have a lot more after last night, some of whom might be more interested in how you looked at the end of your message than what you were saying." He dropped the hand to his side.

Abby turned to the two women. "Is that true?"

"About the number of views?" Lisa blurted. "You're not going to believe it. By the time we got up this morning, you had over twenty-five thousand, and most of your followers hadn't even woken up yet. You should read some of the comments—things like: 'Now I think I understand what God is all about.'"

Jasmine didn't sound nearly as positive. "On the other hand, we're already starting to get some heavy-duty negative stuff as well. They're all over the place. Some folks felt like you were torching the mainline denominations. Things like, 'I love God, but I'm never going to a regular church again.' Others felt like they needed to defend their churches against your attacks. One post even said you were trying to equate modern denominations with the Pharisees in Jesus's day, the guys you told us gave him such a hard time."

"I never said anything like that." Frustrated, Abby turned back to Cliff, "It's not fair."

Cliff twisted his lips. "I agree, but once someone uses that kind of language, it gets picked up quicker than a hot dog and a cold beer at a baseball game." He shook his head. "For the next few hours, a lot of the folks who are going to be offended by what you said will still be in church. After that, I can't imagine what's going to happen."

"And," Jasmine winced, "that may not be the worst part. Some people are saying you planned for all that lighting to go out, that you're trying to make yourself look," she paused, finding it hard to say the words, "as if you were somehow like Jesus—maybe his sister."

Abby heaved a sigh. "So be it. We didn't come here to make friends; we came here to speak the truth. If people heard something that made them uncomfortable, then perhaps they should do a little self-examination—see if they really do think I'm off-base—see if maybe there are a few things they need to change."

Cliff spoke without much enthusiasm. "That would be nice." He rubbed his chin. "And as for the lighting thing, I doubt there's much we can do about it. As a reporter, I can go ask the tech guys what happened and get their answers on the record. Coming from me, though—especially now that folks know I'm associated with you—I don't think we'll get any of the doubters to believe you didn't plan the whole thing, no matter what those guys say."

∽

THE NEXT MORNING, Sunday, Abby and the rest of the team attended the worship service—though Abby had trouble focusing as her mind churned on and on about what had happened the night before. When it was over, she and the others climbed into the van and headed back to Shiprock.

By Monday, the ruckus Cliff had predicted came to pass. As news of Abby's message crossed from social media platforms used primarily by younger people to those which were now populated by older folks, the leaders of mainline denominations began making comments about the things she'd said—comments that were less than supportive. In addition, based on her appearance on *Insight* with Cybil Harris and the video replays of her appearance at Godspeed that were flying around the internet, Cliff was bombarded with requests for Abby to hold a news conference.

Three days later, Abby, Kai, and Cliff walked into the nicely appointed lounge at the Courtyard by Marriott in Farmington. Awaiting them was a small gaggle of reporters and videographers representing all the major networks. For all her experience on television, Abby was still uncomfortable when she saw the temporary lights come on. The notion of standing in front of six microphones was daunting enough to make her wish she had not felt compelled to agree to the event.

After a brief introduction by Cliff, Abby stepped to the small podium. "Good morning. Thank you all for coming today. Before we start, I'd like to make just a few statements." She pressed on quickly. "First, I need to make clear that I have nothing against organized religion and that my only goal is to urge people to do everything they can to experience a truly personal relationship with God. Second, I have no political agenda. Any comments I make concerning the use of people's religious beliefs as a tool for promoting political aspirations apply to everyone, no matter what their political persuasion."

Abby's eyes scanned the room, and it seemed to her that the

event was off to a good start. Then she said, "I'm open to your questions."

The room exploded. Though the number of journalists was small, their intensity and desire to be the first ones to ask their questions turned the quiet and reserved atmosphere into a circus. The reporter's questions filled the room, creating a roar in which Abby could hardly make out their words.

"Abby," a reporter shouted over the voices of her colleagues, "lots of folks are saying you staged the whole lighting fiasco at Godspeed. Would you like to comment?"

"Abby, Abby! Why are you so against people attending church?"

"Abby, is it true you're taking a salary of $10,000 a week out of the New Life Initiative?"

It was only moments before Cliff stepped to the microphone, nudging Abby gently aside.

"Listen! Listen, everyone. Ms. Duncan has come to answer your questions, and she'll be glad to do so, but please, one at a time." He paused, waiting for silence, then pointed to the dark-haired woman who had asked about Godspeed. "Let me be the one to answer your question." He went on to explain that he had spoken to the sound and lighting staff at Godspeed and had determined that Abby had nothing to do with the failure of the lighting that night. The system had simply overloaded. He yielded the space to Abby once again, standing behind her and off to the side.

Abby did her best to answer each question as honestly as she could, realizing that reporters from outlets that had a less-than-positive view of her and her work were making their point, not with her answers, but simply by asking their questions. It was the last question she fielded, however, that made her squirm inside. When Abby pointed to a tall, silver-haired man at the back of the room, one who seemed somehow more sophisticated, more deliberate than the others, he took his time framing his question, then delivered it with a subtle intensity.

"Ms. Duncan, there are those who say you are the epitome of a charlatan using smoke and mirrors to create an illusion that would ultimately bring you fame, and more importantly, fortune. There are others who believe what happened in Amarillo makes it obvious that you are no mere mortal, that you are something," he cocked his head, "how do I say this, otherworldly. Personally, I am not inclined to accept the first premise. But if that's not true, I would like you to tell us, once and for all," the rest of the room became suddenly silent, "exactly who or what you are."

Abby's thoughts careened through her mind. How many times had she insisted she was no one special? Yet, how long could she deny that very special things had happened to her, things she couldn't explain—things that did appear other-worldly? Before she could answer the man whose eyes held her gaze from across the room, she had to answer a question for herself. If she were something special, or at least was being used in a special way, would she know it?

Her hands turning to fists at her side, never breaking the intense connection between her eyes and those of the silver-haired man, she answered slowly, deliberately. "Does anyone ever really know if the things that happen to them or the things they do are truly the results of happenstance or their own decisions? Did you come here today simply because your boss assigned you to this task? Or did some higher power ordain that you be the one to come and ask me that question?" She leaned forward, contin-uing to hold the man's gaze. "And what if you had been held up in traffic today? Would it simply have been because of poor plan-ning on your part? Or is it possible that it would have been God sparing you from being injured or injuring someone else? Could it even have been God making certain you were not kept from being here right at this moment, asking me your question?" She paused, allowing the question to marinate in the intensely silent room, slowly drawing in a breath. "And if something like that happened, if God intervened in your life, do you believe you would know it?"

Abby broke the connection between the two of them, then turned and walked toward the open door behind her. As she did, Cliff straightened suddenly and called out, "Thank you, ladies and gentlemen. I hope this was useful for all of you." He turned quickly and followed, Kai at his side.

Though Abby expected a fresh volley of questions to be hurled at her as she exited, none materialized. The silence made her wonder if one or more of the reporters might be wondering exactly how they had gotten to the day's event.

44

Kansas City, Missouri – *Tuesday, September 21st*

In late September, Abby found herself sitting on the set of yet another TV program. She had been invited to be a guest on *Today is The Lord's Day*, an early morning Christian talk show produced in Kansas City, Missouri. After the reaction to her speaking at Godspeed, and remembering her experience with Billy Comstock, she had been reluctant to accept the invitation. Nonetheless, after watching some episodes of his show, she, Kai, and Cliff had flown to Kansas City with hopes that the host, Adam Gabbard, might allow her the chance to share her message without being directly attacked.

The floor manager counted them down. "In five, four, three . . . ."

As Gabbard introduced Abby to his audience, she took in the man. Like so many TV hosts, he was meticulously groomed, his silver hair complimented by a gray suit, white shirt, subtle blue and gray tie. The voice was rich and deep. But there was something different about him. There was no aura of ego. The greeting he sent out to his viewers, "Welcome, and let us rejoice that today is the Lord's day," rang true—less showbiz, more authentic reverence.

He turned to Abby. "Good morning, Abby. We're truly grateful that you are here with us."

"My pleasure. Thank you for having me."

He started with some of the standard questions to which Abby had become accustomed, adding that his audience was truly interested in what she had to say—eager to understand her message, to glean anything that might be useful in their own lives. As she answered, she watched for the moment he would turn on her. Instead, he said, "So many people who heard you speak at Godspeed, either in person or later on video, have said they thought it was a wonderful message for young people, for anyone, actually —that it was, to a large degree, a restatement of some of the material in Paul's letter to the church at Rome. Was that your intention?"

Abby waited for the next shoe to drop, the transition into attack mode. When he simply smiled and waited for her answer, she let out a deep breath, then responded. "Well, you know, I've done so much reading lately, some of which deals with Paul's letters. Apparently, I just sort of absorbed some of what those wonderful writers were saying, people like Fritz Ridenour, in his great book, *How to Be a Christian Without Being Religious*. I guess those writings have become foundational in my own thinking."

An authentic smile warmed Gabbard's face. "And, it could be that someone your age, somebody with the experiences you've had, might be especially effective in reaching other young people. Are there certain topics you believe are particularly challenging for them, or in fact, for new believers in general?"

Abby grinned broadly. "Excuse me for smiling, but I'm a little surprised that you asked that question."

He raised his chin. "How so?"

"Well, for one thing, it just so happens I was thinking about that very thing before we left New Mexico. If our goal is to help people, young and old, come into a deep personal relationship with God, what are the obstacles that stand in the way? And for another thing, I found something I thought might be especially useful."

Adam rocked back in his chair, subtly ceding the floor to Abby. "Go on."

"So, I was listening to some old music, and I came upon a song that caught my attention. Unfortunately, the recording had been copied and transferred so often, I can't find out who the composer is, but I do know it was written and published sometime in the '90s. It's a song that seems to answer the question, 'Why would God come down to earth in the form of his son?' Now, I know that people well-versed in theology will immediately respond that he came to save the world, to reconcile it to himself as he died on the cross for the forgiveness of sin. But those are rather abstract terms and thoughts for many new believers, wouldn't you agree?"

"Certainly, at times."

She reached into a pocket and pulled out a folded piece of paper. Smiling at him, she asked, "If you don't mind, I'd like to share the lyrics with you and your audience. I think it will add a new perspective to the discussion."

He grinned. "Please do."

After a centering herself, she said, "The name of the song is *Ol' Ben*.

OL' BEN, lives on a farm just outside of town.

Never had much truck with people, never had nothing good to say 'bout God at all.

But the creatures who lived on his land, you know he loved them all.

One night, the sky was clear and the moon was bright, but the weather was not fit for beast or man.

Bitter cold gripped the night, snow that had fallen made a blanket of deadly white.

And the birds in the trees on his land, they wouldn't last the night.

Ol' ben, he opens his door to let them in.

Come share the warmth of my fire, come into my home, do not fear, it will be all right.

But the birds in the trees on his land, they just sat in the night.

Poor Ben, what is he to do, only wants to lead them to the safety of his room?

"How will I ever tell them all I want to do is just love them and be their friend.

If just for a little while, I could be one of them, and we'd talk and then I'd

Lead 'em inside to the warmth of my fire, just to be their friend."

Ol' Ben, lives on a farm just outside of town.

Never had much truck with people, never really knew nothin' bout Jesus at all.

But if he'd opened his eyes that night, he would have seen it all.

WHEN SHE FINISHED, she looked up at her host. She could tell from the expression on his face that he understood perfectly.

45

P *hoenix, Arizona - Saturday, October 9th*
At four o'clock on Saturday afternoon, the New Life Initiative van pulled up outside a large warehouse in Phoenix, Arizona. During the roughly seven-hour trip down from Shiprock, there had been a sense of excitement and anticipation as Abby prepared to speak to another large group. This time it was over 1,500 people, some of whom had come to see the woman who had graced the stage at Godspeed in Texas—the woman who might at any minute shape-shift into an ethereal spirit. Many of them were Christians looking to hear from the visionary who was bringing new insights into the worship of the god they had already chosen to follow. Many others, however, were people who were exploring the notion of accepting there was a god at all.

What Abby and the other members of the team had feared was also there. Though banners welcoming Abby hung outside the building, a group of protestors, upwards of seventy-five people, waited for her as well. As the van arrived, signs filled the air. *False Prophet! Liar! Scam Artist!* read some, and worse, *Servant of Satan! Desecrator of the Faith!*

As Abby put her fingers on the handle of the front passenger door, Cliff grabbed her arm. "No, no. Let the guys out first."

Abby turned and looked at Jamie. He grinned. "We've got this, sister." Nodding at Peter and Rob, he opened the van's sliding door and jumped out. The brothers followed.

As soon as the men were out, Lisa said, "Me and Jas first, and Kai. You slip in between us, Abby."

Jasmine called out from the back of the van, "You take up the rear, Cliff. We've got to make sure she's safe."

With the young men in front, Cliff behind her, and surrounded by the three women, Abby made her way to the entrance of the building. She fell under a withering hail of insults, including several aimed at her Navajo heritage. Keeping her head down, she followed closely behind Jamie and was relieved when some of the event organizers came out to help escort her and her entourage into the building.

Finally inside, unhurt but not unfazed, Abby took her first deep breath and looked around. Though only 1,500 people were expected, it seemed to her that a lot more had shown up. Signs and banners filled the warehouse, almost all of which extolled Abby and her efforts to encourage people to examine their relationship with God—to become aware of their relationship with their creator if they had never done so before. Swiftly escorted to a small space behind the temporary stage area, Abby tried to calm herself and prepared to speak.

At four forty, a local Christian group began playing worship songs and, given the concrete walls, filled the space with more sound than it could comfortably handle. Nonetheless, the people who had come to hear Abby sang and swayed, sometimes closing their eyes or raising their hands in worship. Abby could feel the love in the room—most of it for God, some of it, she feared, for her.

Promptly at five o'clock, a pastor from a local non-denominational church, introduced Abby. He brought her up on stage with the words, "Now let us listen to the message the Lord has for us tonight."

Abby's gut tightened. Yes, she had committed to sharing her experiences with others—what she had learned, what she now believed. But, though she had come to trust her own heart, to believe she was sharing her own truth, she still struggled with the notion of being considered God's special messenger.

Abby took a deep breath, centered herself, and moved to the microphone. "Hello, I'm Abby Duncan." The people standing in front of her couldn't contain the excitement they felt at seeing her in person. A roar reverberated through the warehouse. She waited. "Let me start by saying *I* am not important, I am not here to talk about *me*, but I am here to share what *I* have learned, what *I* believe, and what I hope *you* will consider about your own choices as you try to experience God in your own lives."

Much of what Abby said to this crowd was similar to the things she had shared at Godspeed. She spoke about the difference between religion and having a relationship with God. She spoke about the pitfalls of allowing religion to be used as a tool for political purposes. She even generated a few laughs by asking people what party Jesus would belong to. "Should we show him riding on an elephant or a donkey?" She cocked her head. "Though he did ride into Jerusalem on a donkey." She grinned. "But that's a different story altogether."

She also added thoughts about respecting God's creation. Referring to the questions that had arisen after her address at the Four Corners Generating Station, she replied, "My father has said coal and gas and oil have been here to use for a season, but that we must look toward another epoch, one in which the scars man has inflicted upon creation can be healed."

While she spoke, Abby noticed movement at the back of the room. Distracted by the task at hand, and unable to see clearly because of the bright lights shining in her eyes, she paid the activity little attention.

As Abby finished, she raised her cupped hands, offering her heart to God. Looking out over the audience, she once again saw people mimicking her. She spread her arms wide as a sign of her acceptance and love of both of God and the people in front of her, and the crowd responded accordingly. She said, "May God's grace and love find their way into our hearts—past the walls we humans erect. May we choose to accept him into our lives as he accepts us into his kingdom. Amen."

With that, Abby turned and headed for the stairs that would lead her off the stage. Waiting for her, in a now-familiar configuration, were Jamie and the two brothers, Kai, Jasmine, and Lisa. Cliff was hurrying to pack up his gear, eager to be in place behind her by the time Abby reached the exit.

Moving at a painfully slow pace through the crowd, the entourage made its way to the back of the room. Just before Jamie and the brothers made the turn toward the exit door, Abby called out to them over the buzz of the crowd. "Wait! Wait! Not yet!"

Pushing forward, past her escort, she stepped into the open space at the back of the room. In front of her were several large tables upon which sat piles of posters and T-shirts, all of which bore images of Abby. All she could think of was Jesus chasing the money changers out of the temple.

Shocked, she strode toward them. Walking down the line of tables, she stared at the people standing behind each one, sending a silent message. Finally, she spoke, just barely loud enough for them to hear her in the noisy room—pain in her voice. "Not me," she shook her head, "this is not about me."

Jamie slipped up behind Abby and guided her away, speaking into her ear. "We've got this. We need to go."

Jamie and the women led Abby out of the building and to the van. Kai jumped in first, then pulled Abby inside. "Come on, get all the way to the back and sit down. We've got to get you out of here."

Within moments, everyone else piled into the van, Jamie in

the driver's seat. Still agitated, he called out to his passengers. "Seat belts on! Buckle up! Here we go!"

As he maneuvered the van past the crowd that had spilled out of the building, Abby leaned over, peering between her cohorts' heads. Her heart rose in her throat. In front of them, the crowd of protestors had taken up positions on either side of the driveway. She knew immediately that Jamie was going to have to run that gauntlet, and they might have to face attacks much more serious than the invective she had met with earlier.

She was not wrong. Doing his best to avoid injuring anyone, Jamie pushed the van as quickly as he could through the throng. In addition to the yelling, Abby could hear thumping that told her people were banging on the vehicle, or perhaps throwing things at it. It wasn't until the van reached the public street, and Jamie took off at a rate noticeably faster than the speed limit allowed, that Abby began to feel they were finally out of danger.

46

D urango, Colorado - Friday, October 23rd
At nine o'clock Friday evening, Abby and the whole NLI team sat around the large-screen TV in the cabin. In one sense, it was Cliff's big night. In another, it was Abby's.

Though he had tried to put it off, Cliff's station had pressed him to finish his documentary and get it out to the network. After two weeks of feverish work, he had delivered the finished production and it was scheduled to air that night.

The room vibrated with mixed emotions. There was certainly a sense of excitement, for these people had become inexorably tied together emotionally, trusting each other—counting on each other. Now, Abby, the person around whom they had all coalesced, was about to be the center of attention on a show aired on national TV. At the same time, everyone there was fully aware the program was going to catapult Abby further into the national consciousness—further into a situation that seemed to be increasingly fraught with potential danger.

Abby wondered if those who were drawn to her, who followed her, would be even more enamored of the Navajo woman who spoke so powerfully about an intimate relationship with God, or if something in the show would turn them off? On the other hand, would those who disagreed with her, perhaps despised her, come to accept the value of some of the things she was saying, or would they be further enraged?

The program began with Cliff on screen, introducing himself and describing his initial meeting with Abby. He read a brief excerpt from his first article, then explained that it had been reprinted in the *Arizona Clarion*. That was followed by an interview with Dr. Susan Sterling, from Abby's 'God loves you' experience in Tucson. The first segment also included video of her speaking at the New Mexico Clean Earth Coalition, as well as clips from *The Barbara Ellis Rice Show* in Albuquerque and *The Billy Comstock Hour* on Christian television.

The second half of the program contained excerpts from Abby's interviews with Alex Bennis in London and Cybil Harris on *Insight*, then described the inception of the New Life Initiative. As the program moved toward completion, it showed video from Abby's appearances at Godspeed and the rally in Phoenix. Cliff shared interviews with people who had attended those events, as well as social media postings that showed both the depth of the following she had developed and the level of outrage she had engendered. He closed by saying, "It is not our task to judge the things you've seen tonight, to imply that Abby Duncan is who some people say she is or to discredit her. We have endeavored to bring you as much live video of her actions and words as possible and allow you to make your own judgments. We thank you for joining us and wish you a safe and happy weekend."

As the closing credits rolled over the theme music, every eye turned first to Cliff, then to Abby. Words and smiles flew across the room, surrounding Cliff in a wash of congratulations: "Well done," "Incredible," "Man, was that great."

"I guess," Abby nodded broadly, "those folks at Syracuse taught you well. That was *pro-fession-al* journalism, young man. That's going to get you some notice at the network."

Cliff was all smiles as he graciously accepted his friend's accolades. He turned his attention to Abby. "But here's the real star of the evening. What did you guys think of our very own Abby Duncan?"

Rob was the first to speak. "Incredible. I didn't know a lot of that stuff."

"Neither did I," Peter added. "We were a little late coming to the party."

"Well, how do you think *we* feel?" Jasmine looked over at Lisa. "Abby was already a star by the time we joined NLI. She'd already been on national television with Cybil Harris."

Abby raised her hands, feigning her own importance. "Thank you, thank you, my loyal fans. But I owe all of this to one person." She looked directly at Cliff. "My dearest friend, Kai."

The gang burst into pleasant laughter while Kai walked over to Abby and wrapped her arms around her. She whispered in Abby's ear, "No, sister. It's you who made all of this happen. Or should I say, it's God working *through* you?"

Abby leaned back. "Ain't that the truth?"

Cliff called out over the buzz of the group. "So, is it time for some more drinks? I've brought some beers if anyone's interested, and I know there's always plenty of iced tea in Abby's refrigerator. In fact," he turned to Kai, "any chance we might rustle up some popcorn?"

"Can do." Abby hopped out of her seat. "I'm on it."

As the celebration continued and people drifted into separate conversations, Rob stepped up to Abby. "Can I speak with you for a minute?"

She smiled. "Sure."

He nodded toward the far end of the cabin's great room. "Over here if you don't mind."

Abby followed him to the window through which they would have looked over the beautiful mountain below had it not been pitch black outside. "What can I do for you, Rob?"

"Listen, Abby." His words percolated with excitement. "This is a big night. You may well be on the verge of becoming an even bigger national presence after social media takes off with the stuff on this show. Just think of what you could accomplish if you broadened your work?"

"Broadened my work? What do you mean?"

"Listen, Abby. I know who you are, what you believe. And all this stuff about being in relationship with God, I'm totally with you. But in the next few days, you may have close to a million followers on social media. Just think what you might accomplish if you started talking about immigration, women's rights, all kinds of things."

"How would that happen?" She scrunched her face. "People only think of me in terms of what I've been doing."

"That's my point, Abby. You could be doing so much more. You could have so much more influence."

"How so?"

"By getting involved in politics. By running for office."

Abby recoiled at the words. "Politics?" She shook her head. "No. I don't do politics."

"But you could." Rob leaned toward her. "My dad has connections, and it's the perfect time of year. He could get you on a ballot somewhere. He could get money for your campaign, he could—"

Frustrated, Abby lifted her hand in his face. "I. Don't. Do. Politics. End of story." She walked around him, headed toward the kitchen and spoke over her shoulder to him. "Drop it, Rob. Just drop it."

47

D urango, Colorado - Wednesday, October 27th
Five days later, Cliff showed up at the cabin around five in the evening. Sitting out on the porch with mugs of hot coffee, he, Abby, and Kai got to work. "What's the latest, Cliff?" Kai asked.

"Well, as usual, good news and bad. You've probably noticed you have close to a million followers on social media now, and the money keeps pouring into NLI. In fact, have you seen there are now online NLI pages popping up—people sharing their views on God and religion, talking about their religious experiences?"

Abby smiled warmly. "It's wonderful, isn't it?"

"And here's something else I just heard," he grinned, "groups around the country are actually getting together, meeting in coffee shops and people's apartments, and so on." He continued a bit more seriously. "I don't get the impression they're trying to start their own churches or anything, but I wouldn't doubt there's some prayer and stuff going on at those gatherings."

"How exciting." Kai took a sip of her coffee. "Now, what about the bad news?"

He shrugged. "As I'm sure you've also seen, a pretty strong current of negativity is building up out there as well." He looked at Abby. "I'm afraid you're ruffling an awful lot of feathers."

Kai twisted the ends of her hair. "That's not the worst of it, Cliff."

"What do you mean?"

"I mean, Jasmine called today. She and Lisa were working the social media platforms and found a death threat."

Cliff lowered his chin, his fingers rubbing his forehead, then squinted up at Abby. "I guess that's how it goes these days. People in the public eye are just open to all kinds of rude and scary things from folks on the internet."

Abby shook her head, frustration filling her voice. "I don't get it, Cliff—not really. I mean, all I'm talking about is the difference between going to church and having an actual relationship with God—feeling like he's really a part of your life. Don't you think everyone who considers themselves a Christian, any kind of person who believes in God, would want a closer connection with him?"

A long breath whistled through his lips. "Listen, Abby. First, there are a lot of people who love the traditions, the ritual of religion, the consistency it brings into their lives, the constraints it helps them put on their own behaviors. Many of them don't like you poking around and pointing out problems that might exist in that part of their world."

"I'm not attacking religion," Abby protested. "I'm not telling people to give those things up. I'm just trying to let them know I think God is looking for more than ritual. Not that ritual itself is necessarily bad, we can do things that *represent* our thinking, our feelings; we can do things that put us in a particular mindset, that prepare us to come close to God. But if we do those things, things God actually *wants* us to do—coming together to worship as a community, acting out certain rituals—but lose sight of *why* we do them, then what? If our hearts are not *moved* by them, if those things don't help us experience the presence of God, then what's the point? In fact, we may be further away from a relationship with God than when we started because our communication with God has been stifled by the very acts we've chosen to do in order to be close to him."

Cliff gave her an understanding smile. "I realize that, but people can get pretty defensive about stuff like that, and when they do, they stop listening carefully and simply write you off altogether."

"And what about the denominations themselves," Kai asked. "Shouldn't they be trying to achieve those same ends?"

Cliff sighed again. "I'm sure they would all agree. But if a movement like Abby's results in folks turning to God in new and deeper ways, they're kind of put on notice. If they can be the place people turn to for those things, that would be great. But if people come to see them as an impediment to reaching those goals, then those institutions will wind up in decline. And now we're talking money, and buildings, salaries, and retirement plans—the whole ball of wax. Trust me, it's a tricky bit of business."

He took a sip coffee. "And then there's the other part, the discussions about Abby being more than a mere mortal. We all knew that when the video from Godspeed hit social media, a lot of folks would jump on that bandwagon, and we were right. There's a whole movement picking up speed out there that says they believe Abby is God's daughter—that, in some fashion, she's directly related to Jesus."

Abby's gaze drifted to the forest surrounding them. "Whoa, that's a lot to handle."

Cliff reached out and touched her arm. "I'm sure it is."

Silence fell over the porch as all three of them pondered the huge implications of what Cliff had just said. Finally, he spoke again. "Here's another thing I should tell you about. I got a call from Reverend Lucas Wright."

Kai put her empty cup on the floor near her feet. "Who's that?"

"That, young lady, is one of the biggest hitters in the world of Christian television. I'm certain his programming reaches close to a million viewers, if not more." His head rocked up and down. "He's the big time for sure."

Abby raised her eyebrows, "And?"

"And he wants you to be a guest on his show."

Those eyebrows fell into a furrow. "What do you think?"

Cliff straightened in his chair. "I think the guy is just gunning for you. I don't believe you would find him really interested in what you're saying. If I were you, I'd take a pass on that one."

"Are you sure?" Kai asked. "I mean, all those viewers—and Abby can hold her own."

"I'm sure she can, but what's the point? If the guy just wants to attack her, I'm not sure how much of her message will get through. Again, in my opinion, we just take a bye on it."

Abby stood and walked to the railing. "If that's what you think, I'm okay with that." A long moment later, she turned to face them. "Now, Kai, what do you say we go inside and see if this guy from back East really does know how to make a homemade pizza."

48

T *he Navajo Reservation: Near Rock Point, Arizona - Thursday,*
October 28th

The next day, Abby headed down to Shiprock. After stopping
at Pecos Bill's to say hello to Gus and have lunch, she took off for
the reservation proper.

As she drove through miles of empty land—desert land, but
rich in its own kind of natural beauty—she passed the occasional
house sitting alone on a ridge or tucked into a notch in a small
mountain. Some of those homes were hogans, the traditional
Navajo lodging. Usually round or octagonal, each would contain
four poles, representing the four mountains that demarcate the
Navajo world. They were normally built with logs and had a
dome-shaped roof, representing the sky, and a doorway that
faced east, welcoming the morning sun.

Other members of the tribe lived in trailers or modest homes.
Unfortunately, finding adequate housing on the reservation was a
tremendous challenge; many families were homeless or under-
housed. A surprising number of the modest houses that did exist
were crumbling and in disrepair.

As Abby pulled up to her mother's home, she felt blessed; her mother and aunt Dyani shared a simple two-bedroom, one-bath home in decent repair. She climbed out of her beat-up Chevy Malibu and was greeted by her smiling mother. "Yá'át'ééh."

"Yá'át'ééh," Abby responded. "How are you, Mom?"

"I am well, and yourself?"

"I'm okay."

"It is good to have you here, home, on your land."

"Yeah, Mom, it's good to see you too. Where's Dyani?"

"She will stay with your other aunt while you are here. It makes more room. Can I get you something to drink?"

"Anything cold, Mom."

Abby and her mother spent the rest of the afternoon walking and talking. In the evening, the older woman took a large bowl, filled it with flour, baking soda, salt, lard, and water, then mixed it with her hands. She kneaded it on the kitchen table, rolled it out into a tortilla shape and size, then dropped it into hot oil to cook. The tiny home filled with an incredible aroma as the oil spit and splashed while the two women dodged the tiny droplets of scalding liquid.

A dreamy look crossed Abby's face when she took her first bite. "No one makes fry bread better than you, Mom."

Her mother glanced at her, an accusatory look on her face. "Do you make the fry bread for you and Kai?"

Playfully guilty, Abby answered. "No, Mom. I just can't seem to get it right."

Sitting at the tiny kitchen table, the two talked deep into the night, mostly about Abby's mother's life with her sister, but touching at times on Abby's now-unusual situation. Eventually, Abby told her about all the things that had happened to her in the past year. She admitted how much it bothered her that so many people were angry at her, and then finally asked the question that had been weighing on her heart: "Why do they hate me, Mom?"

Though only in her late forties, Abby's mother spoke as if drawing upon a deep well of wisdom. "Because they think you may be of God."

Abby's eyes widened at the suggestion. "What?"

Her mother's tone remained level, almost detached. "Abby," she paused, "you speak with the voice of God. You are anointed."

Abby cocked her head. "How would you know that?"

Her mother smiled and chuckled. "Just because we're Navajo, do you think Dyani and I sit around rubbing sticks together for fire at night? We may not have wi-fi here at the house, but we go into the village and follow you on social media—what you've been doing. We've even seen that TV show they made about you."

"Mo-o-o-o-om," Abby stretched the word out, "you let me tell you everything you already knew?"

Her mother answered, her voice still level. "I wanted to hear it in your own words."

Abby thought a moment. "Still, the voice of God?"

"Yes, Abby. You speak with the voice of God. And I saw what you looked like in Texas. People may want to deny it, but they fear you are telling the truth, a great truth. They think you are the daughter of God."

Abby braced herself. "And who do *you* think I am?"

Her mother looked deep into her eyes. "Only you know that, Abalone. Only you know."

"But," Abby's tone grew stronger, "I'm just using the gifts God gave me, saying the things I believe he wants me to say."

"Listen, my child, you do not have to turn wine into water to be special, so special that you are like no other."

"But—"

Her mother lifted a finger to Abby's lips. "When the great spirits reach into our lives and touch us, it is not our job to understand, only to accept."

Abby leaned back in her chair, absently running her fingers

through her hair. Eventually, she sat up. "Come on, Mom. I'm a flesh-and-blood human being, just like everyone else. You're my mother, Dad's my father, I'm just a normal human being."

Abby's mother didn't respond. Her eyes drifted away from Abby, to the far end of the room.

"Mom? What is it? Tell me."

Her mother took a deep breath before speaking, her eyes still distant. "I do not believe you know how miraculous your birth was."

Abby tilted her head, but the question remained unspoken.

"You see, while I was still young, before you were born, I developed a raging infection," she looked at her lap, "down there. It left me with scarring in both my uterine walls and fallopian tubes." She shook her head slowly. "There are surgeries for that kind of thing, but out here on the reservation, back then . . . well, you know."

She took a breath. "Anyway, I was told by my doctor that there was almost no chance I would ever be able to have a child. It was something I had to accept. And all that fancy stuff with surrogates and everything—well, it just wasn't going to happen.

"Then, one day, after I hadn't had my time for the longest while, I had the tiniest sensation." She looked up at the ceiling. "I can't say I felt you move in me, but there was just the slightest sense that something was happening inside me.

"Of course, I waited before going to a doctor, convinced there was no way I was pregnant. But then," a warm smile grew across her face and her eyes sparkled, "when I finally did go, she told me that I was with child—that I was going to have a baby. She called it a miracle."

Abby's mother stood, walked behind her daughter, and put her hands on Abby's shoulders, squeezing. "You were a miracle baby. Your birth was miraculous. You were *my* miracle, my only miracle."

Abby sat silently for a very long time. Eventually, her mother simply bent and kissed her on the top of her head. "Yá'át'ééh hiiłchi'į̃. Good night, Abby."

49

T he next morning, when Abby was preparing to leave, her mom emerged from her bedroom. In her hand was a beautiful silver and turquoise squash blossom necklace, a piece of jewelry of special importance for the Navajo people. Spaced between the silver beads were eight large turquoise stones trimmed in silver and set in the shape of blossoms. In the center was the traditional crescent-shaped naja, often thought to represent the womb.

"Mom, I remember that necklace, it was Grandmother's."

Her mother crossed the room and held the necklace up to her as if in a sacred ceremony. "Yes, Abalone, we have passed this down through generations and generations of our family. Now it is time it belongs to you. Wear it when you stand in front of the world and talk about the God we found in church. But remember that it is made of the same material that the Navajo First Man was created from, turquoise and white corn. And remember, also, that your name reminds you that you are a descendant of the Navajo First Woman, made of abalone and yellow corn. Carry both those traditions with you as you go into the world, speaking the truth and power of the one God and remembering the beauty and peace of the others." She reached up and kissed Abby on the forehead, placing the necklace into Abby's hands and cupping them in her own. "Leave now, my child; go with God." She turned and walked back into her bedroom, leaving Abby both filled with spirit and aware of the hole in her heart as she prepared to leave her mother. It was a powerful sensation—a feeling tinged with a strange foreboding.

THE FOLLOWING WEDNESDAY, Jasmine, Lisa, Peter, and Cliff joined Abby and Kai for another work and study session. When Abby asked where Rob was, Peter said, "Oh, he's gone down to Albuquerque. My father has some influential friends down there and Rob wanted to talk to them about something." A vague twitch flashed through Abby's mind.

Cliff must have sensed her uneasiness, because he stepped close to Abby and asked, "Is everything all right?"

Abby nodded toward the balcony overlooking the mountain, and they walked to it in silence. She turned, an uncomfortable expression on her face. "Do you know where the New Mexico Democratic Party offices are located?"

Cliff scratched his chin. "I'm pretty sure they're in Albuquerque, why?"

Abby turned again, looking out the windows to the view below. "That's what I was afraid of. I never told you this, but last week, Rob told me that he thought I should go into politics—that with the following I was developing we could accomplish lots of things."

Cliff seemed surprised, but after a moment, he said, "You know, he's not wrong."

Abby's only response was to shake her head.

"Really, there are a lot of important issues, immigration for one, income equity, health care, not to mention rights for indigenous people."

Abby turned to face him. "No, Cliff. Those are all critical things, but that's not what I'm about." She gently touched his arm. "Listen, you know I've been reading and reading, studying the Bible. And guess what I've learned? Judas," she stepped back shaking her head, "he wasn't some kind of terribly evil man. Scholars believe he was a zealot, mostly motivated by socioeconomic and political factors. People like him believed the Messiah was supposed to help the Jews throw off the oppression of the Romans. It was his disappointment in Jesus not wanting to deal with politics that was one of the reasons he eventually betrayed him. She grinned. "That," she snorted, "and thirty pieces of silver."

She shook her head, turning once again to the incredible view from the cabin. "I don't want any part of it either. If God has somehow given me the task of speaking to folks about finding deeper relationships with him, I can't let that message get lost in the political vortex that seems to be swallowing up our world." She rolled her eyes. "And remember those folks who are mad at me for suggesting that politicians have been using people's religious beliefs to power their ambitions? What would they say about me if I suddenly began turning my followers into the base of some political movement?"

Cliff nodded, turning toward the mountains as well. "I see what you mean. If you believe God has given you this task, then who are you to decide it would be a great idea to tack something else on top of it?"

Abby sighed and dropped her chin. "Now, let's hope Rob hasn't started something that's going to blow up in our faces."

～

OVER THE NEXT FEW WEEKS, Abby had two more short appearances on Christian television, both without incident—both with hosts honestly trying to understand Abby's work and deal with it in the contexts of their own experiences. She also had two more speaking engagements, one in Santa Fe, New Mexico, and one in Colorado Springs. Much to the surprise of everyone on the team except Kai, Abby had changed her style of dress. When asked, she told them that from now on, when in public she would wear black pants and a black shirt, clothing many serious Navajo men and women wore on important occasions. She would also wear the necklace her mother had given her.

The whole team accompanied her on each trip. There was always the chance that in any one of those cities they might be responsible for keeping people from getting to Abby—some out of adoration, others with malice.

While they were at a rest stop on their way to Santa Fe, Abby pulled Rob aside. "Can I ask you a question?"

"Sure."

"The last time we met at the cabin, you didn't join us."

Rob seemed suddenly defensive. His smile resembled a dog's bared teeth. "Why are you asking? Do I need a note from my mom for missing class?"

Abby's face hardened. "Don't get wise with me, Rob. This is important. Peter said you were down in Albuquerque talking to some influential people. They didn't happen to be the folks from the Democratic Party, were they?"

"No," he blurted, then added, "Well, while I was down there, I did happen to run into one of my dad's old friends, Maddi Lightwind. She works for the Democratic Party. But that's not why I went to Albuquerque."

"And," Abby chose her words carefully, "what did you talk to Maddi Lightwind about?"

Rob licked his lips before answering. "Nothing, really. She just asked me what I was up to and, of course, I told her about working with you—about the New Life Initiative and every-thing." He shook his head. "No big deal."

Abby moved closer to him. "Fine, Rob. But remember, I want no part of politics. I made that clear to you. I feel like I'm doing God's work and I don't want it to get tangled up in a bunch of political battles. You've got that, right?"

He nodded. "Sure, sure. I know that. You said that before when I brought it up the first time."

"Okay, then," she gave him a half-smile, "good. Now, let's get back in the van; we still have a long way to go."

In both Santa Fe and Colorado Springs, Abby tried to keep her message simple and focused on seeking a personal relation-ship with God. The one part of the program which she refused to change, however, was the final moments. Stopping, looking inward with her eyes closed, she would cup her hands as if holding the abalone shell that represented her life and slowly offer it up to the Lord. After a moment, eyes still closed, she would spread her arms, welcoming him into her life and sharing the experience with the people who had come to see her. Invari-ably, when she opened her eyes, she would see the vast majority of those around her releasing their cupped hands and spreading their arms as well.

Each time, as she walked off the stage, Abby would need to slip away to a solitary place where she could be alone—away from other people, but not away from the spirit of the Lord with whom she felt she had just communed.

50

D urango, Colorado – Wednesday, November 24th
Four days after Abby's engagement in Colorado Springs, the team met again at the cabin. Usually, Abby would teach first, then they would discuss the progress of NLI. This time, however, Cliff took a different approach.

"Listen, everyone. There's some stuff happening I think we need to deal with." He turned to Abby. "If it's all right with you, can we do that before we get into our discussions?"

Everyone turned their attention to Abby. "Sure. What's up?"

"I've got good news and some troubling news. Which do you want first?"

Abby smiled. "For a change, let's start with the good news. Maybe the bad won't seem so hard to deal with after that."

Cliff described how the NLI movement was growing like crazy. More and more groups were meeting, mostly online, to talk about God and different ways in which to be in relationship with him. Jasmine and Lisa added they were getting a great response to their social media posts, and that Abby had just topped a million followers combined over all the different platforms they were using.

Abby looked over the group, taking in the incredible things that were happening, things that revolved around her in some strange way—even though she felt she was in no way responsible for their success. "What can I say? God is good . . . all the time. And all of you, you're the best."

Smiles went around the circle of friends, then Kai asked, "So, what's the bad news, Cliff?"

He shrugged. "Well, it's not so much bad news as a problem. As you recall, Abby has received several invitations to appear on Christian television with Reverend Lucas Wright, and we've turned them all down. Now it appears he's stepping up his attacks on Abby's work and citing her refusal to join him as proof she's up to no good."

"Can he do that?" Lisa asked.

"Sure, if he's not too blatant—and he knows that. So, mostly his comments are questions, things like: 'I wonder why she won't appear on air with us? Could it be she's really about something else, something we're not able to see right now?'"

Peter jumped in. "It's the oldest trick in the book. He makes a negative statement about Abby by asking those kinds of questions. Then, his viewers start telling everyone they know Abby is hiding something, and they *know* it because she won't be on his program. They're all quite convinced she's hiding something, though they have no idea what it might be."

Jasmine followed up, making air quotes. "*I'll bet she's.*"

"What?" asked Jamie.

"*I'll bet she's.* One person says, 'I'll bet she's a Satanist or a coke head.' Another person says they bet she's taking money from some worldwide conspiracy that's trying to crush Christianity and will arrest anyone who goes to church. And boom, every one of those things starts to stick somewhere, with some group of folks. Abby's reputation is shot without Lucas Wright ever directly accusing her of anything in particular."

There was silence among them for a long time before Abby finally asked quietly, "What do you think we should do, Cliff?"

He pursed his lips. "I hate to say it, but I think you may have to call his bluff."

"Wait a minute," Kai was quick to respond, "you told us a while ago that if she goes on that program, she's just setting herself up to be attacked."

Abby stood. "So he did. But if our work is going to accomplish anything, it will have to stand up to those kinds of attacks—*I'm* going to have to stand up to those attacks." She turned and walked toward the balcony, fully aware every eye in the room followed her.

Looking out over the vista, her words reflecting off the window in front of her, Abby spoke with determination. "And if that's what I'm called upon to do, then so be it."

She turned and faced the group. "Jas and Lisa, I want you to start watching Wright's program every day. Do all the online research you can on him." She looked at the man who had led her through so many challenges already. "Cliff, you use all the resources at KFRM and the network to help us understand exactly what this guy is all about."

Rob raised his hand. "Will you attack him on his own show?"

She shook her head. "No, I have no intention of attacking him at all. I do need to know, however, how he's most likely to attack me—to see if he'll do it directly or try to trip me up." She took a deep breath. "I just want to be prepared."

"Like Daniel going into the lion's den?" joked Kai.

"No," Abby smiled sadly, "Daniel had no plan for surviving being put into that hole because of his refusal to stop worshipping his God. And according to scripture, it was God's angel who came and protected him, nothing Daniel did." She sighed. "I'm not sure I can count on an angel coming to help me." She paused, turning back toward the window. "But honestly, I don't believe I'll be going in there alone, either."

51

S hiprock, New Mexico – Sunday, November 28th
It was past midnight when Jasmine turned her Honda Civic into the parking lot of Abby and Kai's complex. They were returning from a quick trip home to San Diego for Thanksgiving. Lisa grabbed Jasmine's arm. "What's that?" She pointed. "Who is that?"

"I don't know." Jasmine slowly pulled the car to the curb and turned off the lights. Staring into the dimly lit area in front of their apartment, she asked, "Do you think those guys by that Jeep are reporters?"

Lisa shook her head. "I don't think so. It's too late at night." Her eyes widened; her voice rose. "Unless something has happened." Worry tinged her voice. "Do you think something has happened?"

Jasmine let the car idle, but her words picked up intensity. "I have no idea. Quick, get your phone and look. I'll check mine too."

"No, I'll check." Lisa's tone matched Jasmine's. "You try to reach Abby."

Jasmine kept her eyes on the two men standing in the parking lot while she waited for Abby to answer her phone. What she heard made her heart beat a tick faster. The voice was light and welcoming. *"You have reached Abby. You know what to do. I'll get back to you as soon as I can."* The phone beeped.

"You get through?"

Frustration tinged her words. "No, it went straight to voice mail. I'll try Kai." She did, but the results were no more encouraging. Increasingly nervous, she turned to Lisa. "Anything?"

Lisa shook her head. "Nothing. I can't find anything about something happening. I'll keep looking. You try Cliff."

"Wait. Look." Jasmine pointed. "One of them is walking toward the apartment." She put the car in gear. "We've got to get over there."

"No, Jas. Don't. What if . . . ." Her voice leaped. "Oh, my gosh. What is that? What are they doing?"

Jasmine's words filled the car. "It's a firebomb! It's one of those Molotov cocktail things! He set it on fire. No, no. Oh, God, no." She turned to Lisa. "Quick! Record this!"

Though it was impossible for them to make out who the men were, Jasmine and Lisa had no trouble seeing what was happening. As Lisa videoed the scene, one of the men ran toward the apartment and launched a flaming bottle. The women's hearts stopped. It crashed on the ground, exploding into a ball of fire ten feet or so in front of the building.

Both men jumped into the Jeep, then it roared toward Jasmine's car.

"Duck!" Jasmine screamed, "Hide!" Both women turned their heads and crouched down as the vehicle careened toward them. A breathless moment later, it veered past them and screeched onto the street, leaving their hearts in their throats and a ball of flames just feet away from their temporary home.

JASMINE'S PHONE rang fifteen minutes later. "Abby?"

"*Yeah, Jas. I saw I missed your call. What's up?*"

Jasmine calmed herself before speaking. "Listen. First, everyone's okay. No one got hurt. Nothing is ruined."

"*What?*" Abby's voice rose an octave. "*What are you talking about? What happened?*"

Tears welled up in Jasmine's eyes and her voice cracked as she spoke. "I don't know how to tell you this, Abby, but someone just tried to firebomb the apartment."

"*No! Are you okay? Is Lisa okay?*"

"Yes, yes. We're both okay. Some guy threw one of those Molotov cocktails at our place, but he screwed up and missed. It landed on the lawn. Really, the only thing that burned was some grass. But," she swallowed, "but it was so scary. I can't tell you how scary that was."

"*Are you sure? Are you certain no one was hurt; everyone's okay?*"

"Here," Lisa grabbed the phone, "let me talk to her. Abby?"

"*Yeah, Lisa. I'm so glad you're okay.*"

"We're okay, I promise. The police and the fire department are here now, but the fire burned itself out pretty quickly. The police have started asking people questions, but it looks like Jas and I are the only ones who saw anything. And honestly, other than telling them it was two guys in a Jeep, we really can't tell them anything else."

Abby paused. "*Look. You take care of yourselves. Be totally honest with everyone and let me know if you find out anything else. I'm just so grateful no one got hurt.*"

"Yeah, we're fine. We'll keep talking to the police, and we'll get back to you if something turns up. Good night."

"*Good night, Lisa. And listen, let's all just take a minute to thank the Lord for his protection, okay? See you tomorrow.*"

∿

WHEN SHE GOT off the phone, Abby told Kai everything she knew
about the incident in Shiprock. A few minutes later, she called
Cliff at his home in Farmington.

"Abby? It's past midnight. Everything okay?"

Abby went through the whole story again, doing her best to
calmly tell Cliff not only what had happened, but how much it
had rattled Jasmine and Lisa.

"Abby, I'm so, so sorry, and so glad everyone's okay."

"Why, Cliff? Why would someone do that?"

"Honestly, I have no idea."

"And who? Who would do that?"

*"Again, Lord only knows. But listen. We've known all along that
you were ruffling feathers. And as often as you talk about wrapping
religion around politics, there are people out there, on both sides, who
think that you're messing with their right to say what they want to
say, do what they want to do."*

"But, Cliff . . . ."

*"No buts, Abby. We've said this before. Sometimes it's not what you
say that counts, it's what people hear, what they want to hear."*

"I guess."

*"Then again, remember, there are people out there who accuse you
of implying that you have a special relationship with God—that you
may be something special. And that's making some of those folks pretty
crazy."*

Abby's voice turned sarcastic. "Crazy enough to burn me at
the stake?" Cliff didn't respond right away, and Abby wondered if
he was considering just how close to the truth her joke had come.
"Well, at least they missed tonight, right?"

"Right," he said sadly, *"at least they missed tonight."*

52

Oklahoma City, Oklahoma - Thursday, December 2nd
Wearing black clothing and the turquoise necklace her mother had given her, Abby, along with her team, stepped into the studios of the Spirit of Life Worldwide Ministry in Oklahoma City, Oklahoma. The building reminded Abby of the home of Billy Comstock, only grander, more opulent. The chill in the greeting she received reminded her that something pretty scary had happened just four nights ago.

They had arrived the previous evening and had come to the facility two hours before air time, as requested. A round-faced, blonde woman with a warm and welcoming demeanor plastered over a poorly hidden disdain for Abby had greeted them.

She led Abby, Kai, and Cliff to the hair and makeup department while another assistant escorted the rest of the team into the studio. Plush theater seats, raised so that the audience could see over cameras and operators, lined the back of the gigantic room. Without the stage lighting on, the space was downright chilly.

Abby's hair and makeup completed, the trio was led to the green room, where they would have to wait for over an hour.

Abby wondered if they had been put on ice in the hope that she would be frustrated and tense by the time of her interview. She decided to spend a good part of that time in prayer, hoping to calm herself and preparing to present her work in the best light.

"Number five, right?" Kai said.

Abby looked at her. "Excuse me?"

"This is your fifth appearance on Christian television."

Cliff chuckled. "Yeah, but there's a world of difference. Billy Comstock wanted nothing more than to show he was the only true believer on stage, and I'm afraid we're in for a pretty rough ride with Wright. But with Adam Gabbard and those other two shows? Those folks were open and welcoming, truly interested in trying to understand what Abby was all about."

A half-hour before the program was to begin, someone else entered the room, a pleasant young lady in a conservative yellow knee-length dress. "Hi. I'm Gloria Restin." She looked at Abby. "You must be Abby Duncan." Her face broke into a genuine smile. "It's a pleasure to meet you. I'm a singer. I'll be following you on the show today."

Nods and introductions passed around the room, and Gloria took a seat on the couch next to Abby. "Ready for this? They say it can be a little intimidating to be on TV."

Abby chuckled softly. "I hear it can be." She let her own words soak in. "But let's hope everything goes well for both of us."

Gloria filled Abby's last few minutes before the show with small talk until another staff member appeared. "Ms. Duncan? It's time for you to come with me." It was nearly ten minutes before Abby found herself standing slightly off set and listening to Lucas Wright introduce her to his audience.

Abby had watched several episodes of Wright's program, so she wasn't surprised by the look of his long, dark red hair. Tall and lanky with a brighter-than-white smile, he popped out of his seat to greet Abby as she walked onto the set. "Ms. Duncan, so nice of you to join us today. Thank you for making the trip here from," his last words twisted, "Shiprock, New Mexico."

Though she wasn't sure if the condescension she heard in that sentence was a slight directed at the small city in which she lived or the fact that it was on the Navajo reservation, Abby extended a hand. "My pleasure, Reverend Wright." She took a seat on one of the two spacious, wine-colored couches.

"Well, Ms. Duncan," he started, "we don't usually have guests whose purpose in life is to deride organized religion."

Frontal attack. Abby was taken by surprise. She had seen him take some potshots at guests, but this was not his normal style. Clearly, he was not going to pull any punches, and she had better get herself together and respond—but not in kind. "Oh, Reverend Wright, I'm so sorry you think of me that way. It's never been my intention to attack the notion of organized religion."

Before she could continue, he jumped in. "Well, then, perhaps you'd like to explain this New Life Initiative you've started—tell us how encouraging people to meet in groups on the internet and talk about all the things they think the men and women of the cloth are getting wrong is helpful."

Abby smiled, taking her time. "Now, Reverend Wright. Maybe you could help me by explaining exactly what *you* think the purpose of organized religion is?"

The question clearly threw Wright off balance. "Well, uh," he took a deep breath, "that's obvious. Organized religion creates a structure in our lives, helps us as we strive to worship the Lord, keeps us from stumbling into the traps the Enemy sets for us— falling prey to our own lust, or pride, or greed."

"I couldn't agree more," she smiled again. "And the goal of that worship, what would you say that is?"

"That's obvious as well, isn't it?" His consternation glared through his smile. "To let the Lord know how grateful we are for all he has done for us, how we understand that without his grace we would be doomed to eternal damnation—that he is the supreme power in the universe."

"And to bring us closer to him," she leaned in, "wouldn't you agree."

"Certainly, yes."

She pressed her point. "To be in a relationship with him, isn't that what God seeks with us—a personal relationship?"

He leaned in as well. "That's exactly what you have been talking about as you've traveled throughout the country, Ms. Duncan." He almost grinned. "Now, would you like to explain what you think that means?"

Abby was still leaning forward. "Actually, I'd love to if we have the time."

Thrown for the briefest moment, he leaned back as if totally comfortable. "Certainly. You can take all the time you would like."

Abby sat up taller. "Reverend Wright, can you imagine someone who has serious money problems choosing to go to some sort of financial counselor?"

His eyes squinted just the tiniest bit. "Well, that would be the right thing, wouldn't it?"

"Yes, it would. And that financial counselor would lay out a plan for the person, steps he or she might follow to try to reach the goal of financial stability—things he or she should do and maybe not do, correct?"

He nodded. "I'm sure."

"And this person, this man or woman, they would be grateful and try their best to adhere to that advice?"

"I would hope so."

"But when that person went home to friends or family, what do you think he or she might say?"

Wright appeared to squirm. "I assume they would share the advice they were given."

Abby straightened up in her chair. "They might, after a while. But I believe the first thing they would *want* to do is find someone they could talk to, to express their frustration, maybe even guilt, about having gotten into such a mess. If they were lucky enough to have a spouse or somebody else they were very close to, they might pour their heart out—looking first for understanding and acceptance."

Her words flowed quickly. "You see, as humans, the thing we need most is support, personal connections, relationships. And if we're able to get that support, achieve that personal connection, expose who we are, flaws and all, then we are more likely to succeed in following the very valid structures and behaviors which are suggested to us. Does that make sense to you?"

Wright's back straightened. "Well, of course it does. We of the cloth certainly understand the human condition."

Abby bore down on her point. "Then you see that we might think of organized religion sort of along the lines of that financial counseling—instruction in who God is, help in understanding how to function in his world, help in getting to the same kind of relationship people desire from their friends and family—acceptance, understanding, support, only on a deeper level. If organized religion helped them to achieve those things, it would be one of the most important pillars of a successful worldly *and* spiritual life, correct?"

Wright pointed as he spoke. "Yes, it would. Yes, it *is*. That's my point, young lady." He pressed her. "Organized religion, whatever its form, helps us to do all of those things." He leaned in, his smile gone. "Yet you're out there trashing the work of all those who try to achieve the very things you just spoke of."

Abby raised her voice. "No. No, I am not. What I tell people is that the personal relationship I just described is available to them, not only with their friends and family, but with their God. And to the degree whatever religious organization they are involved with leads them to that personal relationship, they should hang onto it, cherish it, drink it in. But if their experience is more like financial counseling than close communication with the God who loves them, if it's good logical advice, dos and don'ts that will supposedly lead them there but leaves them dry, then they must make whatever changes they need to because they are missing out on the greatest of all the human experiences—turning to a God who loves them, who accepts them warts and all. And that God wants only the very best for them, even though it means walking with them through the most difficult of times. He longs to cradle them in his arms when they hurt, rejoice with them when things go well—especially when they move in the direction of accepting his love."

Out of the corner of her eye, Abby glimpsed the floor manager signaling to Wright it was time to take a break. He turned flawlessly to the camera, smiling. "We'll be right back with more from Ms. Duncan."

53

The next few minutes were interminable for Abby. Neither she nor Wright said a word while his assistant came on the set, checked his makeup, and whispered in his ear. Finally, she heard the voice of the floor manager. "Thirty seconds . . . . And we're back in five, four, three, ..."

Abby had no idea where Wright was headed for this second segment, but it didn't take long to find out. "Thank you again, Ms. Duncan," he intoned, "for sharing your thoughts with us on organized religion. Now, I'd like to ask you about something else, your insinuation that somehow you are in a special, almost otherworldly, relationship with our Lord."

Abby braced herself for another attack but smiled back at him. "I don't believe I've ever said any such thing."

"Oh, Ms. Duncan," his tone was condescending, "come on now." He made air quotes. "'My father,' 'My brother,' hearing from God? It appears you've been dancing around your birthright for quite a while. You speak as if you know exactly what God is thinking."

"Don't you?" she asked without blinking.

"Excuse me?"

"Don't you think there are times when you know exactly what God is thinking?"

He shook his head dismissively. "Ms. Duncan. I would never presume to know something like that."

She didn't miss a beat. "Let me ask you a question, then. Someone has a company that produces toxic waste as a by-product. In order to increase profits, they dump their waste into a river, polluting it. Any idea what God thinks about that?"

He huffed. "Yes, but—"

"Or some men see a young man, an effeminate man who is clearly gay. They follow him, grab him, take him into a field. They beat him and tie him to a fence, leaving him there to die. Do you suppose you know what God thinks about that?"

He puffed up. "Ms. Duncan, we all know the Lord Almighty has commanded us, 'Thou shalt not kill.'"

"Okay," Abby shrugged, "let's just say, instead, one of the men walks over to him and says, 'You disgust me,' quoting scripture to him. What is God thinking then?"

"Love the sinner, hate the sin," Wright spat.

She pressed further. "What if the man just tells him he's not allowed to worship the God who gave him life?"

Wright exploded. "Now, wait a minute, young lady. Standards, we must have standards. Who are you to come on this show and throw away hundreds of years of Christian theology, dogma, and tradition?"

Abby moved to the front of her chair, speaking forcefully. "I never did any such thing, sir. Theology is the study of God, of the nature of God, who he is, what we think he thinks or wants. If you recall, I was simply asking you if you thought you could tell what God would be thinking if those things happened. By the expression on your face, I believe you could. So, is it all that amazing to you that I might have moments when I believe I am communicating God's thoughts to people?"

Wright seemed stunned when she stood up, wagging her

finger at him. "No, Reverend Wright, the issue is not whether or not I have a special relationship with the Lord, but whether or not we can open our hearts and minds to the relationship God wants with *us*." She took a breath. "And now, it's time my team and I get right back on I-40 and head on home to Shiprock, New Mexico." Her final words reflected the condescension she'd picked up on earlier.

With that, Abby pulled off her microphone and walked off the set. In her mind, she could hear some director yelling frantically in Reverend Lucas Wright's ear, "Go to commercial!"

ABBY and the rest of the team couldn't get out of the studio fast enough. The looks they got as they passed through the lobby and out into the parking lot ran the gamut from shock and disdain to utter disgust—though Abby thought she also caught a few supportive smiles.

In less than ten minutes, everyone was in the van. Kai pulled the vehicle onto I-40, headed back home. Abby sat in the passenger's seat, the rest of the team settling in on the bench seats behind her.

It wasn't long before Cliff spoke. "Well, my dear, that was quite a performance."

Chuckles ran through the van as the team slowly relaxed, speaking excitedly about what had transpired. Kai said she couldn't believe Abby had put Wright on the hot seat. Jasmine and Lisa spoke gleefully about the phone video they had shot and how all of this was going to look on their social media platforms.

Cliff and the others shared the moments they wondered if they would have to protect Abby from personal assault as they left the building, and again when they drove out of the parking lot.

As they cruised along I-40, past buildings and under bridges, the sounds in the van descended into a babble of several simultaneous conversations. A jumble of thoughts ran through Abby's mind. She, too, was surprised at her behavior—how frustrated she had gotten, how much she had felt the need to shut that man down.

Abby noticed a car pulling alongside them on their right. Something about the way the driver was speaking into his phone sent a shiver through her. For the first time, she wished they had never painted the New Life Initiative name and logo on the vehicle.

She turned to Kai. "Listen, I don't want to make you nervous, but there's a black car next to us and he's kind of giving me the creeps. Do you see him?"

Kai looked to her right. "No, I can't. Lean back."

Abby did what Kai asked. "Can you see him now?"

Kai's eyes bounced back and forth between the car next to them and the road ahead. "I've got him."

"Slow down. Let him get past us."

Kai did, but the black car slowed as well, staying abreast of the van.

"What's up?" Cliff asked.

Abby squeezed the armrest in her door and nodded to her right. "I don't know. I think this guy over here is following us. He looks angry."

Cliff leaned toward the side window, trying to get a better look at the car. "Change lanes, Kai. Let's just try to get away from him."

Kai did what he asked, but the car stayed with them—first two lanes away, then next to us again. "Hang on!" she shouted as she jumped on the gas pedal, pushing their speed to sixty, seventy, eighty miles per hour. The black sedan had no trouble at all staying with them, a sick smile on the driver's face.

The road became a blur. They flew past other cars, swooping

under bridges, but never able to shake their pursuer. As they approached yet another overpass, Abby glimpsed some sort of sign or banner hung from its railings. Almost under it, she finally made out the letters painted hurriedly across the bedsheet: *HERETIC!!!*

Abby's heart froze as she realized those words were meant for her. She braced herself as she caught sight of two men lifting what appeared to be a concrete block over the railing.

The world shifted into slow motion. Abby saw the block leave their hands. Though her brain knew it was careening toward the van, in her mind it appeared to be floating—drifting through the air, right at them. "LOOK OUT!"

A millisecond later, the concrete block crashed through the windshield, directly in front of Kai. The sound of exploding glass was followed by the screech of tires as the back of the van slid left, turning it sideways on the roadway. It was only an instant before the vehicle began tumbling and bounced several times, then crashed into a concrete support that held up the road above them. As the roar of twisting steel and crunching concrete enveloped her, Abby slipped into darkness.

54

klahoma City, Oklahoma – Friday, December 3rd
Abby heard a distant sound, tiny, short—a beep. Her thoughts swirled. Darkness overcame her. She slipped away.

Sometime later, it returned. Then, after a few seconds, there it was again—now regular. She willed her eyes open. Only the right one complied. She lay still, taking in as much of the room as was possible with her one good orb.

A nurse walked in, a wiry woman with a blonde beehive hairdo and a southern accent. "Well, mornin', sweetheart, good to see you back among the living." She chuckled. "I'm not gonna ask how you feel 'cause I know it ain't great. But you can hear me, can't you?"

Abby's voice was scratchy, almost inaudible. "Yes. I can hear you. I know what you're saying." She had to ask. "Everyone else, are they . . . ?"

The woman raised a finger to her lips. "Don't you worry about everyone else. Right now, you just got to keep trying to stay awake, letting your thoughts straighten themselves out. My name's Olivia and I'll be here to take care of you till five tonight. You just try to get some rest," she wagged her finger, "but don't you go taking a nap on me. I need that brain of yours trying to make sense of what's goin' on."

THAT AFTERNOON, the doctor came in, a tiny waif of a woman in a crisp white coat. She told Abby how lucky she was—that besides having lacerations to her face and a concussion, they'd performed surgery on her—removing her spleen. She'd be okay, but for the rest of her life, she would have to be careful to avoid getting infections like streptococcus pneumonia and meningitis. When Abby asked her about the others, she dodged the question, saying there would be time to deal with that later.

THERE WAS a large clock on the wall of Abby's hospital room, so she knew it was a little after four o'clock when she had her first moment of real hope. Cliff came in on crutches, his right leg in a cast above the knee. In addition, a good-sized bandage covered his forehead.

He shuffled to the side of Abby's bed. "Hey, there. How you doin'?"

She licked her lips with difficulty. "Not bad, considering. And yourself?"

He looked down at his leg. "The doc says I won't be playing professional football anytime soon, but in a couple of weeks, I will be able to walk out to the mailbox on my own." He grinned and it warmed her heart. "How about you? What did the doctor say?"

She did her best to give him a one-eyed smile, then told him about her surgery and the challenges ahead. A feeling of dread in the pit of her stomach, she asked, "What about the others?" Her heart froze as she waited for his response.

Cliff backed away from the bed and managed to sit, stiff-legged, in the chair behind him. "Well, miraculously, it's not as bad as it could have been." He looked up at the ceiling. "Let's see, Jamie has a broken collar bone and messed up his shoulder pretty badly. The girls seemed to do okay. They're stiff and sore, and the docs had to shave part of Lisa's head so they could get to the wounds in her scalp, but it will all grow back."

"And the boys?"

Cliff sighed. "Here's the thing. It seems as soon as the van started skidding, the guys tried their best to wrap themselves around the girls, you know, to protect them. That left them pretty vulnerable. Peter wound up with a broken jaw, and Rob may have damaged several discs in his back. He's in traction right now, but they're hoping that if he lies perfectly still for the next week or more, things might work out for him—he may even be able to avoid permanent damage."

Cliff stopped speaking. Abby's heart froze. Finally, she mustered the courage to ask, "And Kai?"

He took a deep breath. "Well," his voice faltered, "that concrete block came right through the windshield. It looks like when the van started tumbling, her head was slammed pretty hard."

"Oh, Cliff, no. NO."

Cliff raised his hands. "It's okay, Abby. It's okay. She's alive." His arms dropped. "But I'm afraid she's in a coma, a deep coma. The doctors, they're . . . they're not all that optimistic—not right now." He sat up taller. "But listen, they say it could go either way. She might be okay. It may just take her a while to come out of it." He stopped.

"Either way?" Tears trickled down her cheeks. "You mean she *might* come out of it or . . . ?"

Cliff put on the best smile he could. "Let's not think about that, Abby. Let's just pray and think about the fact that she might be fine."

ABBY SPENT the next full day in bed resting, visited again by Cliff, Jasmine and Lisa, Jamie, and Peter—who barely spoke because his jaw was wired shut. Rob, of course, was still in traction and would be for the next few days, maybe even weeks.

At the end of the day, left alone with Cliff sitting in the chair near her bed, Abby grappled with her new reality. "It's all my fault, Cliff."

He was quick to respond. "What are you talking about? None of this is your fault."

Her eyes widened as she struggled to sit up and frustration bubbled up through her words. "Yes. Yes, it is. If I had just kept my mouth shut, none of this would have happened. Especially after the fire at the apartment. I should have known I was putting everyone else in danger. But no, I just had to keep going. If only I'd stopped, no one would have gotten hurt, including you," her voice trailed off, "including Kai."

"Wait," Cliff raised his eyebrows, "you shouldn't have said what you said to Lucas Wright? Or you shouldn't have said what you said to all those people in Amarillo or Phoenix?" He shifted awkwardly in his chair, his injured leg clearly still hurting. "Or maybe you shouldn't have said what you said on *Insight* or all those other TV shows?" He paused. "Or are you saying you never should have stood there in Tucson and said nothing but, 'God loves you?'"

In silence, Abby turned her face away from him.

He struggled to his feet and hopped over to the bed, touching her arm gently. "Listen, you never chose this, you weren't looking for fame or glory. This all came to you and you've handled it the best way you knew how—by simply telling the truth to anyone who asked."

She turned back to him. "But what now?"

"What about now? Are you going to stop speaking to people? Are you afraid to go on?"

Her eyes flashed. "I'm not afraid." She let out a short sigh. "It's just that . . . ."

"It's just that what?" His tone became mocking. "That maybe God hasn't been with you this whole time—or he has, but he's bailing on you now?"

"No," she shook her head, her energy rising. "I could never think that. It's not him, it's never him. It's me. Maybe I'm just not the right person for this. Maybe this work is too important to be put in my hands. I mean, if I hadn't screwed up, none of you would be in the hospital, and Kai would be sitting with us right now."

"So you're saying God made a poor choice when he chose you to do something special." He turned away from her, sighing. "I guess even God gets it wrong once in a while."

She smacked him on the arm, a sad smile creeping across her face. "Yeah, right. But still, I feel so out of my depth here. I don't know if what I've done makes sense." She paused. "More importantly, I have no idea how to move forward."

He squeezed her hand. "Listen, when this all started, I was a pretty lukewarm believer myself. Sure, I'd been raised in the church and if you'd asked me, I would have said I was a Christian. But these past nine months or so, they've changed me—traveling with you, watching you, has changed me. And if nothing else, there's one thing I've come to believe in the depths of my heart. There *is* a God. And as the guy who wrote that book, *The Shack,* put it, he's particularly fond of you." He struggled to his feet. "The other thing I'm sure of," he slipped into a southern dialect, "is that the big man's gonna take care of what comes next, you can count on it."

With that, Cliff started shuffling out of the room. "I'm going to get some lunch. Maybe a nice hot piece of pizza and a cold beer." He turned to face her. "Can I bring anything back for you?"

She would have thrown something at him if she had it. "Get out of here, you creep. Anyway, I've got a great lunch coming, dried-out chicken and green Jell-O with yesterday's leftover fruit in it. I don't need any of your decadent pizza."

As she watched him make his way through the doorway and into the hall, she couldn't help but think how nice it would be if only he were right about everything.

55

A bby spent a fitful night worrying about Kai and the rest of her team. By the next morning, she was determined to get out of bed and go visit her dearest friend. It turned out to be easier said than done.

As she swung her legs off the sheets, a sharp pain made her immediately aware of the incision on her side, under her rib cage, through which the surgeon had removed her spleen. Nonetheless, she pressed forward, laughing quietly at how much she resembled Cliff as she shuffled out of the room and into the hallway.

After asking for directions at the nurse's station, and insisting she was going to see her friend no matter what anyone said, Abby found Kai's room. She wasn't surprised to find Kai's mother there, stroking her daughter's head. The aroma of herbs, spices, and tobacco filled the room.

"She's still not awake?" Abby asked.

The woman's voice was raspy, obviously worn from stress and fatigue. "No. They say she has made little progress. There are many natives here in Oklahoma: Choctaw, Cheyenne, Arapaho, but we were lucky; we found a Navajo hatááłii. He has been here and performed a smudging ceremony for her. Still, I am afraid I may never see her smile or the light in her eyes again before I close my own."

Abby realized the most she could offer the woman was silent support. She took a seat in a blue cushioned chair and waited without speaking. In her mind, however, she pled with the Lord to touch her friend, to bring her out of her coma—to bring her back to life.

Eventually, the woman's demeanor changed. "I have to go now. My own mother is staying with me in the hotel down the street, and I must make sure she is well. She is very old and not able to deal easily with living in an unfamiliar place. I will be back later after I have gotten her lunch and made certain she is okay."

In the first minutes Kai's mother was gone, Abby continued to sit quietly in the cushioned chair, vacillating back and forth between prayer and ruminating on all that had happened to her and Kai in the last eleven months. After a while, she stood and moved to the side of the bed.

Laying her left hand on Kai's forehead, raising her right, she closed her eyes and began praying softly. "Heavenly Father, I hold your servant up to you. I know, Father, that you love her and want only the best for her. Father, Abba, your child lies here hurt and broken, and only you have the power to restore her. Take her into your arms and embrace her with your love. Send your healing power through her, for I believe she has come to love and accept you. And if you will allow it, I'm certain she will be your servant for as long as she walks this earth—until you call her home to your perfect love. I pray this in your name, Lord Jesus, Amen."

Abby's eyes remained closed, her hands fixed in the same position. She waited, frozen—unclear why. A long moment later, her right hand felt the slightest tremor, almost indiscernible. Abby's body froze, rigid. Her eyes opened expectantly. Involuntarily, she took in the longest inward breath she had ever taken.

And then it happened. Kai's face twitched and her eyes slowly opened, staring at the ceiling. Almost simultaneously, Abby and Kai each released the air in their lungs, their life-sustaining breath mixing above her body. Still unable to move, Abby wondered what had happened—what would come next.

Moments later, warmth and joy seeped into her being as Kai's head turned slowly and she looked into Abby's eyes. "Abby?" Her voice was tiny. "Abby? What's happening?"

Tears poured down Abby's face as she bent down, kissing Kai over and over again—on her forehead, on her cheeks, on her chin. It was as if she couldn't get enough proof that Kai was okay. She reveled in Kai's breath on her face, ran her fingers ran through Kai's hair, careful to not touch the bandaged part of her head. Finally, she simply dropped her head onto her dearest friend's chest and allowed the sound of Kai's beating heart to fill her ears, her mind.

Long moments passed before Abby stood up and smiled at her friend. "Are you okay? Do you know where we are?"

Kai ran her tongue over her dry lips. "I think. We're in a hospital? Is that right?"

"Yes, we're in a hospital and you're okay. Do you remember what happened?"

Kai's eyes roamed around the room. "Uh, no. No, I don't remember. What happened? Why am I here?" Her eyes shifted focus. "Why are you in a hospital gown?"

Abby shook her head, unable to keep from grinning. "Oh, sister, it's a long story. I'll tell you all about it, but for now, let me go tell the nurse you're awake." The smile on Abby's face continued to grow, as did the sparkle in her eye. "You're alive and you're awake, and God loves us both."

Durango, Colorado - Monday, December 13th

It was another week before Abby and Kai were back at the cabin in Durango. The lacerations on Abby's face still looked nasty, and a bandage protected the large wound on the top of Kai's head. Cliff, Jasmine, and Lisa came to visit, though Jasmine had to drive because of Cliff's broken leg. The two of them had to help him up the tall stairway that led to the cabin, made slicker by the lightly falling snow.

"Hey, ladies," Cliff called as the three of them walked through the door. "Looks like you guys are settling in. Everything okay?"

Abby nodded. "Everything's fine."

"I keep telling her not to," Kai rolled her eyes, "but she's doting over me as if I'm a sick puppy."

Abby was well aware that she often found herself staring at Kai, reliving her fear that she might never watch Kai open her eyes again. She knew she would never forget the moment Kai woke up as she prayed for her.

As the five of them sat drinking hot chocolate and taking in the beauty of the mountain below, Cliff shared several important developments. "First," he said, "what you said on the Lucas Wright show has led to a significant increase in your number of followers. We're well over a million now.

He added that he'd been swamped with requests for Abby to speak, but the group decided it would be best to put those off until after Christmas. Grateful for the extended time to recuperate, Abby told Jasmine and Lisa to take two weeks off and go home to spend the holidays with their families.

Cliff took a sip of hot chocolate, then checked his lip for a foamy mustache. "There is one opportunity I'd like you to consider, Abby."

"What's that?"

"You have an invitation to speak at one of the big churches in Washington, D.C. on Christmas morning."

She looked at him askance. "On Christmas morning? That's weird isn't it?"

"Well," Cliff answered, "I guess they do their sacred service at midnight on Christmas Eve. Then they take a sort of fresh start approach on Christmas morning." He nodded. "It would be a big deal for NLI—a real sense of acceptance by a major non-denominational church."

Abby pondered for a long minute. "Well, I'm not leaving Kai here, and I'm not going alone either. So, if you want me to do this thing, I need both of you to come with me."

"Sure," Cliff shrugged and smiled, "we can fly. Obviously, the guys are still pretty banged up and, now that I think about it, we don't exactly have a van at the moment."

Kai pointed at Cliff's cast. "The question is, will you be able to get into an airplane seat with that thing on?"

Cliff rocked his head back, smiling. "Thanks to modern medicine, it appears I'll be in a much smaller, lighter cast by then. I think I'll be okay. And," he raised his hot chocolate in a toast, "I think this will be an unforgettable Christmas for us all."

56

W *ashington, D.C. - Friday, December 17th*

At ten thirty in the morning, a man in an expensive-looking, dark blue suit and gray car coat walked into the offices of the Republican National Committee on First Street in Washington, D.C. Early forties, a little paunchy, a little bald, he stopped at the receptionist's desk. "Hi. Jimmy Belgin here to see Louise Sunderland."

The receptionist, an attractive blonde woman in her thirties, picked up the phone and pressed two buttons. She waited. "Ms. Sunderland? Jimmy Belgin from the DNC is here to see you." She smiled at him. "You can go right in."

Belgin walked through the door and into the offices of one of the most powerful political operators in the country. Another attractive woman, late fifties or early sixties, with frosted hair, she stood, extended her hand, and gave him a frosty smile. "Jimmy, good to see you."

He crossed the room and shook her hand briefly. "And you, Louise." He took a seat in the armchair across from her desk. Glancing at the well-appointed wood and leather décor, he wasn't surprised to see photographs of many leading current and former

Republican legislators hanging on the wall. The picture most prominently displayed, an autographed image of Ronald Reagan, left no doubt about Louise's political loyalties.

"I'm surprised to see you still in town, Jimmy. I would have assumed that by now you'd have your family out on the ski slopes somewhere or sitting on a beach in the Caribbean."

He gave her a wry smile. "You know me better than that, Louise, I'm always trying to work some angle to get a leg up on my competitor—just like you."

She returned his smile, hers even frostier than before. "So, what can I do for you?"

He straightened in his chair. "It's not what you can do for me, Louise, it's what I can do for you."

She made a gracious motion with her hands. "Of course; go on."

"So, I got a visit the other day from a woman named Maddie Lightwind. She's Navajo, out of New Mexico. Five-foot nothin', but a real powerhouse of a lady. Sharp as a tack, too."

"Okay."

"She tells me she recently had a conversation with a young man named Rob Jacobs. He's one of the crew that's working with Abby Duncan. You know who Abby Duncan is, I assume?"

Louise remained stone-faced. "I'm most certainly aware of who Abby Duncan is. And your point?"

"So this Maddie Lightwind says Rob Jacobs told her he believes he could get Duncan involved in politics—and, of course, that she'd play on our team."

"Interesting."

A broad smile crept across Belgin's face. "Come on, Louise. Don't give me that. This woman has more followers on social media than ten senators combined. She's got people forming small groups, online and in-person, all over the country—talking about her and her ideas. And I imagine you've heard about some guys trying to firebomb her place, and others trying to kill her by dropping a concrete block off a bridge. Once that block video went viral, her numbers shot through the roof."

Sunderland simply nodded.

"Anyway, she's got this New Life Initiative that's been raising tons of money; she's got a well-oiled social media team; and now she's not only got the country's attention, she's got its sympathy. Come on, Louise, this woman couldn't possibly be any better positioned to make a political move if someone like you or I had scripted the whole thing—*and* pulled it off."

Sunderland's demeanor shifted just slightly. "And the reason you're telling me all of this is?"

Belgin leaned forward. "Here's the thing. As you well know, that time of year is right around the corner. The DNC has already spent lots of dollars positioning the guy we're quietly backing to win the primary the Third Congressional District in New Mexico." His smile took a turn toward wry. "And based on how the economy is doing out there, high unemployment and all the other stuff, we're pretty sure he's going to give your girl one heck of a run for the money."

She shook her head dismissively. "Yes, Jimmy. I know all that already. Get to the point."

"Okay. So, if this Abby Duncan were to jump in at the last minute, she could create some serious waves—throw a real wrench into our plans—make things difficult for both of us."

It was Sunderland's turn to grin. "How so? Sounds like she's your problem, not ours."

"Oh, really? Here's this girl who's preaching about God, talking about bringing people into a closer relationship with him, and you're not afraid she might pull some of your evangelicals over to our side?"

She gave him a dismissive snort. "Sure, maybe a little. But with all the things she's said about the LGBTQ+ folks and her attacks on organized religion, I don't see her putting much of a dent in that part of our base."

He pressed. "Louise, think about it. She doesn't have to hurt you that much. She's got support from at least part of the Christian community; she's got support from the tree huggers; she's got support on the gay front; and she's a bona fide Navajo. Hell, she shows up dressed all in black and wearing some special necklace that's supposed to have spiritual powers. Every black and brown voter in the state is going to wonder why they shouldn't back a minority candidate who loves God, loves people, and loves the earth. And I don't mean she loves God the way our candidates make believe they do when they make an appearance at some local church while they're running for office. She really means it. It's what she's all about. It's who she is."

Sunderland slipped out of her chair, stood, and turned her back on him. She looked out the window behind her desk. "So, you believe that if she can suck just enough support away from the evangelicals and pull together a coalition of all those other folks, she just might be able to beat our girl—a woman who's pretty much behind the eight ball already."

"Yes, I do."

She turned to face him. "And you don't want to be the beneficiary of all of that?"

He ran his fingers through his thinning hair as he spoke to her back. "Well, first, it's kind of a risky play on our part. I mean, I think our guy can beat your girl, you know, just head-to-head. But if Duncan gets involved in our primary and wins, who knows how the election plays out."

"Good for us, right?"

"Not if she dings you enough and brings your house of cards down right next to ours. Not to mention, who knows what she'd do if she ever took office." He shook his head. "No, Louise, I don't think this is something either one of us can afford to let happen."

She returned to her high-backed chair. "So, Jimmy, what are you suggesting?"

He scratched his chin, a boyish grin on his face. "One of us has to take her off the table, find out some stuff about her, poke holes in her holier-than-thou persona—do something that makes sure she's not a factor."

A wry smile crossed her face as she shook her head. "Oh, no, Jimmy. Don't look at us to do that. If we got caught, our whole state organization could go down the tubes. Does the name Watergate ring a bell?"

He stood up and leaned on her desk. "And it's too risky for us as well, almost more so. Someone who fits naturally into our party shows up and then the folks in Washington step in and surreptitiously push her out. No way. Seriously, Louise, one of us has to find some serious dirt on this lady, maybe both of us—and not get caught at it. You know what I mean; nothing really bad, just something to tarnish her halo."

He turned and headed for the door. "Just wanted to give you a heads-up, Louise. Who knows, maybe some other group out there is angry enough to do the digging, to find out what kind of skeletons are in this girl's closet. She's already made some folks hoppin' mad—mad enough to throw a Molotov cocktail *and* a concrete block at her." He reached the door, stopped, then turned to face her one last time. "But if I were you, I'd be thinking long and hard about how you're going to handle this. I know I am." He tipped the hat he wasn't wearing. "Have a nice day, Louise."

57

Durango, Colorado – Tuesday, December 21st
Late afternoon, Abby stood on the cabin's balcony, looking out through the picture window. A steady snow fell, covering the trees and the vista before her with a fluffy frozen blanket ready to tuck the world in for the evening. She had spent the majority of the afternoon in conversation with the God she had come to feel so close to—expressing her gratitude, sharing her fears, asking for clarity about the future. And though the conversation might have sounded one-sided to anyone who could have heard her thoughts, it didn't feel that way to Abby.

Kai quietly walked up behind her, standing so close their arms touched. She spoke softly, caringly. "Are you okay?"

Abby thought for a second before answering, then turned and smiled. "Sure. I'm okay. Just thinking about everything that's happened and what I'm going to say in Washington." Her gaze returned to the falling snow.

A long moment passed before Kai spoke again. "About everything that's happened, can I ask you a question?"

"Sure." She turned back to Kai.

"That day in the hospital, when I came out of the coma. What was that like? What was happening before I woke up?"

"You mean medically?"

"No. I mean what happened right then, right at that moment?"

Abby cocked her head. "What do *you* think happened?"

Looking out the window, Kai rolled and bit her bottom lip as if she were about to share something she herself didn't believe. "Here's the thing. Before that, I guess the whole time I was in the coma, I felt . . . tiny, like I was at the bottom of a black hole that was miles and miles deep. And I was paralyzed—so paralyzed that even my thoughts were frozen. Honestly, all I experienced was this whisper of barely existing. I couldn't move; I couldn't think." She let out a sigh. "I couldn't anything."

She turned to Abby. "Then, out of nowhere, I had the sensation I was rising, moving upward through the hole, slowly at first, but then more rapidly. I started going faster and faster, and suddenly it was as if I could feel the wind blowing my hair back as I careened toward the top.

"On and on it went, always rising, always faster. Then, there was a sound—small and far away. I could hardly make it out. Eventually, I realized it was a voice, your voice. And words, 'Father,' 'broken,' 'restore.' Then a glow, a red glow, and this force pulling on me, forcing my eyelids open. Finally, an explosion of light, and your face right there above mine. Your eyes were open wide and suddenly I knew it—I knew I was back—I knew I was alive."

Abby spread her arms and pulled Kai close to her, squeezing her so hard she could feel Kai's back pop. She let go, tears in her eyes, but she had to swallow before she could speak. "Oh, sweet, sweet Kai. How I love you, my dearest friend. How grateful I am that you are back with me, with us." She closed her eyes and buried her face in Kai's hair.

After a long, intimate moment, Kai gently pulled away. "Can I ask my question now?"

Abby chuckled. "Sure. I'm sorry. Go ahead."

"Did you . . . did you bring me back to life?"

Abby stopped. She knew there was a time when she would have laughed at the question—an earlier time when she wouldn't have even understood it. But now she knew full well what Kai was asking, and she was prepared to answer.

"Listen, Kai. I know what you're asking. You want to know if I had the power to bring you back to life. If I am, somehow, special." She licked her lips, searching for the perfect words. "Am I of God? Did he send me here like he sent Jesus?" She ran her fingers through her hair. "I can only tell you what I believe."

She looked out at the snow again. "I remember the first day I met Cliff. He tracked me down after I got into it with that professor, and I eventually let him buy me coffee. I recall him saying to me, 'At some point, don't you have to decide what you believe, who you are?'

She turned back to Kai. "And now, after all I've gone through, I know who I am and that's all that matters. I know God wants me to do his work, to tell people he wants more—not just folks trying to work their way into paradise." She shook that thought off. "No, there isn't any way they can ever be good enough to *deserve* to be with him in heaven. What he wants is for them to think about him often as they go through their day; to talk to him, to ask him for help, to look to him for guidance, to trust him. And most importantly, he wants them to turn to him for comfort, in the same way any child runs to their parents' arms when they're hurt. He wants us to do our best to live a life that pleases him because we are so grateful that he knows us and loves us."

She gently brushed a hair out of Kai's face. "Look, there's no denying what I experienced while you were coming out of your coma was equally strange. See, I knew exactly how you were going to describe your experience to me just now. Because, for me, it was as if God was reaching through my body, pulling you out of that hole, dragging you up through the darkness right toward me. I was merely a portal through which *he* was rescuing you.

She put her hands on Kai's shoulders. "I'm certain of it, Kai. I *have* been, I *am*, being used by God in a unique way. And in that hospital room, praying for you, I experienced for myself what I have been talking to other people about for a year—but on a level I had never known before. I felt myself crawling into his arms, my father's arms, and asking for something I had no right to demand, certainly didn't deserve. I was pleading for the life of the friend I love," she sighed, "and begging for relief from the fear that I had caused her death."

Abby turned and walked toward the small fire they had built in the fireplace. Following her, Kai said, "You weren't responsible for that. You didn't throw that block off the bridge."

Abby curled up on the floor in front of the hearth, her eyes on the dancing flames; Kai sat next to her. "No, I didn't throw that horrible thing, but if it hadn't been for me and my willingness to ignore the warnings, to take on Lucas Wright, you wouldn't have been lying there in that hospital bed all but lifeless, with no apparent hope of ever returning to us."

Kai put a hand on Abby's shoulder. "But I did come back. You prayed for me and I came back—God brought me back."

"You don't understand." Tears formed in Abby's eyes as shapes of red and gold danced before them. "I was also praying for me—praying to be relieved of the responsibility."

Kai's eyes drifted to the floor. "Oh."

Abby sat up. "But now," her voice rose, "I understand. I believe God has led me down this path, has directed me to do what I'm doing, and has shown me two things."

Kai's eyebrows furrowed. "What two things?"

"First," she sounded more confident than ever, "he wanted me to learn that there is often a price to pay for following his calling

—that there may be pain and suffering, sometimes physical, sometimes emotional. Second, that there are times he reaches into the world and uses miracles to achieve his goals, and that we don't always understand what he's doing. We may think he's answering our prayer when, in fact, he has a totally different purpose in mind," she sighed, "something that will only be made clear in his own time."

Kai's response was barely audible. "Wow." She turned away, obviously trying to digest what Abby had said.

Silently, Abby wondered if Kai really understood what she had just said—had even an inkling of what Abby now knew. She reached out, took Kai by the chin and turned her face back toward her.

"And now," she smiled, "everything must change. No more dancing around about who I am, what I'm doing, who sent me. God wants people to see him not only as the Lord of the universe but as a loving Father. And to the degree that following religious practices helps people achieve that, he wants them to give themselves wholeheartedly to those things. But when religion gets bogged down in perpetuating social norms, in asking us to march through repeated activities that have somehow lost connection to their true purpose, he wants his people to rise above that—to seek the deeper kind of relationship I just described."

Abby leaned even closer to Kai. "And this has to go beyond *me*, Kai. This can't be about me; it has to be about him. You, and Cliff, and all the others, you have to take this on as a holy mission, your only desire being to help people connect, truly connect to God—to get them to believe that in his eyes they are worthy of his love simply because they are his creation. And then we have to empower all those people who are already coming together online and in-person. We have to help them move forward—take the risk of really opening themselves up to God."

She looked deeply into her best friend's eyes. "Can you do

that, Kai? Can you promise me that whatever happens, this work will continue?"

Kai wrapped her arms around Abby and spoke softly in her ear. "Yes, Abby; yes, I can. Following you has brought me out of a place of spiritual emptiness. I love the beliefs our people have built their lives on for a thousand years, but it was hard to accept them as part of this modern world. At the same time, I was simply unaware of what was available to me through accepting God, understanding what he wants of me. Now, watching you, learning from you, experiencing him literally rescuing me from death, I'm ready to believe in him—to open my heart and let him in." She pulled back a few inches. "Together, Abby, you, and I, and those who will come after us, we'll do this for as long as he needs us to—for as long as we can."

58

Shiprock, New Mexico – Thursday, December 23rd

Two day later, Abby and Kai packed up the cabin. Their time there had been wonderful, and they were tremendously grateful for having been able to get away from the world. After packing all their personal belongings and NLI materials into their cars, they stood at the bottom of the steps and prayed a prayer of thanksgiving for the gift they had been given and all they had accomplished there.

By early afternoon, they were back at their own apartment. As they walked through the door, Kai said, "Looks like Jas and Lisa did a super job keeping the place up."

"Yeah," Abby responded, "but by the time their two weeks off are over, we're going to have to figure out where they can stay."

Kai turned to Abby, a gleam in her eye. "Unless, of course, those folks will be done using the cabin for the holidays and you and I get to go back there after New Year's."

Abby grinned. "That'd be nice, wouldn't it?"

They spent the day both settling in and preparing for their trip to Washington. Just after twelve, Cliff stopped by with lunch,

and they made plans for Abby and Kai to meet him in Farmington the next morning. He would drive them all to the airport.

Jamie came around six and took Kai to dinner, both of them
glad to be in the same city—even if it was only for one night.

Abby spent the evening quietly, reading and working on the
message she would deliver on Christmas morning. Around
eleven o'clock, however, that changed.

Dressed warmly in her eggplant-colored down jacket, Abby
got into her old Malibu and drove to Pecos Bill's. She walked in,
dusting some light snow off her shoulders, and headed for the
counter. She was surprised that she didn't see a single familiar
face. She caught the attention of a young redhead behind the bar.
"Is Gus around?" she asked, though she knew the answer.

"Sure, he's in the kitchen."

"Can you tell him someone is here to see him?"

"Okay, who should I say it is?"

"Abby Duncan."

The girl's eyes widened. "*The* Abby Duncan?"

Abby shook the question off. "Just tell him it's Abby."

The girl disappeared, and a moment later, Gus came to the
window of the swinging door. Getting Abby's attention, he
motioned for her to come into the kitchen.

Abby yelled, "Door!" as she backed through, an old habit
from her days working there. Within a few seconds she was
enveloped in Gus's arms. "Welcome home, young lady." He held
her out at arm's length. "Let me look at you. Gee, you look great,
and a big star now, aren't you?"

An "aw shucks" expression crawled across Abby's face. "Well,
maybe not so much a big star as public enemy number one for
some folks. How have you been, Gus?"

"You know, same old thing. Smoke the meat, cut the meat, sell
the meat, clean up. Smoke the meat, cut the meat . . . on and on."

Abby smelled barbeque on him, and perhaps a whiff of something stronger. "The place doing okay?"

"Not bad. You looking for work? I could sure use someone willing to help out on Christmas Eve."

Abby gave him a warm smile. "Not this year, Gus. But who knows, I might well be back here and ready to help you out by next Christmas."

"Always a place for you, Abby—always a place."

Abby glanced around the kitchen. "Listen, can you make up some to-go orders for me?"

Gus winked, then broke into a toothy grin. "Bringing 'em to someone special?"

"Yeah, I guess. Give me two Pecos Bill Specials and do it up right, will you?"

"Absolutely, girl. Nothing but the best for you."

Ten minutes later, Abby had said her goodbyes and had walked out of the building with two over-stuffed Styrofoam containers in her hands. Backing out of her parking spot, she turned onto the main street and headed for downtown. After a mile or so, she pulled to the curb, opened the door, and slipped out of the car. She walked a few steps down the alley between an empty retail space and a twenty-four-hour convenience store. Two old friends were seated on the ground, their backs against one of the buildings. She could see her breath as she greeted them. "It's a cold one tonight, isn't it, boys?"

Two scruffy faces stared up at her. "Where you been, girl? Haven't seen you in a dog's age."

She nodded. "Yeah, I guess I've been a little busy." She held out the containers. "Listen, seems Pecos Bill cooked too much barbeque tonight. He asked me if I could do him a favor and help him get rid of it. Me being a vegan and all, I can't eat it myself. Any chance you two good-hearted Samaritans could help me out?"

The thinner one spoke to the other. "Looks like she's got herself a problem, Sonny. Think we should give her a hand?"

Sonny nodded. "Seems the Christian thing to do, don't you

think?" He reached up. "Hand 'em down here, girl. We'll do the best we can for you."

Abby's heart filled with warmth as she placed the clean white containers into two pairs of dirty gloves. "And listen, the Surgeon General says it's dangerous to eat that stuff without drinking something warm. Be all right if I get you guys some coffee?"

"Got to follow the rules, girl. Do what the general says."

A few minutes later, Abby emerged from the convenience store, bent down, and gave each of the men a tall, hot cup of coffee. As she did, she took two hundred dollar bills she had taken from NLI petty cash and stuffed them into the men's coat pockets.

She stood. "Good to see you, boys. Hope it won't be so long before we get to do this again. For now, can you do me a favor?"

Mouths full of barbeque, the men looked up at her with yellowed eyes and silently nodded.

"Just remember one thing. God loves you." She bent toward them, hands on her knees. "Seriously, please believe me. God truly does love you."

She straightened, turned, and walked to her car, ready to drive back to her apartment. A mix of joy, acceptance, and sadness filled her heart.

59

Washington, D.C. – *Friday, December 24th*
Abby and Kai had reached Farmington by seven o'clock the next morning. By eight-thirty, they were on a plane with Cliff and on their way to Washington, D.C.

When they arrived at Reagan National Airport, a two-man security team they'd hired for the weekend picked them up and drove them to the Herald Hotel—a small boutique establishment on E Street. Though surrounded by some older and seedier buildings, it offered nice accommodations in a less public and potentially more secure location than one of the larger upscale hotels. They had booked three rooms: one for Abby and Kai, one for Cliff, and one for the security team.

Using a nondescript hotel had made sense from a security perspective. Once the church at which Abby was to speak had announced her appearance on Christmas morning, word had flown around the internet, and there was tremendous interest in seeing her in person. When the team landed in D.C., they were dismayed to find that news about their hotel had also leaked out.

"How did that happen?" Abby asked as they waited in line to check into their rooms.

Cliff shrugged. "I have no idea. Jasmine and Lisa certainly wouldn't share that information, and the folks at the church didn't even know which hotel you were using."

Nervous, Kai twisted the ends of her hair. "Should we change our plans?"

"No," Abby shook her head. "It's probably too late, and we wouldn't want anyone to think we're hiding from them." She put a hand on Kai's shoulder. "Don't worry. We've got a security team that's already checked this hotel out, and nothing's going to happen." She smiled, "We'll be okay."

As they rode the elevator up to the second floor, Cliff turned to Abby. "Listen, now that people know where you're staying, you can count on them showing up outside. They'll want to see you in person. Maybe we should announce a short appearance in front of the hotel sometime tonight."

"I wouldn't do that," said Bobby, the larger of the two security guards that had accompanied them in the elevator—a blue-eyed man with a shaved head and ham hock hands that revealed serious tattoos below the cuffs of his sports jacket. "Too risky."

Abby thought for a moment, then looked at Cliff. "You're right about needing to do something. Any other options?"

Kai moved closer to Abby. "There's a balcony on the third floor that has access through a guest lounge. Maybe you could just step out on that and say a few words."

Abby heard Bobby's loud sigh. She turned to him. "You don't think that will be okay?"

He replied as they left the elevator and walked down the hallway to their rooms. "Listen, folks like you, people who hire us for protection, are always trying to balance privacy and safety with the need to be seen by their audience—whoever that is. I absolutely can't go along with you being down on the street in front of the hotel. Jamal and I could never guarantee your safety. Standing on the balcony? I'm not in favor of it, but it's certainly the better option."

Cliff took over. "I'll contact Jasmine and tell her to put out a notice that you'll be appearing there a little after ten. Then we'll wait until ten fifteen, just to be certain everyone who's coming has shown up. You wave, say a few words, then Bobby and I make a big show of pulling you back inside. It should all be okay."

It was past five o'clock by then, and they were all starving. Bobby and Jamal had urged them to avoid going out in public, but Abby and Kai had never been to Washington and wanted to experience at least one nice meal in the nation's capital. Along with Bobby, they took an Uber SUV to a famous seafood restaurant named Pesce on P Street North West.

On the drive home, Cliff leaned over and spoke softly to Abby. "You were pretty quiet at dinner. Everything okay?"

She gave him a tight smile. "Sure. Just thinking about tomorrow and what comes next."

"Don't worry," he squeezed her knee, "it's going to be great; it'll open so many doors for you. Think of all the people you'll be able to reach after that."

"It's not about me, Cliff," she snapped at him, "it's about the message." The brief interchange left Cliff momentarily stunned and chastised.

Bobby stepped out of the Uber first. His eyes roamed through the surroundings, looking for any sign of danger. As he reached to open the sliding door, Abby caught a glimpse of the handgun he wore under his sports jacket. It sent a shiver down her spine.

BY TEN O'CLOCK THAT EVENING, Christmas Eve, several hundred of Abby's admirers had filled the street in front of the hotel. Looking out her window, Abby could see that more people were showing up by the minute. She turned to Cliff. "What do we do now?"

Bobby didn't hesitate. "Remember, you can't get anywhere

near that crowd. Just stay with the plan. And, for the record, you're doing this against my best advice."

Abby walked to the window and looked pensively out at the people below. After a long moment, she turned back to Cliff. "I have to do this. Without a microphone, I won't be able to address them, but at least I can show my appreciation for their support." She turned to Bobby. "It'll be okay. I promise not to stay out there very long."

Cliff walked to the window as well. "Okay, but remember this: you step out on the balcony, shout a few words, wave, let them take pictures, and we come and drag you back in. It'll look like you wanted to stay out there longer, but we didn't let you."

She smiled sadly. "I *do* want to stay out there longer, Cliff," her voice dropped off, "but I hear what you're saying."

60

Abby and the others waited until ten ten before they took the elevator up to the third floor. As she walked toward the balcony from which she would greet the crowd, Abby steeled herself, whispering under her breath. "Lord, everything we do we do for you. I ask your blessing on all that comes next."

At exactly ten fifteen, Cliff opened the door. Bobby stepped through first, took a quick, careful look around, then waved Abby onto the balcony.

Abby walked out, Cliff and Kai at her side. She was overwhelmed when she realized how many people had braved the cold on Christmas Eve just to see her. Kai spoke softly in her ear. "This is the real beginning, Abby. Who knows where the Lord is going to lead you—all of us?" She squeezed Abby's arm and smiled. "Go. Let everyone know how much you care about them —how much God cares about them.

Abby stepped to the edge of the balcony. It had gotten colder, and the wind was driving the bitter air directly into her face. She didn't care. Her heart was warm, bursting with love for the people who were out there to see her, to support her—love for the God who had led her to this place. As they cheered for her, Abby struggled with how to direct their attention *through* her, and up to that God. It came to her in moments.

She shouted down to the smiling faces. "Thank you so much for coming! We are all here to praise God on this special night!" Unfortunately, she could tell the wind was carrying her words away, that it was unlikely anyone had understood a single word she'd said. Still, she knew exactly what to do. Stepping as far forward as she could, she looked down and brought her hands together, cupped as if they were holding an abalone shell.

Slowly, very slowly, she raised her hands to her waist. As she did, she noticed many people in the crowd copying her motions and smiled inwardly.

Taking a deep breath, she lifted her cupped hands chest high, presenting her imagined abalone shell, the illusory physical representation of her life, to the Lord. Without looking, she knew the people below her were doing the same thing, trying to capture Abby's sense of reverence.

Finally, with yet another deep breath, she lifted her arms above her head then spread them as wide as she could, opening herself to the Lord and to the people who stood in front of her. An image flickered in her mind—Christ on the cross.

A flash of light from across the street caught her eye. At the same instant, a loud crack split the air. An unseen force pounded her in the chest.

Kai screamed, "Abby!!!"

It took a second, but suddenly, Abby's torso felt on fire.

Bobby leaped in front of her, his weapon drawn, searching for the source of the gunshot. Simultaneously, he was on the phone, calling his partner, while Cliff awkwardly grabbed Abby's elbow.

Screams filled the air as the people below realized what had happened. Pushing and shoving, they ran for cover.

∿

ACROSS THE ROAD, in the Foster Hotel, the shooter sat in his wooden chair. The rifle still resting on the window sill, smoke from the gun's discharge drifted upward. He lifted the weapon's bolt and pulled it back. As one spent shell was ejected into the air, another round rose out of the rifle's magazine. He slammed it into the firing chamber.

As he had expected, he would have to find a shot past the security guard. Watching carefully, his finger on the trigger, it took only a few seconds to get the opening he needed. Release the breath, squeeze, BLAM!

WOBBLING, Abby felt a second blow, higher, closer to her throat. Her knees buckled, and as Bobby pointed his weapon in the direction of the shooter, Cliff wrapped his arm around her and gently lowered her to the cold, concrete balcony floor.

Under her open jacket, blood oozed its way through Abby's sweater, creating two large pools of red which quickly ran together. Cliff gently pushed Abby's hair out of her face, and in a heartbeat, Kai was kneeling next to them. Both her hands grasped one of Abby's—squeezing. "Stay with us, please, Abby, stay with us."

WITH MECHANICAL PRECISION, the gunman dismantled his weapon and slid it into the guitar case. Two quick clicks and the case stood on its side, ready to go.

He pulled the window closed, lifted the rag he had already laid out, and wiped down the window sill. With another quick motion, he spun the chair and placed it where it had been when he had stepped into the room.

Thumbing the switch on his hand-held vacuum, he bent and

pocketed the spent casing from his first shot. He lifted the guitar case and backed toward the room's entrance, vacuuming away any possible evidence he might have left as he walked through the room.

When he reached the door, he slipped on the wig, then carefully vacuumed the spot where it had been lying—making certain no artificial hairs would be left to indicate to investigators he was not, in fact, a blonde-haired woman.

Tucking the vacuum under his coat, he grabbed the guitar case off the floor, turned, and peeked into the hallway. Finding it empty, he slipped out of the room.

~

ABBY'S EYES reached out to Kai, imploring her to lean closer. "It's yours now, Kai," she licked her lips, "the work is yours."

"No!" said Kai fiercely, tears streaming down her cheeks. "Don't say that. You're going to be okay. We're going to get you help. Hang on, Abby, hang on."

The tiniest smile crossed Abby's lips. "Go, Kai. Go and do God's work. Go tell the world he loves them."

~

MOVING SWIFTLY DOWN THE HALLWAY, then the stairs, the man in the blonde wig and feminine ankle boots walked quickly through the lobby, down the front steps, and into the street. Joining the throng of panicked admirers, he walked the four blocks to the 13th Street station, hurried down the steps, and disappeared into the crowd waiting for the next train. Three tense minutes later, he was on his way out of the city.

~

CLIFF LEANED OVER ABBY, visibly struggling to stay calm. "She's right, Abby. Help is on the way. Hang in there, please." His words came to her through clenched teeth. "Please don't give up."

Abby licked her lips again and struggled to swallow. Her lips barely moved. "Cliff, come here."

He cocked his head at first, unclear what she was saying, then understood. He leaned closer, their faces almost touching, then turned his ear to her mouth.

"Kiss me."

He raised up to look at her, his eyes searching hers.

A tiny smile crossed her lips. "Please?"

Cliff leaned closer. Abby felt his breath on her face, felt his lips touch hers. They kissed gently, a long, lingering kiss. Abby's heart gave in to the warmth and acceptance, the love that permeated that physical manifestation of all she felt for him—and which she now knew he felt for her.

Cliff pulled his lips away from her, lifting his head, his eyes glued to hers.

A rich, satisfied smile crept across Abby's face. She closed her eyes.

Bobby knelt and placed his fingers on Abby's bloody throat. A moment later, he looked at Cliff and simply shook his head.

61

K ai cracked her puffy eyes open around eight thirty the next morning. It had been a long and painful night. She had seen Abby placed on a stretcher and taken to the hospital well after she'd stopped breathing. Then she, Cliff, and Bobby had talked to the police for more than an hour about what had happened on the balcony and the events leading up to it.

After returning to her room, she and Cliff talked late into the night, trying to come to grips with what they had witnessed—what life would be like going forward.

Still lying in bed, Kai looked across the room at Cliff. Fully dressed, he lay under the duvet on the other mattress, his feet sticking out, his shoes still on. He appeared sound asleep.

Shellshocked, her body stiff, her eyes aching, Kai rose and walked to the window. She pushed the heavy curtain aside and peeked out. An inch or so of snow had fallen, giving the Christmas morning scene a lovely, storybook appearance. The image of a winter wonderland clashed with her memory of the night before, creating such a dissonance in her mind it literally made her dizzy—nauseous. She turned away, shuddering.

Kai wandered around the room, trying desperately to land on

some thought that wasn't excruciatingly painful. Her gaze fell on Abby's Bible, lying open on the dresser, the turquoise squash blossom necklace spread across its pages. Running her fingers lovingly along the stones, Kai realized the Bible was open to the very last chapter of the book of Mark. Her eyes followed the blossoms to verse fifteen; her fingers traced the words as she silently read: *Go into all the world and preach the good news to all creation.*

"Morning." Cliff's words broke the silence.

Her reddened eyes still on the Bible, Kai responded, "Morning." She turned to face him. "You all right?"

He slid his legs out from under the duvet and sat up at the edge of the bed, running his fingertips across his chin. His voice sounded raw and dry, as if he had been screaming at some imaginary adversary all night long. "Yeah." He let out a deep sigh. "Okay, but not okay." He rubbed his forehead with his fingers, squeezing and releasing. "Though right now it feels like I'm never really going to be okay again."

Kai walked across the room and stood beside him. She wrapped her arms around his head and pulled him close to her. "I know, I know," she whispered as she rocked back and forth. "I just wish . . . ." Her next words eluded her.

"You just wish what? That this isn't Christmas morning—that Abby wasn't murdered on Christmas Eve?" She could hear the anger bubbling inside him. "That some monster hadn't taken her from us?"

Without speaking, Kai ran her fingers through his hair. She felt his body shudder while she held him. She knew he was crying the way some men do—silently, desperately. She gave him all the time he needed.

Eventually, Cliff calmed and gently pushed her away, still struggling to speak. "Listen, I've got to get up and," he swallowed, "call those folks at the church. Who knows whether they've heard or not? I need to tell them," he licked his lips, "Abby won't be there today; *we* won't be there today."

"No," Kai shook her head, stretching her arms over her head, "let them know about Abby, but don't say we won't be there." Turning away from him, she walked back to the dresser and looked down at the necklace and Abby's Bible. Her words tumbled gently into the silence. "Tell them I'll be speaking today instead."

"Really?" He rose stiffly and walked up behind her.

Touching the turquoise stones reverently again, Kai spoke with a newfound determination. "Really. I've heard Abby's message over and over. I know what she would want me to say." Picking up the necklace, she turned and gave Cliff the bravest smile she could muster. "And somehow," she lifted the necklace in front of his face, "I'm pretty certain I won't be alone."

AUTHOR'S NOTE AND
ACKNOWLEDGEMENTS

As I'm sure you can *imagine*, many people have asked me about the genesis of this book. "Where did it come from?" "Why did you write it?" It's a tricky question.

There are, however, two things I know for sure: First, the initial idea of writing a book about a woman who could possibly be seen as a "sister" of Jesus came to me while sitting in church. Second, as I worked my way through the book, I would wake up early each morning with a clear sense of what needed to be written that day.

Does that mean that I was *led* to write this book? It's difficult to say. As Abby might put it, "Aren't there times when there are words in your mind, words you hear in your own voice, but that you are not sure are really your own thoughts?" My answer to that question is yes. And as regards this book, I have made the decision to put in the time and effort to write it and bring it to publication because, as a matter of faith, I *do* believe I was led to write it.

Though many writers work in solitude, doing their very best to bring a novel into existence, that is not how I work. From the beginning, my efforts have been supported by a team of people who have been committed to making this book the very best it could be. That list includes Judy and Granville Thompson, Kristin Morford, George McCormick, and of course, my wife, Denise Messina. Without their help at every stage of development, this book would not tell quite the same story, nor have quite the impact I hope it does.

In addition, several people have shared their time and efforts as advanced readers. That list includes Deb Lutz, Karen McBrinn, Sonnia Ferb, Nicki Trabilsy, Nancy Sherman and Kerry Bastow, as well as my dear friends Mike Kennedy and Alex Vangellow. There was also one reader whose special insight, based on years of training and study, has been particularly important: Dr. Mark A. Smith.

I also want to thank Dean Thomas Bennett of the Navajo Nation's Diné College for his assistance and Ms. Marisa Sosa, a student at that fine institution, for serving as a sensitivity reader for the project.

Finally, the person who had the most significant impact on the way this book "reads," is my professional editor, Jennifer Barricklow. You can thank her for every sentence that reads smoothly and every grammatical error you didn't find in this book. And one final "tip of the hat" goes to the person who set me on the road to knowing how to write fiction at all, my dear friend Edie Maddox Torok.

Note: If you are interested in hearing the original recording of "Ol' Ben, " written and recorded by Doc Messina, please search for "Ol' Ben" or "Doc Messina" on YouTube.

ABOUT THE AUTHOR

After a long career as a professional musician and educator, Frank Messina turned to writing fiction in 2015. He holds degrees in music education and television as well as a Doctorate in Education from the University of Massachusetts at Amherst.

A native of Long Island, New York, he moved to Lexington, Kentucky, in 1978 and lives there with his wife, Denise, two of his four daughters, and one of his five granddaughters.

Though *Imagine: A Tale of Faith and Courage in a Dangerous World* is Frank's first literary venture into the realm of spirituality, he is also the author of *The Bluegrass Files*, a murder mystery series set in the beautiful Bluegrass region of central Kentucky.

You can follow f j messina at:
On Facebook@fjmessina ;
On Instagram@fjmessina_author
Or at fjmessina.com
Or contact him at:
fjmessina.author@gmail.com

And a personal request . . .
If you have found this book enjoyable . . . or significant . . . or you believe that this is a story that should be shared with people who <u>need</u> to hear it, please tell as many people as you can about it.

Thanks – f. j.

OTHER BOOKS BY F J MESSINA

The Bluegrass Files: Down the Rabbit Hole

The Bluegrass Files: Twisted Dreams

The Bluegrass Files: The Bourbon Brotherhood

The Bluegrass Files: Mirror Image

The Bluegrass Files: Revenge

and coming soon

The Bluegrass Files: Broken Glass

Reviews by Amazon Readers:

5.0 out of 5 stars You can share this book with your children July 29, 2020

". . . an easy read (that) will pull you into the chapters . . . . Also, this is the type of book that you can share with your children without fear of bad language."

5.0 out of 5 stars Fantastic new mystery series I will eagerly follow! January 26, 2019

"I thoroughly enjoyed the first book in this new series . . . a series which I hope will have many books to come . . . ."

5.0 out of 5 stars It's 3:00 AM! April 6, 2018

"I purchased this book earlier today and talked myself into reading "just one more chapter" Thus, here I am at 3:00 AM because I couldn't put it down."

Made in the USA
Middletown, DE
23 October 2021